BLACK PEARL

BLACK PEARL

A *Richard Mariner* novel

Peter Tonkin

This first world edition published 2013
in Great Britain and the USA by
SEVERN HOUSE PUBLISHERS LTD of
19 Cedar Road, Sutton, Surrey, England, SM2 5DA.

British Library Cataloguing in Publication Data

Tonkin, Peter
  Black pearl. – (A Richard Mariner adventure ; 27)
  1. Mariner, Richard (Fictitious character)–Fiction.
  2. Africa–Fiction. 3. Adventure stories.
  I. Title II. Series
  823.9'2-dc23

ISBN-13: 978-0-7278-8284-4 (cased)

All Severn House titles are printed on acid-free paper.

Severn House Publishers support The Forest Stewardship Council [FSC],
the leading international forest certification organisation. All our titles that
are printed on Greenpeace-approved FSC-certified paper carry the FSC logo.

MIX
Paper from
responsible sources
FSC
www.fsc.org   FSC® C018575

Typeset by Palimpsest Book Production Ltd.,
Falkirk, Stirlingshire, Scotland.
Printed and bound in Great Britain by
MPG Books Ltd., Bodmin, Cornwall.

For

Cham, Guy and Mark
As always

And, with thanks, for
Graham Stanley,
Olga Tarasenko
and
Michaela van Halewyn

Black Lake

1973

M izuki Yukawa stumbled through the rainforest in the heart of the West African country of Benin La Bas, which stretched from the west coast towards the interior of Central Africa, whimpering with terror. Her ribs seemed too frail to contain the beating of her heart. Her skull seemed too small to contain the pictures of the brutal attack that had destroyed her jungle home and led to the slaughter of everyone she worked with. She was certain that only flight could save her from the horrific fate her friends had suffered. She was running for her life. She had twenty minutes left to live.

As Mizuki battled through the dank grey-green ferns that stood as high as she did and filled the ground between the enormous tree trunks that dwarfed and terrified her further, she relived the horror she had just experienced in a series of disorientating flashbacks. Pictures of a dozen Japanese biologists all formed up dutifully beside her in a cheerfully expectant line along the reed-fringed edge of Lac Dudo – *Black Lake* in the local Matadi language of the place. Dressed in tracksuits and trainers like Mizuki herself, ready for their morning tai-chi, the fitness programme undertaken by all employees of the Yakimoto Freshwater Pearl Company back home in Takashima City.

Pictures of the square, solid, grey-haired Dr Koizumi standing framed against the timberline, beside the greenhouse that contained his collection of orchids, ready to lead them in farming the black pearls in the lake. The dreary vegetation rising in a wild wall close behind him, the upper canopy brushing the sky and hiding the enormous volcanic crater of Mount Karisoke, on whose vast flank they stood.

She pictured the way the nearest bank of ferns had parted silently to reveal an astonishing number of soldiers, who seemed at first surprised to find the facility here. Strange young men armed with rifles and fearsome, iron-bladed matchets almost long enough to be swords. Their faces as black, hard and cold as Dr Koizumi's priceless black pearls. The soldiers had raised their guns and almost casually taken their aim.

Mizuki carried on running as she visualized the lakeside reeds that had formed a flimsy wall between her and the slaughter in the facility, behind which she had thrown herself at the first sight of the fearsomely armed men, and through which she had glimpsed even more shattered, kaleidoscopic flashes of horror.

Dr Koizumi standing with his back against the front of the orchidarium, hands raised placatingly. The others, so conveniently lined up for the tai-chi, going down as though before a firing squad, beneath a withering hail of bullets from the automatic weapons. The sound of their shots like slaps against her delicate ears.

Then Dr Koizumi collapsing like a burst balloon in front of the shattered greenhouse, his clothes a shocking red. Bullet holes in his T-shirt, black-rimmed and smoking. The bodies hacked disgustingly to pieces under the rain of matchet blows.

Dr Koizumi's head rolling free of his bright red torso and bouncing down the slope towards her, still spraying blood, his eyes wide with shock and horror. The soldier who had chopped it off looking up, his face a mask of tribal scars, his wide eyes seeming to see right through the reed wall. His powerful arm raising his dripping matchet and his blood-flecked boots stepping down the bank towards her as she turned to run.

Now the tiny passage leading from the lakeside reed bed to an outcrop of the jungle proper seemed to jump and rock crazily in front of her as she fled along it, certain that the scarred man was close behind her. It was a passage she had never followed alone before for fear of what might lurk there.

The ferns were rising in sombre waves in front of her, spitting icy drizzle into her face, whipping and tripping her as she plunged among them. Echoes of the gunshots were taken up by the jungle creatures all around her, stirring noisily with the dawn. Birds and monkeys were calling in the upper canopy, while sloths and lemurs were further down, adding their hoots and howls. Fruit bats and flying squirrels flitted from creeper to liana above her, shrieking and shrilling. All invisible – there only as part of an unnerving cacophony or a flicker in the outermost edge of Mizuki's vision, until she burst out of the trackless jungle on to a narrow path which she did not recognize as an elephant trail. She paused, gasping hoarsely, looking right and left, trying to calm herself sufficiently to think, to reason. On her left the path seemed to rise – leading up towards Karisoke's distant fiery peak. On her right it fell – leading, she prayed, down round the end of Lac Dudo and on towards Cite La Bas, the local government centre where there were authorities. Regular army. Police. Safety.

Mizuki turned, therefore, and ran downhill towards her hope of safety. She had covered perhaps a hundred yards before the gorilla charged her. It came out of the jungle wall to her right without giving any warning at all. Like her, it had seen much of its troop slaughtered by the soldiers and was in no mood to give ritual warnings. It towered two full metres high and weighed two hundred and fifty kilos. Its arms extended two and a half metres fingertip to fingertip, ending in hands nearly thirty centimetres wide – and they reached for the screaming woman as it charged. The Japanese doctor stood a little over one point five metres. She weighed forty-four kilos. The only thing that saved her was that the gorilla had been wounded in the leg and so he collapsed on to all fours before he could reach her. She ran full tilt down the path, spurred on by his roar of frustration and the thunder of his huge palms beating against the massive drum of his chest.

The elephant track ended abruptly at the wall of a fallen tree, whose trunk rose nearly six metres in front of her. She turned left because the gorilla had attacked from the right and followed the great brown wall of the tree trunk along a narrow sunlit path cleared out of the canopy three hundred feet above by the destructive force of its fall. She followed it for a hundred metres before being beaten back into the undergrowth by the shattered limbs of its branches. And here, at last, her luck ran out.

Just as she had blundered unawares into a gorilla troop, Mizuki ran into a chimpanzee community that was still disorientated, angered and coming to terms with the random slaughter visited on them by the soldiers. Dr Koizumi had never included chimpanzees in his warning lectures and Mizuki at first found the pink, clown faces, wide mouths, ridiculous ears and round brown eyes reassuring. But then the largest of the males ran forward aggressively and reared up, screaming, less than thirty centimetres ahead of her. He stood one point seven metres tall, seeming to tower over her. He weighed over seventy kilos, almost twice as much as she did. No sooner had he arrived in front of her than half a dozen others, almost as big, joined in. And when he screamed again, shaking his head from side to side, filling her nostrils with the stench of his breath and her face with a rain of hot drool, she saw just how long and sharp his black-edged teeth were. Felt how unbelievably strong his grip was as he grabbed her by the throat and the upper arm. Her choking screams of terror and agony were lost in their blood-curdling snarls of threat and attack.

Had Mizuki been one of the other smaller primates the chimpanzees normally hunted – a colobus monkey, a lemur, a bush baby, a youngster from another group – they would have torn her corpse apart and eaten it. As it was, they left her there with her throat ripped out and half her face chewed off, missing fingers, toes, and one or two other soft body parts.

As the cool of the morning began to fade, a black panther, returning from a night's hunting, stopped to sniff at her. He was a massive beast, more than two metres in length to his tail tip and weighing one hundred kilos. When he snarled, he revealed teeth that were the better part of twenty centimetres long. But all he did was lick her drying blood and pass on.

As noon approached, a cloud of iridescent blue-winged butterflies descended on her and made the horror she had become seem unutterably beautiful. For a long, lingering moment, she was transformed into the most delicate work of art, covered in trembling shards of bright blue lapis lazuli as they, too, feasted on her, as thoughtlessly and randomly as the soldiers had massacred her friends.

Within a day there was nothing left of her but bones.

2003

Mizuki's skeleton was never recovered. Nor was Dr Koizumi's head. Both lay undisturbed through the succeeding decades as the Yakimoto Freshwater Pearl Company pulled out of Africa and went into liquidation. What little could be found of the other bodies was respectfully returned to Japan but the facility was left to moulder. Unknown to anyone, the orchids in the ruined orchidarium and the pearl-rich oysters on the bed of the black lake flourished. The creatures Mizuki had blundered into did not. Through more than thirty years of sporadic war, with well-armed armies marauding hungrily to and fro, they all became bush meat – or vanished eastward over the mountains as the creatures they relied on in their food chain became bush meat in turn.

The gorillas went first. The huge hands of their leader were sold in the great Ahia market of Cite La Bas as ashtrays. His hide became a rug, his head a massive paperweight. His flesh was smoked and eaten along with that of the rest of his troop. The murderous chimpanzees were worth nothing as ornaments in The Ahia so they too were smoked and sold for food. The black panther's snarling head ended up on the wall of the minister of the interior in his offices in faraway Cite Matadi before even that great folly fell to ruin. His midnight-coloured pelt graced the floor of a Lebanese diamond trader in Granville Harbour. His bones were sold as tiger bones and followed Mizuki's colleagues back to Japan.

As the turn of the millennium came, the last of the creatures in the high canopy were blasted out of existence, either by random gunfire from below or by strafing runs from above as warplanes and attack helicopters sought to terminate the uncontrolled comings and goings of the armies, to bring an end to the anarchy that followed so destructively in their wake as their names went into nightmare folklore: Simbas, Interahamwe, Boko Haram, M23, Lord's Resistance Army, Army of Christ the Infant.

The rainforest became empty and silent, as did the whole country, from the volcanic chain at its heart right the way down to the delta. Even the mosquitoes and butterflies died out, for there was no blood for them to feed on. Moreover, the natural breeding ground of the mosquitoes in the warm, still waters of Lac Dudo were forbidden them by another form of invasive plants. Water hyacinth spread relentlessly upstream from the delta and managed to cover the obsidian surface of the lake in great mats thick enough to keep even mosquitoes at bay.

Eventually there was nothing living on the western slope of Karisoke above Cite La Bas and the black lake except the water hyacinth, the gigantic plant life of the virgin rainforest and such creatures as could find food in the plants but could not furnish sustenance for the endless succession of starving armies. Who then began, in the time-honoured tradition of the place, to eat each other.

The scarred man who cut off Dr Koizumi's head was called Ajani, which is Matadi for *'he fights for what is his'*. In some ways the three decades after the massacre by Lac Dudo had been kind to Ajani – he was alive and relatively wealthy; he had a job and a shanty to live in. In other ways they had not – he was crippled and in constant pain, doomed to eke out the last of his days working as a cleaner in the main hospital in Cite La Bas. Unable to apply for what little social help there was – not with a past like his – nor able to afford the drugs he saw dispensed around him, he eked out his meagre wages by a little pilfering. Which saved doctor's fees as he healed himself, and allowed a little extra income from street trading what was left over in The Ahia, where anything could be bought and sold. That was where he had bartered his battered AK-47 and rusty machet when he had finally escaped from the Army of Christ the Infant after twenty-five years of brutal service.

Although he was only in his early sixties, Ajani moved like an eighty-year-old, pushing his broom along the corridors with a stooped back and an unsteady gait. Increasingly regularly now he reeled and staggered as though the floor was heaving. Sometimes this was because of his pain but more often it was because of an overdose of self-administered painkillers.

Ajani was staggering badly as he began the last hour of his life. His legs were hurting unbearably. He had swallowed several handfuls of high-dose Keral tablets stolen from the already ill-supplied pharmacy. He was light-headed and thought his sense of balance must be failing him. But, in fact, the ground was quaking, an effect emphasized by the fact that Ajani was working on the topmost floor of the hospital, twelve stories above street level. The corridor he was sweeping so unsteadily ended with a panoramic window looking north across the city towards the volcanic caldera of Mount Karisoke. Ajani noted dreamily that the unsteadiness beneath his feet seemed to be matched by a disturbing amount of activity up there. He saw much more smoke than usual issuing from the massive crater, but there was no eruption. Karisoke often fumed and smoked – she had done so right throughout Ajani's entire life. However, she had never yet erupted. He was not unduly disturbed.

But Karisoke was playing a trick on Ajani and his fellow citizens in Cite La Bas. She was not erupting – she had not done so this century. Instead she had been quietly filling the huge caldera on her crater with a lake of molten lava, some seven hundred and fifty million cubic metres in volume, fed by a magma chamber nearly twice as large below. The lava was largely composed of melilite nephelinite – light rare earth elements which made the molten rock almost as liquid as water.

The tremors that Ajani felt as he staggered towards the panoramic window and looked north up the vertiginous ten-mile slope towards the volcano's rim were the effects on the lower slopes of a massive collapse in the southern wall of the caldera. The effect of the collapse was that of a dam bursting. Molten lava sprang out in a red-hot river more than two kilometres wide. The boiling rock was at a temperature in excess of one thousand degrees Celsius. Because it was so liquid, it ran like a tidal wave, guided by the heaves and folds of the mountain side round the eastern end of the lake and down through the blazing jungle towards the city below. It came down the mountainside at one hundred kilometres per hour. And that was the speed it was still going when it came flooding into the eastern suburbs of Cite La Bas.

On the twelfth storey of the hospital, Ajani was too high above the streets to see individuals. The window was double-glazed and the air-conditioning fitfully alive, so he heard nothing of their panicked flight southward. All he really saw was a wall of flame-footed smoke that swept incredibly rapidly into the city on his right. He reeled unsteadily, fighting to take in what his eyes were revealing to him in a kind of drug-enhanced slow motion. Fire ran relentlessly through city blocks. Vehicles of all sizes were swept aside, burning, exploding. Buildings reeled, collapsed, ignited. Petrol stations detonated as though hit by bunker-buster bombs. Power went out. The air-con choked – then the back-up generators kicked in and gave it the kiss of life. Ajani bashed his forehead against the glass as he strained to see more. He watched, unbelieving, as the red flood swept through the airport, covering the runway and sweeping at last into the massive avgas storage tanks. The explosion as they blew apart shook the hospital more force-fully than the collapse of the volcano wall had done.

Ajani fell backwards and hit his head on the floor. He pulled himself erect and reeled to the little cubicle in which he kept his equipment. Here he vomited so forcefully that the whole world seemed to shake and swirl. He passed out into a coma deep enough to block out the shrilling of the hospital's fire alarms and the bustle of rushing feet. During the time he was uncon-scious, the building was evacuated. All the patients assembled, in beds and wheelchairs as necessary, in the car park outside, well away from every danger of the molten lava except for the sulphurous stench of it. Here they waited expectantly for help. But the flawlessly executed procedure proved useless. For Karisoke was joined by Lac Dudo in another grim little joke.

The floor of the lake, like the floor of the caldera high above it, was hollow. Beneath a thin crust on its southern side was a chamber, sealed for centuries. This did not contain magma but a range of gases, mostly consisting of carbon dioxide but also hydrogen sulphide and sulphur dioxide. As the caldera emptied, pouring lava past the lake's eastern shore, so the bubble burst. The southern section of the lake – far away from Dr Kuozomi's oyster beds – boiled fiercely for several minutes as millions of cubic metres of gas burst up into the air. It rolled in an invis-ible cloud down the hillside beside the lava, also guided by the various folds of the mountain's topography – and, indeed, that of the valley at its foot where the city lay trapped in a deep depression. It flooded into the western suburbs of the city that the molten rock had left untouched. Heavier than air, it swept into the streets and buildings in an invisible wall five stories high. It filled rooms, apartments, corridors, ventilation systems and lift shafts. It flooded into basements and tunnels. It filled the city's once-vaunted underground train system. It washed through the south-western suburbs and out on to the farmland that clothed the foothills of the next mountain range, then, dammed there, it washed back and settled. It filled the streets and parks, the gardens and the open spaces. It filled the car park where the patients, doctors and nurses were waiting and smothered them all in moments. Everywhere it went it snuffed out life as efficiently as if the entire area had become one huge shower stall in Auschwitz.

So that, although he never knew it, Ajani was the last man left alive in Cite La Bas when he came staggering out of his tiny cubicle and started to look around. The fire alarms were still ringing. The air-conditioning was still wheezing. The lights and signs were all still illuminated. Ajani knew the procedure well enough. If the alarms were on, the lifts were out of bounds. But the thought of going down the twenty-four flights of stairs that would take him down twelve stories was more than the staggering man could contemplate. He hit the button on the nearest lift, therefore, and leaned against the wall, listening as the car wheezed asthmatically up towards him. Apart from that mechanical gasping and the shrilling of the alarm, the whole place – the whole city – seemed silent. Ajani decided that as soon as he reached the ground floor he would check out the pharmacy. With any luck he would be able to get his hands on more drugs. From the look of things there would be a ready market for anything he could steal. Though The Ahia was, like the airport, somewhere under whatever had come blazing down the mountainside.

The door hissed open. Ajani stepped in and hit the ground-floor button. The door slithered closed. Ajani looked at his reflection in the mirror on the back wall. His eyes were watering, he noted with some surprise. Then he noticed that his adenoids were burning. His nostrils twitched strongly enough to make the scars of his tribal Poro initiation writhe

like snakes beneath the skin of his cheeks. Abruptly it seemed
as though the whole area behind his nose was prickling uncomfortably. He sneezed; dragged his hand down over his face.
Sneezed again and gasped. Abruptly, he realized his throat
was hurting also. He frowned, shaking his head. Perhaps he
had picked something up, he thought. The other cleaners were
always getting infections from the wards and the patients.
Ajani never had – perhaps because the medications he took
were strong enough to keep everything else at bay, along with
the pain. He looked over his shoulder. The lift was at the fifth
floor. Not long now, he thought dreamily. But the pain in his
throat had spread with unexpected swiftness into his chest and
he was suddenly finding it hard to catch his breath.

Then, between floors five and four, the lift stopped, so
abruptly that Ajani fell to his knees. *Damn*, he thought. *Now
I'll have to call for help. That means I won't be able to get
to the pharmacy so easily.* He reached up for the alarm button
but he couldn't quite reach it. He took firm hold of the handrail
which ran at waist height round the car and started to pull
himself up. Only to find, with some surprise, that he no longer
had the strength to do so.

A sudden realization stabbed through him. He might be in
really serious trouble here. He sucked in a good lungful of air
to call for help, but all he could do was cough and choke. He
gathered his knees up to his chin and hugged them as hard as
he could. The whole of his torso seemed to be on fire. Like the
volcano Karisoke, burning wildly on the inside. He never really
understood that he was being smothered by poison gases. Hardly
even registered, in his dreamy, drugged-up state, that he was
dying. The lights went out and a huge, dark silence seemed to
close over him like the waters of the strange black lake so close
to where he had slaughtered the Japanese workers so long ago.

2013

Then, a decade later, the rains came. Torrential, unrelenting,
month after month. In a vicious meteorological irony, all the
areas of East Africa where huge populations tried to scratch a
living were almost totally destroyed by drought. But on the

empty and forsaken forests surrounding the Central African mountain chain that is the headwater of the great River Gir – which fed the black lake – five years' rainfall tore down in less than a month. There were mudslides on Karisoke's upper slopes powerful enough to tear down even the deserted virgin jungle. More huge trees joined the monster beside which Mizuki's bones lay. The wide black path of the lava flow – as slick as a highway two kilometres wide even after a decade – was transformed into a wild torrent. Great rocks tore the lower sections into a black moonscape. The deserted, half-buried ruin of Cite La Bas was briefly flooded. And Lac Dudo burst its banks.

As well as his precious orchidarium, Dr Koizumi had overseen the construction of a series of dams and sluices to protect his priceless oysters and the black pearls he hoped they would bear to enrich the ill-fated Yakimoto Freshwater Pearl Company, which had employed him and sent him and his little team out here to seed the black lake with Japanese Biwa oysters. But they were no match for floods such as these. As the lake burst free of its natural boundaries, so it burst out of the doctor's system as well. The raging torrent tore away the reed bed through which Mizuki had fled, and uncovered the grinning skull which was all that was left of Dr Koizumi. The flood rolled the skull like a boulder into the ruined orchidarium where the precious plants had continued to blossom untended through all those years. It swept them on to a black-foaming crest and washed them on to a bed of water hyacinth.

But the power of the deluge was so massive that it ripped away the floor of the lake as easily as it tore free some of the plant-choked surface, so that Dr Koizumi's skull was joined on the floating bed of hyacinth not only by his beloved orchids but also by a dozen or more of his huge black pearl-rich oysters. And that bed of hyacinth, a thickly woven mat of stems and roots almost as big as a barge, stayed coherent as it was swept down into the river system that the waters from the black lake fed. Miraculously, the orchids, the oysters and the skull remained wedged in place as the hyacinth barge slid over waterfalls and cataracts, through races and rapids until it sailed safely out on to the broad stream of the main river. The river that was the life's blood of Benin La Bas, the great River Gir.

The hyacinth-laden barge swept swiftly downriver, through what had once been prosperous farms and plantations. Past the ruins of fishing villages and mining towns which, like Dr Koizumi's facility, had flourished in the seventies only to die during the relentless onslaughts of the eighties and nineties. Every now and then there would be something newer – projects that had died at birth under the dead hand of the bribe-crippled kleptocracies that had run the place through into the noughties and early twenty-tens, before the IMF, World Bank and interested economies from Chile to China discovered that money invested in Central Africa was even more at risk than that invested in Iceland or Ireland.

Until, at last, the great river entered the inner delta. A stream that had been as broad as the Amazon at Manaos suddenly fractured, shattered, running away into the swampy jungle in a maze of lesser streams. The barge would have been lost, too, but for the force of the flood which held its floating island in midstream so that it followed that tap-root of the River Gir straight into the heart of the inner delta. Here the flood had all but swamped even the hardiest mangroves. But they still reached out, like deadly reefs, until one at last snagged the matted roots of water hyacinth. The mares' nest of vegetation swung inwards towards the shore and became more firmly anchored.

It had reached its final resting place, seemingly almost as high as the simple wooden cross on top of the missionary church, which was the first sign of current human habitation half a kilometre inland on a knoll miraculously above the floodwater. Then the flood beneath the chapel crested and began to recede. The force of the falling water sucked at the hyacinth raft with sufficient force to start breaking it up. The mangroves tore at it as the current began to release them, ripping at it as they sprang back like the claws of the great panthers that had once hunted here, with branches as powerful as the arms of the huge gorillas that had once ruled the jungle on far Mount Karisoke. The raft came apart. Dr Koizumi's skull rolled away into the receding waters. The rest fell into the mud of the river's shore.

The rains eased. The water fell. The river at last resumed

its accustomed river course, running gently enough to allow the first couple of orphans from the church school near the chapel to come down to the bank and begin to explore the aftermath of the flood, like creatures recently released from the Ark. And it was they who found the oysters lying like a bunch of misshapen black grapes in the mud of the riverside. They took the oysters to the women who ran the place, Celine Chaka, estranged daughter of the current president of Benin La Bas, and Anastasia Asov, disowned daughter of one of the richest and most powerful businessmen in Russia. It was Anastasia who opened them and discovered the huge black pearls within.

Anastasia gave the largest of the pearls to her father, Maximilian Asov, who was in the country planning to do a deal with President Chaka. She would have given them all to Richard Mariner – in the country on the same mission – for she trusted him more than she trusted any member of her family. But Max Asov had a famously successful jewellery business and promised to get her top dollar. It was a promise she and Celine were happy to rely on as they fought to rebuild the finances and infrastructure of their ruined orphanage.

Intrigued by the colour of the pearl, Max had it tested. And so he found that the mud which gave the oil-dark pearl its unique colour – the mud that formed the bed of Lac Dudo, was the purest form of coltan yet discovered. Suddenly the apparently primary interest in the mysterious black pearls became secondary to what had made them black in the first place.

Columbite tantalite – coltan for short – is a black metallic ore only found in major quantities in the eastern areas of the Democratic Republic of the Congo, not far to the south of Benin La Bas. Max had contacts who could refine the ore if he could get at it. They were experts in extracting the niobium, which was used in a range of modern equipment from MRI scanners to nuclear power stations. And also the far more precious metallic tantalum, a heat-resistant powder capable of holding a high electrical charge, a vital element in capacitors, the electronic elements that control current flow inside miniature circuit boards. Tantalum capacitors lie at the heart of cell phones, laptops, pagers, flat-screen TVs and almost every other electronic device, from the radar that keeps the international airplanes safe to the control panels that keep the Internet alive. The technology boom of the noughties caused the price of coltan to skyrocket. Max's experts estimated it would fetch in excess of two hundred and fifty US dollars a kilo, though it had reached more than four hundred dollars a kilo in the past. Even at two-fifty, that meant it was worth a quarter of a million dollars per metric tonne.

According to the latest maps they could get hold of – those prepared by the Yakimoto Freshwater Pearl Company for Dr Koizumi in 1972, Lac Dudo's bed was a million square kilometres in area. The depth of sediment on the lake bed, according to the careful Japanese map makers, averaged ten metres, which meant that the lake could contain ten trillion cubic metres of coltan sediment. A cubic metre of sediment weighs roughly a metric tonne. It took Max Asov almost no time at all to calculate that here could be two trillion, five hundred billion dollars' worth of coltan, therefore, all just waiting for anyone who could get to it and manage to set up an extraction facility on the ruins of Dr Koizumi's doomed black pearl oyster farm.

Richard

'Look, Max,' repeated Richard Mariner, raising his voice over the thunder of the Kamov's rotor. 'Just getting up here in a chopper has taken months of planning. You must see how much tougher it will be to get a permanent team this far by water or on foot. It'll be a long, hard, dangerous undertaking. You'd be mad to even think of leading it yourself.' He leaned forward forcefully, frowning with concern, his ice-blue gaze probing his associate's square Russian face.

'For two trillion dollars I'd *crawl* up here myself,' answered Max. 'Especially, as you say, after everything I have invested in the project already.'

'Besides,' added Max's business partner Felix Makarov, suavely leaning forward to confront Richard, his eyes, like Max's, alight with the promise of two trillion US dollars, 'there may be alternatives to coming up the river by boat. Look how far we have managed to come by chopper, for instance. Maybe we could just drop a team in place . . .'

'Admitted,' Richard agreed, leaning back into his comfortable seat, one long finger thoughtfully stroking the razor-straight scar on his cheekbone as he thought through Felix's statement. 'But hopping up for a look-see in the company Kamov is one thing. Setting up a facility to extract the coltan is quite another. Besides, an aircraft of any kind is only useful if you can land it. And at the moment I'll be damned if I can see anywhere suitable down there.'

The three men grouped round the table at the front of Max's executive Kamov which belonged to his mining company Bashnev/Sevmash, looking out of the window at the relentless green of the jungle's upper canopy. From this angle the virgin rainforest looked like head after head of broccoli to Richard – countless thousands of them; maybe millions reaching to the horizon on their right, where the borders with the countries of Central Africa lay hidden, and to the horizon on their left. Behind them it seemed to reach in an unbroken carpet to the coast, but Richard knew this was an illusion. And ahead of them, the jungle mounted to the ragged, flood-damaged tree line high on the slopes of the huge and restless volcano called Mount Karisoke and the border with the neighbouring country of Congo Libre. But it was hard to get a grip of the fact that each one of the apparently numberless green humps of foliage was standing about a hundred metres above the actual ground, encompassing a cubic area larger than a cathedral.

It had taken the Kamov eight hours' solid flying time to get here from Granville Harbour at the distant mouth of the River Gir, powering through the low, humid sky above the great waterway at its maximum speed. Eight hours that did not count the layover every two hours in increasingly remote wilderness areas where Max had set up fuel dumps. The whole project had taken six months to get even this far – the first sortie up to the fabulous lake itself. A trip that *biznizmen* Max and Felix insisted on leading themselves – and which the Mariners would not have missed for the world. Here, as in their dealings all over the globe, from the oilfields of the Arctic to those off the shores of Benin La Bas, whatever Bashnev/Sevmash discovered, drilled or mined, Heritage Miner shipped for them – and usually by water.

The last executive seat was occupied by Richard's wife and business partner, Robin. 'Even so,' she said now, shaking her golden curls and frowning as she picked up on Richard's point, 'you're looking at two thousand kilometres in from the coast. Two thousand kilometres from civilization to this Lac Dudo. And that's as the crow flies. It must be another five hundred or so if you follow the river. Always assuming you can follow the river. What with the waterfalls, cataracts and white-water rapids we've flown over during the flight so far. And then there's still *this* at the end of it.' She gave a shudder, looking down.

'But there is civil infrastructure down there already,' insisted Max, straining round and unsuccessfully trying to catch the eye of whichever local government historian present on the Kamov had described the transport system in its seventies heyday to him. 'There are roads, a railway, the whole communications network built in the late sixties and early seventies when this place was booming. There's a twelve-lane highway joining Cite La Bas with CiteMatadi, then going straight on down to Granville Harbour and the coast.'

'I've seen it – been on some of it,' countered Robin. 'It's useless. Cite La Bas is dead and CiteMatadi is not much better. Cite La Bas was never all it was cracked up to be in the first place. They talked it up as the New York of West Africa – a buzzing twentieth-century hub. But it was little more than a frontier town with big ambitions.'

'More like Tombstone in the Wild West rather than Tokyo, perhaps,' offered Richard grimly. 'Aptly enough, all things considered . . .'

'Very witty, darling. Moreover, Max, the infrastructure between them hasn't been touched for forty years. It's all just jungle now. As far as I know the only way along your twelve-lane highway is by motorbike and on foot. God knows what's happened to the railroad. Don't fool yourselves, either of you. You'd need to start from scratch.'

'It's as though we haven't just come up the river,' added Richard thoughtfully, 'it's as though we've gone back in time! It's like Jurassic Park down there.'

'Robin!' laughed Max. 'Get a grip! And you, Richard – Tombstone . . . *Jurassic Park*! I ask you!' But for once the booming Russian's confident tone sounded a little hollow. For the last two hours there had been nothing to see other than the jungle, and that had been depressing enough. But now they were coming over the deserted suburbs of Cite La Bas.

After an hour's flight at maximum cruising speed they were nearly three hundred kilometres from the River Gir now, approaching Cite La Bas from the south-west, so they were confronted at first by the stunted overgrowth of secondary jungle that had developed exponentially in the years since the gas cloud had killed those who had survived the eruption and the lava flow. City block after city block was literally running to seed. Plants burgeoned everywhere, given gigantic expansion by the rainforest climate. It was hard to see most of the houses, draped as they were with ivies, creepers and lianas. Huge trees rose, not only in gardens but through entire dwellings. It was hard not to see the secondary jungle as a living thing ruthlessly reinvading the land that humanity could no longer defend.

Awe-inspiring though this huge destruction was, it shrank to insignificance beside the utter devastation of the north-eastern suburbs. Here everything was black instead of green. Starkly, gauntly dead instead of threateningly fecund. Even after all these years – and after all that nature had dealt it, cars stuck up out of the cinder-black ground, half buried, frozen in place. All of them battered and rusting, many of them burst open like obscene flowers where their petrol tanks had exploded. Buses, trucks, lorries, pantechnicons stuck up like toys thrown on to an ash heap. Richard's eyes swept over the devastation almost unbelievingly. A black-throated pit appeared, seemingly leading halfway to the centre of the earth; big enough to make him wonder if this was an offspring of the volcano itself.

'That must be where the avgas tanks went up,' said Max, who had read the report prepared for the government in the months after the disaster, when the international community had been throwing money, aid and volunteers at the place. Before it became obvious that almost nothing was getting past ex-president Liye Banda's venal clique, who were growing fat while the dwindling survivors up-country were simply wasting away. And there was precious little that could be done in any case, especially in the face of the marauding Interahamwe, the Lord's Resistance Army and the Army of Christ the Infant. Before they all pulled out again and left Benin La Bas well alone. 'The explosion took out all the airport buildings and everything on the apron, so it says in the report.'

Richard just shook his head, beyond speech. He glanced at Robin. Her grey eyes were wide and full of tears. The state of the once-great city emphasized the point she had been making about the country's infrastructure more powerfully than any words ever could have done.

'Damn,' said Max. 'I'd hoped we could land on the runway at the airport or – at the worst – on the lava itself. The government report said the shield was flat, like the flows in Hawaii.' He swung round, glaring at the experts cowering down the length of the cabin behind him. The two nearest glanced up guiltily. But in fact they were looking at the Japanese map and the GPS handset and were unlikely to have been the ones advising Max on the state of the lava flow.

'You'll never find a place to land there,' said Robin. 'What was Plan B?'

'The lake,' answered Richard. 'Didn't you see the floats on the undercarriage? The plan is to land on Lac Dudo.'

But Lac Dudo never appeared. The Kamov followed the pitted path of the lava flow until one of Max's experts – the one with the map – called out and the helicopter swung westward. They all craned to see the surface of the volcanic lake. But there was nothing to see. The broccoli heads of the virgin rainforest opened out into a huge prairie of lighter green, but there was no water.

'This is the place, Mr Asov,' called the expert with the GPS, already nervous at having got the blame for the lava flow's unexpected condition. 'We are immediately above the position that the Japanese map makers recorded.'

'But there is no lake here!' snarled Max.

'It looks like a big meadow,' said Felix. 'Put us down here and we can explore,' he called through to the pilot. The chopper began to settle.

Richard looked out, his mind racing. 'This is weird, even for Benin La Bas,' he observed to Robin. 'One minute there's a black lake, the next there's a big meadow. What on earth is going on?'

Robin knew the river best, so she understood what they were looking at first. 'Stop!' she called to the pilot. 'Take us up again! Max, for God's sake tell him before it's too late! That isn't grass – it's water hyacinth!'

The pilot responded to her call, and under the extra pressure of the rotor's downdraught, the apparently solid prairie rippled and began to heave.

'Thank you, Robin,' said Max soberly. 'I believe you have saved us all from an unexpected swim and a very long walk indeed!'

Richard and Robin exchanged meaningful glances. They both knew that if the Kamov had tried to land on the deceptive-looking meadow it would almost certainly have broken through the mat of vegetation and sunk. And anyone trying to find the surface once they were below the water hyacinth would have been doomed to drown as though trapped beneath a solid layer of ice.

Chopper

'Right!' said Max. 'Now that we have found the lake, let us explore a little further. I am not about to let some floating weeds stand between me and two trillion dollars' worth of coltan!'

'Good idea!' added Felix. 'But where shall we start? I doubt we have enough fuel left in the chopper to simply circle round and round . . .'

'Excuse me, Mr Asov,' hazarded the expert with the map a little nervously. 'The area in which the Yakimoto Freshwater Pearl Company constructed Doctor Koizumi's oyster-harvesting facility is marked most precisely on this map. Apparently there was a relatively large section cleared of jungle there.'

'Excellent!' boomed Max. 'Go and give the pilot the coordinates. Once I get a toehold,' Max continued, 'then I'm in. I'll bomb, burn or poison that floating garbage and get at the lake bed no matter what.'

'It might be worth taking it carefully to begin with,' warned Robin. 'If you leave the oysters alive, then you could have a second income stream in pearls.'

'Huh,' grunted Max. 'We'll have to see whether they're worth more mounted or strung – or crushed to get at the coltan dust within them!'

Felix reached down for the briefcase that was standing beside his right ankle. It went on to the table and opened to reveal, among other things, a slim bottle of Stolichnaya *Elit* vodka and four shot glasses, one inside the other. 'Let us leave such thoughts to the future and drink to our continued success,' he suggested, handing shot glasses over to Max and Robin.

Robin put her glass upside down on the table with a disapproving *snap* and glanced at her teetotal husband. But his mind was elsewhere. Richard was not used to following along in someone else's plans. He was a natural leader. She wondered what he was thinking up now. Max held his glass out as Felix unscrewed the top of the bottle. 'Success!' he said. 'A good toast!'

'Success!' toasted Felix cheerfully. Both Russians tossed the spirit back, then repeated the procedure and seemed to become a little more expansive and relaxed at once. They leaned back. Loosened their seat belts. 'It will be good to see what is left of Doctor Koizumi's facility in any case,' rumbled Max. 'It would make a satisfactory base for our own people.'

'There won't be much there, surely,' said Robin. 'Not after what happened. I mean, I'm a bit sketchy on the history of the place but I know they were all slaughtered. Bodies were brought back but no one ever really sorted out who was who. They were chopped to pieces by those terrible matchet things the men all seem to carry here. In any case, the buildings were all destroyed. Apparently there was some woman there who was never found.'

'Doctor Mizuki Yukawa,' confirmed Max, who had clearly read more than just the report of Cite La Bas's destruction. Not for the first time, Robin made a mental note never to underestimate Max's professionalism and willingness to do the basic groundwork. He might be a bullying sexist bastard who'd disowned his daughter Anastasia while bed-hopping through a series of mistresses young enough to be her sister. He might show a weakness for vodka and occasionally become dangerously unpredictable as a result. But he had built a massive company. And he hadn't just done that by luck, bribery, strong-arm tactics and buying up massively undervalued ex-nationalized facilities in the months after the collapse of the communist system. He was nobody's fool. He did the groundwork. And the fact that he knew about the deaths of the Japanese was a case in point.

'She's out there somewhere, whatever's left of her,' Max continued, his tone darkening. He gestured with his left hand, striking the knuckles against the window as he tried to encompass the entire rainforest on Karisoke's southern slope. 'Unless the people who killed the others took her with them.'

'If they did, then she's probably somewhere nearby,' said Robin sadly. 'They won't have taken her anywhere very far, I'd have thought.'

'And, like Shakespeare's Richard III, they *won't have kept her long*,' added Richard grimly. 'Whoever they actually were.'

'Apparently the best guess was that it was an early manifestation of the Army of Christ the Infant,' continued Max. 'Pre-Moses Nlong days. Before they hit the headlines like Joseph Kony and the Lord's Resistance Army. They say the Army of Christ has been coming and going through here for decades in one guise or another, slaughtering villagers and animals, taking boys into their fighting units and making women and girls their sex slaves.'

'If they caught her they'd have raped her, killed her and eaten her,' said Robin matter-of-factly. 'As Richard says, they won't have taken her far. And they won't have wasted time and food keeping her alive unless they thought she was worth a good solid ransom. But if they were going to ransom anyone, logic dictates that it would probably have been whoever was in charge.'

'Doctor Koizumi,' nodded Max. 'They never found much of him either – certainly not his head.'

'Nice!' muttered Felix ironically. He threw back another shot of vodka. 'More chopper work – with those matchets. Very nice.'

There was another short silence. Both Richard and Robin felt the weight of the knowledge they all shared but nobody was willing to discuss at the moment. Max's estranged daughter Anastasia had been one of those attacked by Moses Nlong and his Army of Christ the Infant – and had been miraculously lucky to have survived the capture and slaughter visited on her friends. It had been a narrow escape, with a hair-raising ride down the great river in a tiny motor boat. Not to mention the equally spine-tingling return with Richard, Robin and an army bent on the rescue of the living and revenge for the dead. Anastasia was at the front of it all, armed to the teeth – ready, willing and able to execute her personal vengeance on Moses Nlong, the brutal army's cannibalistic leader, only to see Odem, his right hand man, vanish into the jungle. But Max never talked about Anastasia, whom he had disowned and disinherited in the most brutally public manner possible the better part of ten years ago. So the silence lay there between them, like a dead thing on the table. Max threw back another shot of vodka.

'You'll want to be up on that,' observed Richard grimly, breaking the tension at last. His narrowed eyes swept over both Max and Felix. 'You'll need to know pretty precisely what madmen are marauding around here nowadays. Moses Nlong may be dead but the Army of Christ is still out there somewhere. Like the situation with Kony and the LRA. Whether he's dead or not, they still seem to be going, and not too far south of here either, come to that.'

Robin nodded to herself. So that was what Richard was thinking about as his bright blue gaze had been quartering the jungle all around them. And wisely so. Until the area could be secured against the anarchic militias that had infested the place for the last forty years or so, there was absolutely no point in investing anything up here – no matter how great the promised prize. And there were only two ways in which absolute security could be guaranteed: either the country itself needed a settled government that was able to guarantee security throughout its dominions, or Max was going to have to come up with an army of his own capable of outgunning the Army of Christ and whoever else came cruising by, drawn to Max's promised trillions like sharks drawn to blood.

'And this is the kind of place they come to, to regroup if for no other reason,' emphasized Robin, running with Richard's idea as though she had been able to read his mind. 'Not that there's much for anyone up here, heaven knows! Unless they can get across the border into Congo Libre or one of the other neighbouring states who don't mind supplying arms and expertise in the hope of fomenting a little trouble along the border. They can regroup and rearm there, then come back and start all over again here. But even so, unless they have a very powerful agenda indeed, it's hard to see that there's anything worthwhile for anyone in this godforsaken place.'

'Except for us,' exulted Max, brightening up suddenly, unexpectedly. And, given Richard and Robin's concerns, not a little disturbingly. 'Except for us! For us there is *two trillion, five hundred billion US dollars*!'

'We're there, Mr Asov,' called the map man from the cockpit.

'Right over Doctor Koizumi's facility. At least, where it's marked on the map. But I'm afraid I can't see any buildings or anything . . .'

'Right,' said Max. 'Tell the pilot to take us down. But do it carefully!'

Felix screwed the top back on the vodka bottle and replaced it in his briefcase, much to Robin's relief. Richard strained to see out of the window, hoping for a clear view of whatever lay immediately beneath them, wondering what the odds against finding a hostile army hiding in the undergrowth were.

Robin looked further away as the helicopter settled below the level of the upper canopy. The great branches reached out, laden with broad green leaves, festooned with pendant mosses, even at this upper level, bound with massive ropes of creeper and liana. Below them were cavernous, shadowy spaces. Then the lower, secondary canopy – thinner, robbed of light by the huge upper leaves, seemingly strangled from below by the creepers, the parasitic orchids and all the other plant life fighting desperately for a share of the sun and the rain, feeding off each other like vegetable vampires.

As the Kamov obediently settled further, Richard's gaze fastened on the huge grey ferns of the jungle floor which came piling out into the sunlight like breaking waves. Immediately in front of them, a wall of reeds and rushes as wide as a highway and as tall as a bungalow defined the edge of the lake. The reeds reached towards the belly of the helicopter, and Richard frowned with concentration, seeking clearer ground beside them. But there was nothing.

Where Max had no doubt imagined an open area of grass the size of a football pitch conveniently placed for the Kamov to land safely, there was instead a stand of bamboo the size of Wembley Stadium. Many of the bamboo tops were covered with feathery leaves, but by far the majority of them were tipped with fearsome points, like spears. And the bamboo stood as tall as the lakeside reeds – at least three metres. There was no sign at all that any human had ever had the temerity to come here. Dr Koizumi and his facility might be as much of a fairy tale as the monsters Richard had brought to mind when he likened the place to *Jurassic Park*.

'You'll never get down here,' said Richard grimly. 'This place is locked tight shut against any kind of aircraft. The only way in is on foot, Max.'

'You're right,' admitted Max. 'I just hate admitting defeat.' His fist crashed on to the tabletop. 'Take us up again,' he called to the pilot.

'At least, now that we're here, we can try to follow the tributary stream to the main river,' said Richard. 'Anyone coming in on foot may well want to follow it upstream – as a guide, at least. It'll be as well to get a good idea what the terrain actually looks like.'

As the helicopter rose back into the sky above the treetops and turned away towards the distant River Gir, the largest of the ferns parted and a man dressed in army camouflage cargo pants and a green vest stepped out. He wore a green beret and wraparound sunglasses with mirrored lenses. He carried a Desert Eagle in a green webbing holster on his right hip. On his left he carried a matchet with a stainless steel blade more than a metre long. In his high-laced right boot he carried a black-bladed Russian military Stalker knife. Around his chest he wore a webbing bandolier carrying half-a-dozen double clips of five point forty-five ammunition for the brand-new AK-74M with GP-30 forty millimetre grenade launcher that he cradled like a baby in his muscular arms.

Silently, he watched as the helicopter filled the increasingly narrow band of sky between the treetops that stood astride the river as it followed the flow of black water away. Then he moved his head infinitesimally, and started moving noiselessly forward into the stand of bamboo. At once he was surrounded by the better part of fifty soldiers, varying in age from ten to forty, all as well armed as he was, the largest and strongest of whom fell in a step or two ahead of him, using their massive matchets with practised ease to clear a path through the vegetation, following the vanishing chopper down the black stream from the black lake towards the distant River Gir.

Edge

As the Kamov followed the river course, Robin's attention was torn. It was impossible to see much of the dam system immediately below, but it was all too easy to see the overhanging greenery of the canopy on either side. Far more interesting was observing Richard as he worked his magic on Max and Felix.

Even as Richard leaned forward, Felix reached down for his briefcase once more. This time, as well as the vodka bottle, he pulled out a slim laptop. He opened it and turned it so that the screen covered the lower half of the window. He tapped a couple of buttons and it lit up, showing video feed from the camera mounted under the Kamov's nose, but Robin still looked out of the window. If she looked up, she could see the leaves of the canopy fluttering in the wind of their passage. If she looked down she could see their roots standing out like huge knotted talons as they gripped the steep banks on either side of the precipitous young river beyond the dam system. Below them, much reduced since its overpowering spate, raced the strange dark tumble of the black water rushing downwards so eagerly to join the stately flow of the distant River Gir. But, as far as she could make out, the jungle itself was deserted. Apart from the plant life, it was dead.

After a moment, Robin's attention switched back to Richard. Of course, he would be looking for an edge, she thought. The owners of Heritage Mariner might be apparent spectators here, but Richard never did anything without an ulterior motive and he was as aware as his associates that there was a fabulous fortune to be made. And Heritage Mariner could well do with a share of it.

On one level, the fact that the Russians had returned to Felix's vodka bottle might make Richard hope to get past their defences, Robin calculated wryly. But on another, they just became more suspicious and argumentative the more they drank. 'You've just seen for yourselves,' Richard was saying. 'Getting upriver is hard.' He gestured at the laptop screen, which was showing a waterfall that looked to be taller than the hundred-metre trees surrounding it, tumbling beneath the natural bridge of a fallen tree into a lake that was as thick with water hyacinth as Lac Dudo itself had been. 'Even something like that will take a good deal of time and effort to climb. And I think you'll find there are more – and bigger – waterfalls between here and the main river. Cataracts and rapids too, I shouldn't wonder.'

'Point taken,' allowed Max. 'We can go through the video record in more detail when we get back to base. Have a really good look at it. Digitally enhanced. Make proper use of some of these experts I ferried up here at such expense. But on the other hand, if it doesn't look too difficult down below us now, we can still come upriver anyway. Two-pronged attack. Once we get to the lake we can clear that jungle rubbish away, set up camp and really get to work.'

'There's a time limit,' insisted Felix. 'Word of this is bound to get out, and then . . .'

'The Chinese,' said Richard. 'Yes. I'd worked that out too. Chinese suppliers to Japanese and Korean manufacturers who can't live without tantalum processors for their laptops, mobile phones and flat screens – let alone the new markets for electric cars and so forth.'

'It's Sony, Toyota, Cannon, Honda, Mitsubishi, Sumitomo, NTT, KDDI and all the others from Kagoshimo to Sopporo,' Robin emphasized forcefully. She had read the same reports. 'But the Japanese manufacturers are supplied by Chinese mining companies such as Beijing Jinshan, Dongguan Benyuan and Fuyang Zhongyu to start with just a few of the legitimate ones with interests in the areas closest to this.'

'Right,' said Richard at his most forceful. 'Everything from Anhul Beijing Chenzhou Developments to Xin Yingkou Zenjiang by way of Han Wuhan Extraction! At the last count our commercial intelligence department at London Centre listed more than fifty Chinese companies applying to set up mining concessions in nearby countries within easy reach of Benin La Bas – just to the north or the south. The only reason

they're not here yet is that the place has been too dangerous
– far too hostile to strangers under the last couple of govern-
ments anyhow – and apparently too worthless up till now. We
are the only people who know about Lac Dudo – so far. Once
they hear about this two point five trillion dollar honey pot,
will they ever come swarming round!'

'But of course we have an edge,' purred Robin.

'How do you reckon that?' asked Max morosely, his eyes
fixed on the laptop screen, no doubt thinking about the tantalum
processors that made the microelectronic circuitry work as he
watched the picture showing all too clearly another vertiginous
waterfall that would be hell on earth to climb.

'We already know where the deposits are located,' answered
Richard matter-of-factly. 'You're already in tight with the
president. And so are we.'

'*And* we're in tight with the leader of the opposition,'
concluded Robin. 'However the upcoming elections go,
someone will have their foot in the door. And,' she added
again, leaning forward, 'the fact that the leader of the opposition was damn near killed by the Army of Christ the Infant
means that even during the hurly burly of an election campaign,
the best of the country's special forces will be on their way
up here any day now on a mission to make the jungle safe.'

Richard couldn't resist a *Blues Brothers* joke. '*A mission
from God*, even if it is against the *Army of Christ*,' he said.

'And, with luck,' added Felix thoughtfully, 'I'll be able to
sell the president a couple of my Zubr hovercraft to get his
troops upriver at top speed.'

'Which would, if we time things right,' said Richard,
lowering his voice as though fearful of being overheard in his
shocking deviousness, 'liberate the Zubrs to take you on upriver
as far as the first major waterfall and give you a good head-
start if you want to follow the river route in.'

'A win-win situation,' mused Max. 'I like this!' He reached
down on to the floor by his foot and produced a briefcase
identical to Felix's, which turned out to contain an identical
bottle of Stolichnaya *Elit*. 'Now that's the kind of edge I
approve of!'

Talk

The president's office, inherited from the more grandiose days of the kleptocratic President Liye Banda, was based on the White House Oval Office of the Bush administration, rather than the more conservative Obama makeover. Even after all the years of General – later President – Julius Chaka's dominance, little had changed. Richard might have been waiting in that exclusively privileged environment to be speaking with the present occupant of the White House – except that instead of a Rose Garden outside the French windows there was now a precinct made slightly disturbing by the inverted red claws of hundreds of huge Flame Lilies. It was a national flower Benin La Bas shared with the nearby Democratic Republic of the Congo. But it still looked like the blood-covered talons of recently feeding vultures to him.

'I haven't much time to talk, Richard,' warned President Chaka as he strode in from his private quarters and closed the door decidedly on the anxious countenance of his chief of staff. 'I'm due at an election rally in forty-five minutes.'

'I'm aware of that, Mr President,' countered Richard calculatedly. 'But I know you plan a dramatic entrance by the helicopter waiting in the garden and it's only a ten-minute flight from here to the National Stadium.'

Julius Chaka threw up his hands. 'Touché. Now what can I do for you?'

'It's important, Mr President, or we wouldn't be disturbing you. Robin is just coming with something I think you should see as a matter of urgency. It's on a laptop and she's just having it all checked by your security people. I came on ahead to explain the background as I know you're pressed for time.'

'Very well.' President Chaka leaned back against the presidential desk.

'You are aware that we went up to Lac Dudo yesterday?'

'Of course. Not altogether successfully, I understand.'

'Not in terms of exploring the area in any detail, no sir. But we brought back a good deal of information that will be of use to us in preparing our negotiations with your ministerial team when the time comes.'

'Hmmm,' purred President Chaka.

'We took video footage of everything the Kamov flew over.'

At this point Robin entered, clutching the laptop that had shared Max's briefcase with the vodka bottle.

'If you would just take a look at this, Mr President, I believe our point will become self-evident,' said Richard.

Robin placed the laptop on the desktop and opened it. The screen came alive at once with the picture that the Kamov's camera took of Lac Dudo just at the instant it turned and headed down the river towards the Gir. As the pilot dipped the chopper's nose to follow the valley down past Dr Koizumi's dam system towards the first of the waterfalls, the camera caught a flash of what was happening behind the fuselage. Richard's long finger pointed to the centre of the screen where, frame by frame in slow motion, the ferns parted and a figure stepped out. Richard pressed zoom until it filled the screen in close-up from beret to belt buckle.

'Who is this man?' demanded the president.

'You may need to check with the leader of the opposition,' said Robin. 'Celine's the one who got the closest look at him the last time the Army of Christ the Infant invaded Benin La Bas, but I think that's Colonel Odem, the man who replaced Moses Nlong as their leader after their last incursion into Benin La Bas. But there's more . . .'

President Chaka held up his hand, went behind the desk and sat at his own computer. He engaged Skype and contacted the leader of the opposition. She answered on her mobile, her face betraying surprise that the president should be calling her up instead of heading to the rally she was clearly at herself. 'I want to talk to you as my daughter for a moment,' said Chaka. 'Not as the leader of the opposition and my political opponent.'

'Of course, Father,' answered Celine guardedly.

'Robin Mariner is just about to send you a picture. Can you identify it?'

Chaka looked up and Robin sent the picture from her laptop.

Celine gasped. 'That's him!' she said. 'That's Odem! When was this picture taken? Where is he?'

'We'll talk after the rally,' decided the president. 'And we'll talk as father and daughter, not as political opponents.'

'As you wish,' she answered, without hesitation this time.

They broke contact. Chaka looked down for a moment. His campaign chief came in without knocking. 'Time's getting tight, Mr President,' he said in his gentle Harvard accent. 'Everyone's waiting.'

Chaka stood up; he seemed to expand in size and stature. Within a second he had moved from concerned parent to magisterial president. Once again, the power of his personality filled the room like a magnesium flare.

'You said you had more to show me,' he snapped at Richard, gesturing for the campaign chief to open the French windows.

'Yes, Mr President,' answered Richard.

'Come aboard my helicopter, both of you. You have ten more minutes to brief me further.'

The Mariners joined Chaka and his campaign chief in the executive section of the presidential chopper, whose interior was laid out like the Bashnev/Sevmash Kamov although it was a Chinese Harbin equivalent of the EC175 Eurocopter. Richard sat beside the president next to the window, so he would get the first bullet if there were any snipers about. Robin sat opposite him, looking down at the two government ministers on the ground below whose places they had usurped and whose undying hatred they had earned in so doing. *I hope Celine wins the election,* she thought as her downward gaze met their upward enmity. *If those two stay in office then Heritage Mariner is simply dead in the water.*

'The next point is this, Mr President,' Richard was explaining. 'It's a communication from my commercial intelligence people at London Centre. A photograph, in fact, snapped on a digital phone. It was forwarded to me under our highest company security because there is a legitimate business concern roused by the meeting of these two men in the centre of the picture. It is filed under our Company Most Secret.' He leaned forward, making sure the campaign chief saw nothing of the picture on the screen. 'Are the men in the picture familiar to you?' he asked.

'These two are,' answered the president unhappily. 'This one is Bala Ngama, whom I recently replaced as the minister of the outer delta and removed from my government altogether. This other is Gabriel Fola, the prime minister of Congo Libre, our nearest neighbour inland.'

'The gentleman whose influence begins where yours ends, sir,' Richard emphasized. 'On the north-eastern slope of Karisoke.' He paused for a moment, making sure his point had soaked in. 'And have you any idea about the third man?' he asked.

'No,' answered President Chaka. 'Who is he?'

Richard looked pointedly across at the campaign chief. President Chaka frowned, then gave a brief nod. 'Go and check on the security squad,' he ordered. 'I want things smooth when we land.'

Richard waited until the Harvard man was well away before he continued, in little more than a whisper, 'He is Chen Shufu, Doctor Chen, chairman of Han Wuhan Extraction, the most cut-throat and ruthless of the one hundred and fifty Chinese mining companies currently working in Africa – fifty of whom, I may say, are working within a five hundred kilometre radius of Lac Dudo. They may not have permission to work on your land, sir, but as Odem and his army prove, there's no one there to stop them crossing your borders at will, probably from Congo Libre.

'It's an open secret that Han Wuhan are the people behind the majority of the conflict mineral extraction in Rwanda and the Democratic Republic of Congo during the last few years. They've admitted they have contacts with both the FDLR – Rwanda's army – and the FARDC, the Congo equivalent. Both have been accused of participating in this bloody business – even after the Dodd-Frank legislation in the US which banned the trading of conflict minerals in the United States – but which of course doesn't apply to Han Wuhan directly. And they have, so it is believed, been funding the Lord's Resistance Army and several other unregulated militias who have been involved in supplying this kind of thing.' He leaned forward even more forcefully. 'Doctor Chen is up to his armpits in conflict minerals. Conflict diamonds. Anything, profitable, in fact. No matter where it comes from or no matter how it was obtained!'

Robin leaned forward too. 'I know this is something that would come from Richard under normal circumstances,' she said quietly. 'But they don't call him *Dr No* like in James Bond. They call him *Dr Yao*, which is Mandarin for *Yes*. Yes to *anything*, no matter *what* . . .'

'You were quite right to bring this to my attention,' said President Chaka, pulling himself erect and consulting his watch once more. 'This Doctor Chen sounds like an extremely dangerous proposition. But I'm not certain it was worth interrupting my preparations for the rally.'

'I agree, Mr President. And if that was all I would have brought it to the attention of Colonel Kebila, your chief of security and, via him, to Mr Ngama's replacement as minister of the outer delta. But there is more.' Richard took a deep breath, then continued. 'If we zoom into the background of this picture as we did to the picture of Lac Dudo . . . There. You see? A fourth man, trying very hard to remain in the shadows. And I'm sure you can recognize him, now.'

'Odem,' said President Chaka. 'It's Colonel Odem. Once again.'

The Kivu Gambit

Richard was woken the next morning by the only piece of communications equipment in the Granville Royal Lodge hotel's Nelson Mandela suite which did not require tantalum processors. He put the handset of his old-fashioned bedside phone to his ear after the third ring. 'Mariner?' he said sleepily.

'This is Andre Wanago, Captain Mariner,' said the precise voice of the general manager. 'I have Colonel Laurent Kebila here and he wonders if you could spare a moment to talk to him. The matter is as urgent, apparently, as that with which you disturbed the president's plans last evening.'

Richard sat up, frowning thoughtfully. Benin La Bas's chief of security was clearly on his best behaviour. In the past he had simply come banging on the suite's main door with a squad of soldiers at his back. They had first met like that in the bad old days, when Liye Banda had been president, Celine Chaka had been a political prisoner in the regime's torture chambers and her father had been the general commanding an irregular army in the delta, seemingly little more politically powerful than Odem's Army of Christ the Infant. It was in Granville Harbour's central police station, shortly after Kebila had arrested him, that Richard first met Celine – in the days before her father took over the country and it emerged that young Captain Kebila had been the only reason she had survived her arrest and interrogation. The only reason they had both survived.

Robin stirred sleepily. 'Who is it, Richard?'

'Kebila,' he answered.

She sat up at once, pulling the duvet over her pink-tipped chest like an outraged Victorian virgin. And putting one hand to her golden curls to assess whether they were fit to be seen. *'Here?'* She looked around, half-expecting the colonel to be standing at the bedroom door.

'Downstairs,' he reassured her with a chuckle. 'He wants a chat.'

'Tell him we'll be five minutes,' she said, flinging the duvet aside and returning to type as she headed for the bathroom. Richard forbore to point out that she hadn't been invited.

Fifteen minutes later the three of them were seated at an exclusive little table in the corner of a deserted coffee lounge overlooking the hotel's main swimming pool, which was designed to resemble a lake surrounded by jungle. Richard, having just come back from Lac Dudo, was struck by how much it did *not* look like a real lake surrounded by actual virgin jungle.

It was the lake, in fact, which Kebila had come to talk to him about. The colonel's slim, muscular frame was clad in an immaculate uniform identical in cut and perfection to General Chaka's, differing from his only in the matter of pips and badges of rank. Laurent Kebila and his cousin, Naval Commander Caleb Maina, always reminded Robin vaguely but excitingly of Denzel Washington. Younger and a little leaner, perhaps. One clean-shaven and one with a pencil moustache. Punctilious to a fault, he rose as they arrived and gave them a precise salute. Then he sat silently as coffee was left on the table beside his uniform cap and swagger stick before he started to talk business.

'I have no doubt you have as clear an idea of the opposition's likely plan as I do myself,' Kebila began, his clipped Sandhurst accent coloured ever so slightly by the rhythms and intonations of his native West African Matadi dialect – like Igala, Edekiri and Itsekiri, a subspecies of the Yoruba spoken so generally here. The emphasis he gave to the word 'opposition' made it clear he meant Congo Libre rather than Celine Chaka. 'It is, so to speak, a variant of the Kivu Gambit, if I may call it that.' He glanced across at Richard and Robin. 'The way that Rwanda, in the fairly recent past, fomented restlessness in the Kivu region of the DRC immediately across their border.'

'The point being,' emphasized Richard, putting down his coffee cup and reaching for the cafetière, 'that Kivu is a major source of diamonds and coltan, which Rwanda did not have. The trouble in Kivu allowed them to get across the border and gain access without actually invading. It was – still is, to a certain extent – the core of diplomatic problems not only between Rwanda and the DRC but also between Rwanda and the rest of the diplomatic world. It very nearly became a pariah state. No outside contact except with some selected neighbours. No World Bank support. No IMF. Scarcely even any Oxfam, Save the Children or Medecin Sans Frontieres. No tourism. No inward investment. Even the Chinese are unlikely to go in there.'

'Only one company currently on the record,' emphasized Kebila. 'Han Wuhan, in fact. As opposed to forty in the DRC. The same number in Nigeria. And now we have a good number beating a path to President Chaka's door.'

'As many as will beat a path to the door of President *Celine* Chaka after the elections,' chimed in Robin.

Kebila looked at her, his eyebrows raised. One finger stroked his moustache thoughtfully – a habitual gesture like Richard's tendency to stroke the scar on his cheekbone when he was thinking. 'Quite so,' he said after a moment. Then he switched his attention more exclusively to Richard. 'I have seen the picture of Ngama with Fola, Chen and Odem. How easy it would be,' he persisted gently, 'for our own neighbours in Congo Libre on the far side of Mount Karisoke, where there is no black lake full of coltan but a great deal of poverty, to send in someone like Colonel Odem with his Army of Christ to secure the area around Lac Dudo. Establish a bridgehead, so to speak. Secure a safe route over the mountain and across the border, such as might permit the illegal but unstoppable transport of coltan by Han Wuhan out of Benin La Bas.'

'But not *their* troops,' said Robin, understanding his point at once. 'The Army of Christ, working under their orders, equipped and supplied by them.'

'A well-established terrorist army whose roots are already deep in Benin La Bas,' agreed Colonel Kebila gently. 'As you say, with material and logistical support from over the border. And with advisors from Han Wuhan Extractions, of course. And the connivance of someone who knows the ground and the ropes, so to speak. An ex-government minister, say. Ex-Minister of the Outer Delta, Bala Ngama, perhaps.' Kebila leaned forward and refreshed his coffee cup with a steady hand, then lifted it, sat back and continued. 'He still has contacts in the government – no doubt he will have heard about Max's discovery. A fortune for Gabriel Fola and all his tribe, family and his government – which are, of course, the same thing. And nothing for ours – whether it be Julius or Celine Chaka in the president's palace. Nothing to be passed on to the people of Benin La Bas in the form of infrastructure, medical and educational facilities, the rebuilding of our social and financial economy.'

Richard nodded, his mind fixed on the beginning of Colonel Kebila's speech. It was as he had already calculated it. One glance at the familiar faces in the secret photograph had been enough for him. 'But no pariah status for Gabriel Fola and his nation,' he said. 'A perfect scapegoat instead – just another marauding militia out of control and behaving as they want. No international condemnation. Just two and a half trillion dollars' worth of coltan there for the taking.'

'Unless we can stop it,' said Kebila.

'*We . . .*' said Richard, his voice alive with speculation.

'Consider the vital elements of our own version of the Kivu Gambit.' Kebila ticked them off on his fingers as he enumerated them. 'A willing government happy to take a few chances. A well-equipped force led by men who know the territory; who will stop at nothing to achieve their mission and overcome their enemies.' His eyes crinkled with the smallest of smiles and the edge of his clipped moustache lifted infinitesimally. 'A ruthless business enterprise led by men of questionable reputation who are happy to cut corners – and are not averse to a little backstabbing.'

'And?' said Richard, who suspected that he was just about to be compared with ex-minister Ngama somehow – as Bashnev/Sevmash had just been compared with Han Wuhan; Kebila and his men with Odem and his, and the Chakas with President Fola.

'And a *wild card*,' concluded Kebila. 'An ace in the hole that we cannot quite fathom as yet. Whose involvement may mean nothing. Or everything.'

'Is there,' interrupted Robin, 'a *Mrs* Ngama anywhere in this parallel?'

Kebila laughed. It was a surprisingly pleasant sound. 'The

ex-minister is famous for his taste in beautiful women,' he said. 'But the last I heard, he was still . . . ah . . . *tasting*. So no, there is no Mrs Ngama. However, let us not let my love of rhetoric unbalance the drift of my argument. Your involvement could well be as crucial as your husband's. Were I to suggest that *he* might be a unique liaison between the president and Bashnev/Sevmash, then *you* – to begin with – could perform exactly the same service between Bashnev/Sevmash and the leader of the opposition.'

'So it's a race for the coltan,' said Richard, at his most forthright. 'Chaka – father and daughter – will sanction an expeditionary force to go upriver as fast as possible. It will be led by you and its main objective will be to find and stop Odem. Any inconvenient red tape will be cut in order to allow Bashnev/Sevmash to assay and annexe the lake – on a commercial basis, while you leave enough men to handle the security.'

'And, frankly, to keep an eye on your Russian colleagues, who are to be given the green light now because they are the only opposition to Han Wuhan that we have to hand,' added Kebila smoothly. 'There will be certain carefully negotiated provisos with regard to long-term extraction rights, of course. Perhaps, at a later date, an open bidding process . . .'

'That goes without saying,' said Richard, cutting to the chase. 'But in the long term, we're all dead, as John Maynard Keynes observed. In the *short term*, Chaka wants to put Bashnev/Sevmash in there before Han Wuhan can get a foothold, with you to keep an eye on their security and their behaviour. Longer term to be negotiated as and when, after an increasingly hard-to-call election. And you want Robin and me to be liaison on the ground, oiling the wheels between all concerned – aware that there might well be unexpected additions to the situation that will have to be handled – like I said – *as and when*.'

'A very precise summation,' nodded Kebila. 'Are you game?'

Richard exchanged glances with Robin. She nodded infinitesimally.

'Right,' said Richard. 'You're on. And we're in.'

Patience

Ten minutes later, Richard was hammering on the door of Max Asov's presidential suite. Robin and he had discussed the best way forward as they rode up in the lift. Courtesy really demanded that they phone Max and Felix to arrange a meeting rather than banging on their doors, but it was by no means first thing and Richard was certain that news as good as this warranted immediate action. So they emerged from the lift, swept past the security guards and took a door each.

The door half opened and Max's bleary-eyed face appeared on Richard's third knock. 'Richard! Only you . . .' Even as Max reluctantly answered Richard's knock, Robin, a little way down the corridor, started pounding on Felix's door.

'Max. We have to talk . . .' snapped Richard.

'Who is it, Max?' came the voice of Max's current companion – the model Tatiana Kolina – from the bedroom. At least Tatiana seemed a little more mature than usual. Most of Max's girls would make better companions for his daughter Anastasia. Some of them, indeed, were even younger than Anastasia.

'It's just Richard, Tatiana,' Max called back, without looking round.

'What is so important, Richard, that you must disturb us so early?'

'We're off!'

'Off? Who's off?' demanded Max. 'Where to? Richard! What are you talking about?'

'We are! Bashnev/Sevmash and the whole of your team. Off upriver. As fast as you like, as far as you want; but back to the lake at least. With an escort of soldiers armed to the teeth, and carte blanche from the president and the leader of the opposition.'

Max's eyes narrowed. His face lost that sleepy look and became calculating. 'Carte blanche?'

'For anyone and anything you need. Any provision or permission the country can give. No limits. Just get up the river and take hold of the Lac Dudo on behalf of your company and the Benin La Bas government while an elite force sorts out your security and makes sure your people are safe.'

Max stood gaping as his brain clearly tried to calculate the full implications of the sudden change in President Chaka's position. The door swung wide. Tatiana padded out of the bedroom behind him wearing a nightdress that was more or less transparent. She caught Richard's eye, which was not – to be fair – difficult, gave him a wicked smile and a wave and vanished again.

In the brief silence, Felix's door opened. 'Robin,' he said breathlessly. 'How nice.'

'Felix!' said Robin, gazing over Felix's shoulder into his room. 'Is that a *multigym*? How in heaven's name did they get something as big as that in there?'

'Piece by piece. Now, why have you called me away from it?'

Max caught Richard's wandering gaze again. He shrugged. 'Felix gets his morning exercise one way. I get mine another.'

'Get dressed,' said Richard again. 'We have to talk. My suite in ten minutes; I'll order breakfast. And check whether Tatiana's game for a safari.'

Twenty-four hectic hours later, Richard, Robin and Felix were down at the Granville Harbour docks in the office of ex-minister Bala Ngama's replacement Minister of the Outer Delta, Patience Aganga. Max was up at the airport bidding a regretful farewell to Tatiana who, it transpired, would not be available for a safari into the interior after all. Especially not a safari likely to involve a good deal of hardship and danger – even before Colonel Odem and his Army of Christ the Infant were added to the picture.

The minister's office was in one of the smart new government buildings that had been erected on the land which had housed the shanty towns and slums under President Liye Banda's kleptocratic regime. What had been a mess of shacks and tents constructed of clapboard, bamboo, timber pilfered from the wreckage of the nearest suburbs and ubiquitous plastic sheeting was now, under President Chaka, a carefully planned complex of manicured public gardens and municipal offices. The position of this particular office could hardly have been better from the new minister's point of view. The broad front of the building opened through a series of glass doors on to a convex curving veranda that seemed to command a view of everything for which she stood responsible.

To the left, the mouth of the River Gir opened, as wide as the Thames at Greenwich. Where the jungle used to cluster right up to the edge of the city as recently as ten years ago, now there stood river docks, bustling with river craft, some freighters, more dredgers and a pair of the neat little Fast River patrol boats. And a marina, filled with pleasure craft of all sorts, from pirogues to gin palaces, that could have been transported here directly from San Francisco or St Tropez.

Straight ahead, on the far bank, the jungle of the delta itself swept out across the bay. But where in the old days that had been an environmental disaster of oil-polluted mangroves peopled with restlessly dissatisfied freedom fighters, now it reflected order and care. The pipework looked new. Distant figures were working there, wearing a range of coloured overalls, clearly about legitimate business. Richard remembered that it had been part of ex-minister Bala Ngama's plan to repopulate the delta with a huge number of wild animals – most of them extremely dangerous. He had planned to set up a tourist park that would rival the Masai Mara and the Virunga Impenetrable Forest.

To the right, the bay itself stretched away to southern and western horizons, ringed with rigs – the farthest visible only as columns of smoke and flame. Vessels moved busily among them, and Richard found himself wishing for binoculars as he strained to see the tell-tale house colours of Heritage Mariner. Hard right, looking north-west along the city's coastline, there stood the new dock facilities. Richard's most vivid memory of the place was as a blazing ruin after the late president Liye Banda's helicopter had caused a supertanker to explode with near nuclear force. Now it was all rebuilt.

The port frontage extended right down to the office complex

itself; the minister of the outer delta's waterside office seeming
to stand as the dividing point between seagoing and river-going
vessels, between commercial craft and pleasure boats. Right
at the hub of Granville Harbour, at the heart of Benin La Bas.
But Richard, Robin and Felix were not here to admire the
view, or to appreciate the bustling industry of the anchorages
in front of them. They were here to dot a few 'i's and cross
a few 't's. Because, although they had Kebila's assurance that
he would be supplying men and material, Heritage Mariner
and Bashnev/Sevmash wanted to provide transport. For the
first stages, at any rate.

'It's the biggest hovercraft ever built,' said Richard easily to
the new minister for the outer delta, Patience Aganga, as two
of the Zubrs he was describing came into view cruising across
the harbour. 'It's just under sixty metres long and twenty-five
wide. It has a displacement of five hundred and fifty tons but
when the cushion is up it has a draft of less than one and a
half metres, though it sits just over twenty metres high. It can
carry more than one hundred tons – three T80 main battle
tanks, for instance, and it goes at nearly fifty knots – that's the
better part of sixty miles per hour. It's bristling with rocket
launchers, thirty-millimetre cannons and air missile defence
systems. Or it would be if Mr Asov and Mr Makarov were
permitted to import fully-functioning armaments. It has an
armoured command post and sealed combat stations for when
the going gets tough. That's almost as much firepower as a
naval corvette on a platform that moves as rapidly as a fast
patrol boat, with a draft only half a metre deeper than what a
patrol boat has. The Russian and Ukranian navies have them
and so do the Greeks – though they'll probably have to put
them up for sale soon – and the Chinese navy has half a dozen.
Max has been negotiating with the government to supply these
vessels. But the removal of your predecessor put things back.'

'I am aware of the basic statistics,' answered Minister Aganga,
her square face folding into the faintest frown. 'I have only
assumed ministerial responsibility relatively recently but I have
taken the opportunity to go through my predecessor's papers.'

'Pay no attention to him, Minister. It's just boy toy talk,'
said Robin, who had bonded with the dumpy, bespectacled

schoolmarm at once. She received a grin in reply. Then Patience Aganga put her serious face back on and straightened her glasses.

Richard shook his head gently, watching his ghostly reflection in the minister's panoramic office window. Then his eyes refocused. The huge hovercrafts were speeding full ahead now, skipping across the water like skimmed stones. Each one threw up a massive wall of spray to port and starboard of its long, lean, grey hull, which was almost thick enough to conceal the three great turbofans that powered each of the huge vessels. Almost high enough to cloak the tall bridge houses that sat midships like the command bridges of the corvettes that the hovercraft so nearly resembled.

'The bottom line is this, Minister,' persisted Felix. 'We can crew these vessels and use them to transport Colonel Kebila and his command as well as our own expedition up the river. They have, as you may know, already been used successfully to navigate right past the outer and inner deltas as far as the orphanage and refuge run by Mr Asov's daughter and – until quite recently – the leader of the opposition, the president's daughter, Celine.'

'Indeed,' answered Patience dryly. 'Who has not heard of the great battle that led to the defeat of the Army of Christ the Infant and its leader, the murderous Moses Nlong.'

'But, as is the nature of such things,' rejoined Richard, turning back, 'the winning of a battle is not the same as the winning of a war. And Moses Nlong might be dead, but he's been replaced.'

'By Colonel Odem.' Patience nodded. 'Yes. The president held a ministerial security briefing. Colonel Kebila addressed us in some detail. I am aware of what is at stake. And I have been directed to afford you all the help I can. You may therefore arm your huge hovercrafts. You may use your own trained crews or crews our navy will be happy to supply. Of course, you will be taking Colonel Kebila and his command aboard, but you may also expect to take anyone else you can fly in on time – or anyone else we can assign to you from our own personnel. We are to treat this as a war situation. Before it becomes a war, in fact.'

History

The space inside the Zubr *Stalingrad* was massive, echoing like a hangar. Twenty-five metres wide and fifty metres deep from the bow ramp at the front to the stern ramp at the back. The floor space was twelve hundred and fifty square metres. It stood eight metres high so the cubic capacity was just on ten thousand cubic metres. And it was still only about a third of the width of the whole vessel, because there were bulkheads on either side, behind which were the main power plants, troop compartments, crews' quarters and a range of battle-orientated life-support systems. Richard strode up and into the huge space as soon as the front ramp was fully open and resting on the concrete of the slipway at his feet. He walked purposefully across the echoing vacancy to the nearest companionway, talking statistics to Patience Aganga as she followed him. The booming of his voice echoed, like his brisk footsteps, as though this were a massive cave.

Felix trailed along behind the minister, seemingly content to let Richard, motivated by nothing other than his relentlessly boyish enthusiasm, deliver an uncalculated – but clearly effective – sales pitch. None of them was having any trouble keeping up, either physically or mentally. The minister seemed fit and fleet of foot in spite of her dumpy figure and advancing years. Nor had she seemed unduly overcome by the sheer size and power of the huge hovercraft as it had come sailing up the slipway in preparation to take them aboard for a quick tour, in spite of the fact that it was preceded by a gale of dust and spray that battered them until the vessel's bulging black skirts finished deflating, and the minister could at last let go of her own too dangerously inflated skirts and try, a little pointlessly, to restore some order to her coiffeur. Robin, wise to what was coming and careful of her clothing, dignity and hairstyle, had made her excuses at the end of the meeting and was heading back to the hotel through the bustle of Granville Harbour's seemingly permanent rush hour.

Richard ran confidently upwards now, therefore, counting off the deck levels in his head until he had no option but to cross inwards to a stairway and lift shaft midships before climbing more companionways up the centre of the bridge above the weather deck. Finally, he walked forward and found himself in a strange, almost circular command bridge, amid a bustle of officers and crewmen. He turned to Patience Aganga. 'This is where we really start our tour,' he announced. 'The heart and the head of the ship.'

Captain Caleb Maina was standing beside Captain Zhukov, commander of the huge vessel, and only the fact that he was clean-shaven really made it possible to distinguish him from his cousin, Colonel Laurent Kebila. The captains' heads, one dark and the other grey, were close together as they went through some kind of manifest on a laptop. Caleb Maina, a captain in Benin La Bas's navy, was almost fully trained now as a Zubr captain and was as capable as Zhukov of commanding the sister vessel *Volgograd* sitting on the broad slipway beside this one. He looked up as the little group arrived, threw Richard a companionable smile, then snapped to attention and saluted the minister formally. Zhukov did the same, his white walrus moustache quivering. But it was hard to tell whether his salute was aimed at the minister or at Felix.

'Now, Minister,' said Felix, taking over from Richard much more calculatedly and pointedly, 'I expect the two captains are just checking the most vital elements aboard. Especially under the present circumstances, that would be armaments, of course.'

'Hopefully you won't need them,' said Patience Aganga. 'But I'm aware of the basic armaments of the vessel and can expedite the movement of ammunition from our naval stores. As far as I can see, much of what the Zubrs carry is compatible with what we have aboard our corvettes, as I'm sure Captain Maina will confirm if he hasn't done so already. Beyond that, the president's plan is simply to expedite the movement of Colonel Kebila's men and let them sort out the problem of Colonel Odem and his Army of Christ with minimal interference, while you proceed further upriver towards Lac Dudo.'

The minister showed every sign of wanting to get back to her office, but Felix clearly thought the opportunity of building on Richard's persuasive introduction to the Zubr was too good to miss. He seemed set on turning what had been proposed as a short fact-finding mission into the full guided tour with the relentlessness of a used-car salesman. Perhaps fortunately for Patience Aganga, her Benincom cell phone began to ring even as the Russian was shepherding her off the bridge towards the high-temperature gas turbine engines, already launching into an explanation of how they powered two sets of fans, one set of which kept the skirts inflated while another provided the propulsion.

'I have to take this,' the minister said. 'It's Colonel Kebila.' She turned away, talking rapidly. Then she stopped and turned back. 'I know it's a long shot,' she said, 'but do any of you know a Russian by the name of Yagula?'

'We both do,' said Richard. 'He's the chief prosecutor of the Moscow law enforcement system – of the whole of the Russian Federation, in fact. Lavrenty Mikhailovich Yagula. What does Kebila want to know about him?'

'No,' said Patience, her dark brow furrowed. 'This one's called Ivan. Ivan Yagula. And he's not in Moscow. Or even in Russia. He's in detention at the airport for trying to smuggle a sizeable arsenal of weapons into the country.'

There was a stunned silence. Richard looked at the minister, who was looking at him. They both ended up looking at Felix.

'Ah,' said Felix, with the closest Richard had ever seen him come to a blush. 'I think I might know what's happening . . .'

In one of life's irritating little inevitabilities, Max had just left the airport and was caught in traffic on his way back to the hotel when Felix got through to him. There was no chance that he could get back and sort out matters between Ivan Yagula and the airport authorities. Though, from the tone of what Richard could hear coming out of Felix's cell phone, Max wasn't too happy about the situation either.

'I'll have to go myself,' the Russian announced to Patience

Aganga. 'I'm sorry. I'm afraid your tour of the vessel may have to wait, minister.'

'I believe I will survive the disappointment,' she answered with every evidence of relief. 'But if Captain Zhukov will supply paper I will write a letter of authority for you to take with you, and I will call the airport formally myself when I get back to my office.'

Richard, who had never seen Felix wrong-footed, let alone flustered, found his interest piqued. 'Mind if I ride along, Felix? Robin's taken my car anyway, and I'd love to know more about this chap.'

Probably because he was still a little off balance, Felix agreed and did not even seem to regret his decision until their saloon was snaking out on one of President Chaka's new highways towards the airport. 'So,' said Richard in the cheery tone he knew irritated Felix most. A tone he usually reserved for when he thought Felix had stepped over one of the lines that defined their relationship. 'Another Yagula? Father? Uncle? Cousin? Brother?'

'Son,' answered Felix grudgingly, the way he tapped the minister's envelope against his immaculately tailored knee betraying his irritation.

'Really? I never knew. Though I do realize the federal prosecutor has a reputation with the ladies that almost rivals Max's . . .'

'Son and heir. Acknowledged and legitimate. Mother dead,' said Felix.

'I never even knew Yagula had been married,' said Richard more soberly.

'One marriage, one christening, one funeral. Old story.'

'OK,' temporized Richard as he watched the inbound A380 from Paris begin to settle on to its short finals, swooping lazily towards their own destination. 'So why is he here?'

'We asked him to come,' said Felix. 'We and Lavrenty Mikhailovich.'

That gave Richard pause. His mind raced. Whole new vistas of Muscovite mendacity opened before his inner eye. 'Lavrenty Mikhailovich,' he said. 'Don't tell me. The federal prosecutor has a finger in the Bashnev/Sevmash pie!'

'You were bound to find out eventually. Or work it out, now that Ivan has arrived. I'm surprised you didn't know – you or your spies at London Centre. But what's to tell? He was born, what, twenty-seven years ago. Brought up at home until his mother died. Sent to school by his busy father. Came back to Max's in the vacations, friends with Max's two . . .'

'Anastasia and Ivan Asov, yes.'

'Indeed. Anastasia and the two Ivans. Until Ivan Asov died.'

'Drugs overdose at his eighteenth birthday party. Yes. London Centre was on top of that one.' *And more than that, too*, thought Richard – who was little short of Anastasia's godfather.

'In the meantime Ivan Yagula had transferred to the Moscow Military Commanders Training School. Then into special forces. He resigned three years ago and now runs Risk Incorporated, one of Moscow's most successful security firms. It is a subsection of our business, of course.'

'Risk Incorporated,' said Richard. 'Catchy.'

Felix just gave a curt nod and continued. 'Anastasia and Ivan Asov had gone to private school in Moscow too – The Hope School, before you ask – so the three of them continued to meet. But the parental trajectories were different. Ivan Yagula was being trained to take on a military career and parallel what his father had done in the law-enforcement world. Ivan Asov was always going to take over Bashnev/Sevmash – especially as I have no children. It was a dynastic – Russian – thing. Passing the keys of the kingdom from father to son. When he wasn't at school, Ivan Asov was being shown how to run our business and Anastasia just went along for the ride because the two of them were inseparable, as you well know. The three of them, in fact, when young Yagula came home from Commanders Training School.'

'Then Ivan Asov died.'

'And Max blamed Anastasia – she arranged the party, employed the entertainment, a band called Simian Artillery which was briefly notorious back in the early noughties. And they apparently supplied the drugs that killed Ivan. So Max became increasingly isolated from her. Disowned her in the end. Hasn't spoken to her in years, as far as I know. You probably know as much as I do. And he has been trying to replace his son and heir ever since.'

Richard thought of the number of nubile – fertile – women Max had slept with during the years of their acquaintance. 'Drug overdose. Tragic,' he said. 'So young Ivan Yagula has, what, replaced the deceased heir-apparent in the scheme of things? Until Max manages to make another baby boy?'

'To a certain extent. His father has always been . . . Something of a . . .'

'Sleeping partner?' suggested Richard innocently. 'The only kind that Max isn't trying to get pregnant?'

Felix gave a grunt of laughter. 'You could put it like that. What do the French call it? *Eminence grise?* The man behind the scenes who pulls the strings. Yes, Yagula would approve of that. He is our *grey eminence*. And his son, in this expedition, given the size and importance of the objective, will be the grey eminence's eyes.'

Ivan

I'd *have known you anywhere, Ivan Yagula*, thought Richard. And, unless your late mother stood six foot six in her stocking feet, was bald as an egg and built like a Ukranian combined harvester, then you are most definitely your father's son. After his conversation with Felix, he had half expected camouflage cargo pants, green sleeveless vest, dogtags and a range of military tattoos. But the young man huge in statue standing serenely surrounded by well-armed soldiers and outraged security staff was suited in single-breasted, elegantly tailored, mid-grey gabardine, shirted in white cotton, and boasted a gold silk tie with a Windsor knot between the pearly dots of his button-down collar. The huge black brogues shone like mirrors, and Richard knew from bitter experience that footwear that large just had to be handmade. The gold tie had no regimental crests, but there was the familiar *Batman* logo of the *Spetsnaz* special forces honourable discharge pin on the lapel above Ivan's heart.

The eyes that glanced up from beneath slightly shaggy, dark sand-coloured eyebrows were mid-blue and twinkling with unexpected good humour. The full, rather sensual lips quivered towards a smile as Ivan saw Felix and the surprisingly fine nostrils flared. 'Sorry to do this to you, Felix,' said an unexpectedly light baritone voice with a clear Muscovite accent that did not strain Richard's basic Russian vocabulary too much. 'It's the price of following orders, I'm afraid.'

'Whose orders?' demanded Felix as he and Richard hurried across the room.

'The federal prosecutor's,' answered Ivan easily.

Not *my father's*, thought Richard. *The federal prosecutor's.* Interesting.

'Lavrenty Mikhailovich probably doesn't realize his word isn't law down here. Yet,' Felix answered easily.

'Oh, but it is,' interposed Richard, hoping his Russian accent was as polished as everyone else's. 'Show them the letter, Felix.'

The sandy eyebrows rose. The delicate mouth widened into a ready grin as Felix, who appeared to have forgotten the minister's letter, went to show it to the officers.

'Captain Mariner, I presume?' said Ivan in impeccable English stepping forward, as light on his massive feet as a professional boxer, seeming to lead with his large shoulders.

Richard extended his hand. 'Your English is perfect,' he said. 'Oxford?'

'Sandhurst.' The handshake was short, carefully gentle but full of latent power. Their eyes were almost on a level, Richard for once in his life looking slightly upwards. 'A brief second-ment many years ago.'

'Of course. I should have guessed.' Richard stepped back a little, still holding eye contact. 'How is your father?'

'The federal prosecutor?' Ivan shrugged. 'Much as usual. Prosecuting.'

'We have to wait,' said Felix unhappily. 'They're expecting someone else with Ivan's luggage.'

'Of course,' soothed Richard, turning away from Ivan just enough to meet Felix's frustrated gaze. 'Colonel Kebila is on his way, no doubt.'

'A full colonel?' said Ivan, reclaiming Richard's full attention. 'Either I've gone up in the world or they really do have Mickey Mouse armies down here.'

'You've gone up in the world, believe me,' Richard informed him shortly. 'Mickey Mouse is the last thing these people are.'

Colonel Kebila arrived a minute later, followed by two porters trundling a sizeable luggage trolley loaded with massive suitcases. Clearly no twenty-kilo limit for young Ivan, thought Richard ironically. Two hundred kilos looked nearer the mark.

Everyone in the room straightened respectfully as the dapper soldier entered, even Felix and Richard. Ivan came very close to full attention; A fact which Kebila noted, along with every-thing else. 'Senior Lieutenant Yagula,' he began, also in clipped Sandhurst English. 'I have inspected the contents of your luggage. And find that I am informed by at least one government minister and indeed the president himself, that they contain nothing that presents any risk to my country. Or that contravenes any of our stringent import laws.'

'That is very understanding of all concerned, sir. Please forward my thanks and best wishes as you feel appropriate,' replied Ivan in the equally clipped tones of the Royal Military Academy, Sandhurst, Camberley, England.

Ye Gods, thought Richard. They'll be exchanging visiting cards next. Inviting each other round for tea and cucumber sandwiches. Or calling for seconds and duelling sabres . . .

'*However,*' continued Kebila smoothly with the curtest of nods at the pleasantry, 'you should be aware, *Stárshiy Leytenánt,* that it is my job to guard the people who have just given me my orders, whether I agree with them or not. And if I find I'm having to guard them against you or any of the weaponry I have recorded as being in these suitcases, you can rest assured I will come looking for you. Personally.'

Ivan's smile broadened microscopically, just enough to reveal a flash of pearl-white teeth. 'And I am sure you will know where to find me, Colonel. That, I am certain, would be true even were we not, as I understand it, ordered to undertake the same mission, side by side. But it is, in fact, my very real hope that the equipment I have imported – and which you have so carefully catalogued – will help protect you and your men, when the going gets tough. Somewhere upriver. Sometime soon.'

No doubt there was further family news to swap and more social catching-up to do, but Richard reckoned that if whatever was in Ivan's luggage had upset Kebila so much, it would probably give the manager of the Granville Lodge Hotel a heart attack. 'What did you bring in those cases?' he asked as the limo fought its way through the eternal rush hour south of Granville Harbour International twenty minutes later.

Ivan reached into the inside pocket of his beautifully cut jacket and passed over a carefully folded piece of paper.

'No wonder Kebila's jealous,' said Richard as he finished

scanning it. 'He's just upgraded his men to Ruger MP nines. As I expect you noticed.'

'It was the first thing that struck me,' admitted Ivan. 'But that's a fine semi-automatic. We've kept with HK MP fives, though, as you'll see from the list.' Ivan leaned over to slide a perfectly manicured finger down the column of writing. 'I like Graches, though, I must admit. I carry the four-four-six Viking myself nowadays when I'm at work, but it doesn't take the hot rounds. It's civilian spec, of course. I like the fact there's only seventeen parts. And that the hot nine mil loads will go through body armour like butter. Is body armour a problem? I thought it might be, though I've only had real experience in Chechnya. I've been in Africa, but only in a support role. No combat. But I reckoned *better safe than sorry*, you know?'

'Body armour has been a problem in some areas,' said Richard carefully. 'Certainly the leadership of the hostiles we're likely to face tend to wear it. The foot soldiers, though, are either hopped up on coke or brainwashed into believing Poro magic. Or both.'

'I guessed as much,' said Ivan. 'If a guy's coming at you wearing a wedding dress and a fright wig, you don't need armour piercing, right?'

'That's about the size of it.' Richard nodded, speaking feelingly from personal experience. 'But both cocaine and magic can make them hard as hell to stop, hot rounds or not.'

'Talking of hot rounds,' interrupted Felix, 'you haven't brought ammunition for all these weapons as well, have you?'

'Only the special stuff,' answered Ivan. 'I'm relying on the fact that everything I've brought will take standard military loads. If you guys haven't got enough then we'll have to take it from the hostiles. They'll have plenty if the intelligence is accurate. That's the *head shed* to you, Captain Mariner, I believe. As we seem to be using special ops jargon.'

Richard laughed. But as he did so, he thought back to other conversations he had had like this. And remembered who he had shared them with: Max's daughter Anastasia, in fact. 'You take all this kit upriver with you,' he said easily, 'and you'll certainly have a lot to talk to Anastasia about.'

Ivan flinched as though Richard had struck him. But he recovered like a boxer as well as moving like one. 'Yes,' he said. 'Though, given our history, Anastasia and I never seem to be short of topics for conversation. I would be grateful, however, just for the time being, you understand, if you did not mention me or my presence in any communication you might have with her.'

OK, thought Richard. More along those lines later, perhaps. If it becomes relevant. Or any of my damn business. He shrugged in answer. Nodded a curt affirmative.

In the meantime, 'Felix,' he said, 'I think you'd better tell the driver to head straight for the docks. From the sound of things, almost all of Ivan's luggage needs to go aboard the Zubr *Stalingrad*. And we'll need to ask Captain Zhukov to put it in secure storage with the rest of his arms and armaments.'

After a few moments of reflective silence Ivan asked, a little nervously, 'Now that you've mentioned her, are we likely to see Anastasia?'

'Certain to, eventually,' answered Richard. 'Didn't anyone tell you? Our first base of operations is the orphanage she runs just upriver of the inner delta.'

Plan

'This is a plan of the river,' said Captain Caleb Maina quietly. 'I use the term *plan* rather than chart because as you can see it focuses on what lies along the banks more than the depths or state of the water itself, and even then it shows the land features in very little detail, so it is hardly a map. And, again, as will be obvious to you, the hand-drawn additions show municipal and structural works in progress. Where they are inked in, the project is effectively complete. Where they are in pencil, the project is still in progress. Where the lines are dashed or dotted, there are plans in place but nothing substantial yet on the ground. And, I should add – perhaps a little melodramatically – that some of what I am about to tell you has until recently been what you might term a *state secret*.'

'Does Benin La Bas have an Official Secrets Act?' asked Ivan cheerfully. 'Will we have to sign it?'

'As a matter of fact, yes it does,' answered Caleb. 'But no, you will not have to sign it.'

Richard looked down at the plan which lay spread across the main mess table in the crew's dining room aboard the lead Zubr *Stalingrad*. It showed in little more than sketch outline Granville Harbour and its inner bay, the mouth and main course of the River Gir from its tidal openings to its Central African origins, including Lac Dudo and the chain of volcanoes with Karisoke at its heart, from which the main river sprang. There was a line along the watershed that lay on the mountain chain's highest ridge, beyond which was written *Congo Libre*. Nothing immediately struck him as looking much like a state secret.

Stalingrad was Captain Zhukov's command, but it was Captain Caleb Maina who had produced the long, thin outline plan of his country and its volcanic central feature. And it was Caleb who was delivering this update, revealing, somewhat to

Richard's surprise, that he had a background in intelligence as well as in ship handling. An all-round Ian Fleming, Richard thought. But that thought only made him look forward to the briefing even more. It would be the first, Richard hoped, of several increasingly detailed seminars before they all went charging up the river like gangbusters.

'So some of this planned development is a work in progress,' he observed. 'And a secret work in progress.'

'Yes, Captain Mariner. That makes two important points,' answered Caleb. 'Since the president settled into office and gained the backing of the IMF, the World Bank and other international institutions and NGOs, work on the country's infrastructure has proceeded at a great and gathering pace.'

Particularly, thought Richard, since the president's national heroine daughter arrived as the leader of the opposition – and a competition for hearts and minds really got under way.

'So even modern maps are out of date within a month,' Caleb persisted. He glanced around the table, his attention focused primarily on Felix and Richard. 'I am aware that many of you will have flown over the river – along much of its length on several occasions recently,' he continued. 'But you may not have been fully alive to the changes that have taken place on the ground. Changes that will affect our progress radically and, I hope, positively. Changes which are detailed on this plan.'

The conference had started as an attempt to bring Ivan up to date. Felix had gone through the basic situation in the car coming down here from the airport, but Ivan still felt he needed filling in on some of the background to the Army of Christ the Infant – its history, its likely objectives, and what precisely had been the involvement of Anastasia Asov in the overthrow of its last leader, the mad, cannibalistic black magician General Moses Nlong.

But when it became plain that Ivan remained ignorant of several basic factors that the others were taking for granted, Caleb agreed to a more detailed explanation of the background to the current situation in his country as a whole. Even Felix seemed surprised by some of the more recent developments along the river and further upcountry. And, for some reason, now was the appropriate moment to start filling them in on matters that everyone had remained ignorant of until recently. Or everyone except a very select few at the top of the government, the defence and the intelligence services, by the look of things. So Caleb had led them down to the deserted mess hall, laid out his plan and started filling them in while the main object of the visit – the safe disposal of Ivan's arsenal – was achieved by a cheerfully awestruck armaments officer.

Richard was paying particularly close attention because he knew Robin would be frustrated at missing a briefing like this and would want a detailed explanation of whatever Captain Caleb told them. He was supported in his endeavour to remember what Caleb was saying by the fact that his memory was very nearly photographic, and he would be able to recall the sketch map itself in astonishing detail simply by closing his eyes and concentrating.

'The work on the harbour which you can see marked here . . . has proceeded upriver,' Caleb was saying. 'We have kept the basic rule of the road for the tidal section at the river mouth where, as you see, the main channel is divided into two by a series of small islands. The rule is to "keep right". So, upriver shipping passes to the south of the islands, and downriver to the north.

'We have cleared both channels of the water hyacinth that made them difficult to navigate in the past. And, as you see here, the main road along the north bank has been restored. There was an old casino twenty kilometres upriver on the northern bank – just at the end of the tidal section – that is now a river pilot station whose additional function is keeping the water flowing down to the harbour free of floating obstructions. Especially water hyacinth. The road along the northern bank has in fact been cleared and re-metalled as far as the township of Malebo, more than sixty kilometres into the delta. This is particularly important as the spiralling number of citizens in Granville Harbour need feeding, and we cannot do it all by importing what we need and paying for it with our oil and gas sales. No. Clearing the road and river for commercial access has allowed the growing number of farms in the inner and outer deltas to get their produce to our city markets – and

by extension of that to allow increasing numbers of people
who would otherwise be unemployed to go into the hinterland
and find agricultural work. A benign spiral, you see, and one
extended further inland, as we shall also see in a minute or
two. Therefore, the government is working to clear the next
section, right through the inner delta as far as the Father
Antoine and Sister Faith Memorial orphanage here, where we
are working to broaden the scope of our farming activities
exponentially.'

'Still nothing on the south bank, though?' asked Richard,
thinking *nothing very secret so far*. 'Nothing but mangroves
and delta jungle?'

'Not quite,' answered Caleb. 'The government has been
busy there too. If you look carefully you can see that we are
bringing back the oil pipework that was there and clearing the
jungle itself. There was some talk of a wildlife park there –
that's marked here in dotted lines – and the idea was to make
it a tourist attraction. But it was abandoned when the men
who thought it up, Bala Ngama and his brother – ministers
for the outer and inner deltas – were dismissed for demanding
bribes and using promises of land both in the deltas and further
upriver to build their private power base.

'Minister Ngama had also assembled a considerable
menagerie that was supposed to go into the wildlife park but
as soon as he was dismissed he apparently arranged to have
it all sold off. It was paid for by the ministry, but he is
supposed to have pocketed the proceeds himself. It was
typical of the man and of the activities that finally made
President Chaka run out of patience with him. Then he and
his brother vanished, leaving their families to face the music.
And it is they, in fact, who seem to have sold to our enemies
and competitors some of the facts that I am revealing to you
now. Facts whose importance will be immediately obvious,
I'm sure. Facts which had been secret until the Ngama
brothers crossed the border. In many other countries the
reprisals would have been terrible. Here, they are simply the
subject of an investigation *in absentia*, and their families are
currently at liberty on bail.'

'And there's a deserted town there too,' observed Richard,

focusing on Caleb's overdrawn plan once again as he mulled this new information over. 'A big place, but a deserted ruin now, just inside the inner delta. What about that?'

'It is Citematadi,' answered Caleb. 'It was built, flourished briefly, was abandoned and then died during the nineteen seventies and eighties of the last century. We have sent army engineering units up to see what of the infrastructure can be cleared, made safe and used. Granville Harbour is becoming overcrowded, as you will readily appreciate, and we do not want it to turn into another Lagos. *And* – you will welcome this particularly, Captain Mariner – the engineers were ordered to blow up the piles and starlings of the collapsed bridge there and clear the river, making it navigable for larger craft right up to the orphanage and the new farms beyond it.'

'The orphanage,' said Ivan. 'You mentioned that. What is it and why is it important?'

'Here, on the north bank. The Father Antoine and Sister Faith Memorial orphanage is now at the heart of a considerable new settlement. It is not really large enough to warrant a municipal authority or a name, but the suggestion has been made that it be called *Chakaville* after Celine Chaka, who was wounded defending the orphanage against the Army of Christ the Infant some time ago, before she became leader of the opposition. And that the first municipal leader should be Anastasia Asov, who runs the orphanage itself.'

At the mention of Anastasia's name, Richard felt Ivan stir once again, and was opening his mouth to ask about their relationship when the door opened and Anastasia's father strode in.

'Someone mention my name?' he asked, having heard the last few words.

'No,' said Richard. 'We were discussing Anastasia and her orphanage.'

'Oh,' said Max, his voice flat, his tone somewhere between disinterest and disdain. Then his whole demeanour changed. 'Ivan,' he said. 'Ivan, my boy . . .'

What started as a handshake turned into a bear hug, and in among the whispered greetings Richard was sure he heard the phrase, 'Uncle Max!'

'The point is,' continued Caleb, when the two men finally pulled apart, 'that, just at Malebo, there is now a decent docking facility there. Fuel, supplies and so forth. Any expedition proceeding upriver can expect to refuel there and at the orphanage. And, even as we speak, further fuel dumps are being ferried upriver, nine thousand kilos at a time by the Super Pumas of the Benin La Bas army's support command.' He looked around the table, smiling briefly at the curt nods of approval. Then he continued. 'As well as the fuel and ancillary equipment, we will be leaving a security contingent at the orphanage to guard the place. And that is a happy coincidence, because, as you can see if you look a little to the north and east of the encampment, here is the first of the large nationalized farming cooperatives.

'The land north-east of the inner delta is raised savannah and is particularly well suited to a range of farming activities. President Chaka has set up, in parallel, an agricultural college in Malebo and the cooperative you see marked. Unlike earlier schemes – such as the ill-fated Million Acre experiment in Kenya and the attempted restitution in Zimbabwe – chance has offered us a clean slate here and now. Almost all the original farmers in this area were driven off during the last thirty years by the kind of dangers that closed Doctor Koizumi's pearl factory and cleared the jungle all around it. If there are any survivors with legitimate personal, family, clan or tribal claims to the land, they have yet to come forward. The best experts we can find, therefore, have been brought in to assess what of the most in-demand crops might be farmed there to feed not only our own people but also a global market. And it seems that everything from watermelons to wine is in demand. From beans to Burgundy. As well as the sweet potato, yam and manioc that are the staples of the area.'

'You have people up there farming already?' asked Richard, impressed.

'Indeed. The government has instituted a three-pronged recruitment scheme. We have experienced farmers from the older generation who know the land and are willing to return to it while the next generation are being trained up in the agricultural college. And any shortfall or stopgap is filled by experts recruited from our near neighbours – or from further abroad – who help and advise in the meantime.'

'Experts from the far side of Karisoke?' asked Richard, as he felt something beginning to stir in his mind.

'Indeed. Bala Ngama, before his removal, negotiated a most successful agreement with President Gabriel Fola. There are several of his farming experts involved in the project. But we also have Kikuyu farmers from the Great Rift Valley, Masai herdsmen, Bantu vegetable growers from Kenya who are expert in growing onions, tomatoes, cabbages and avocados, as well as fine green beans for export. Hutus and Tutsis from nearer at hand. Bantu again and Luala from the DR Congo, south of us. It started in secret because of the influx of experts from outside the country and the Matadi tribe, but anyone who reads the government-sponsored press will soon learn the details.'

'OK,' said Max. 'But the main objective remains to get up the river to Lac Dudo first, before this Army of Christ the Infant gets a good firm grip on it – whether they know about the coltan or whether they are just reconquering their old stamping grounds – and lets the other bad guys in through the back door. It looks as though we may have to sort out how many bad guys – fifth columnists – are here already. Where they are, what they're up to and how in hell's name they fit into Gabriel Fola's and Colonel Odem's overall plan.'

Richard nodded. 'But that's not all,' he added. 'I'm pretty certain Colonel Odem has a grudge he wants to settle with Celine Chaka, for instance, so she's involved, like it or not . . .'

'Not too likely she's at any risk,' shrugged Ivan. 'Leader of the opposition, in the middle of Granville Harbour. We're talking Army of Christ, not Smersh assassins . . .'

'*But,*' said Richard forcefully, his eyes on Ivan and not on Max, 'he also has an account to settle with Anastasia Asov, who is effectively alone and unprotected. And out there in the middle of nowhere.'

Du Lac

'Anastasia says she's fine,' said Robin, gesturing towards the Skype screen on her laptop. 'All quiet on the eastern front. And no – before you ask, I did not mention your mysterious Ivan Yagula.'

It was later that evening and they were getting ready for bed. The day had been spent in preparations for getting the Zubrs, the equipment, Kebila and his men up the river. But the job needed to be planned carefully and done right. It was all a frustratingly slow process. Over a light but exquisite dinner, they had talked the situation over.

Their conversation over dinner in the hotel's new *Bistro Bamidele* had started with Ivan, who was not present at the moment because Max and Felix had dragged him out to a less sedate, more actively Russian dinner at a dockside bar and grill called OTI, which was more famous for its massive selection of vodkas than for its actual food. And, for Robin, a bottle of lemony Chablis. Richard explained in detail Captain Caleb's briefing. He was aided in this endeavour first by using the tines of his fork to draw on the starched snowiness of the linen, then his pen on some paper napkins purloined from a passing waiter and finally in perfect detail with a pencil on several overlapping pieces of A4 paper all supplied by the long-suffering manager Andre Wanago. But it was over dessert, presented with a powerful NV 'Alcyone' Tannat, Vinedo de los Vientos, that they had discussed Richard's worries about Anastasia. Worries that had only seemed to darken over coffee. Worries that seemed to persist, even after Robin got through to the orphanage on Skype.

'We still have to move pretty quickly,' insisted Richard, easing off his suit jacket and crossing to hang it in the wardrobe. 'It's like a multiple pile-up. She'll be fine till the wheels come off. Then she won't be fine at all. All within a second or so. You know how quickly it can happen.'

'Don't I ever!' answered Robin, with feeling. She beckoned him back so that he could unzip her dress for her. As Richard pulled the long zip down, his mind was miles away from the warm, silk and lace-encased flesh that the parting teeth revealed. Robin had been kidnapped – with Anastasia – some years earlier in Benin La Bas, before Chaka took over and restored order. One moment she and Anastasia had been going to a party, the next they had been helpless prisoners, and it had taken all of Richard's courage and cunning to get them safely back.

'But give the woman credit,' Robin continued a little ruefully as he moved back to allow her to step out of the crumpled material, clearly lost in thought. 'She lives here. Has done for ages. She knows the score – probably better than you do. And she can look after herself. Better than most, I might add.'

'Even so . . .' countered Richard, pulling his tie off. 'She can be unexpectedly fragile. Look what happened the minute she got back from the kidnapping. She went off the rails completely – hanging out with that rock group Simian Artillery, then going on drugs and what-not.' He began to undo his shirt, frowning with paternal concern.

'As I understand it, she developed quite a passion for the lead singer . . .' Robin remarked as she hung up her dress.

'Even though the band themselves had been involved in the drug-related death of her brother . . .' He nodded, pulling the crisp cotton out of his waistband.

'No explaining the vagaries of the female heart, my love . . .' she observed wistfully, sliding her half-slip down with a wiggle of her hips.

'Says you, Mills and Boon and Barbara Cartland!' he said, loosening his belt.

'Says me at least. And when the lead singer blew his brains out, she was the one who found him.' She folded her slip over the back of the chair and paused, looking across at him, regretting the sheer tights. If she had been wearing suspenders, she thought, it would have been easier to get him in the mood. But then again, it was never too hard once he realized what was on her mind.

'Or what was left of him,' he was saying as he put one foot up on a chair to untie his shoelaces.

'Splattered all over the bathroom walls, floor and ceiling. You can see why she went off the rails. And, I think, why Max just gave up on her and let her get on with it.' She slid out of the treacherously unromantic tights and kicked them across the room.

'That's as may be. But we pulled her out of all that so we're *in loco parentis* now. We're responsible for her.' He stepped out of one shoe and turned to the other.

'You worked in China too long,' she observed, reaching behind her to unhook her bra. 'Isn't that what the Chinese say? You save someone then you owe them, not the other way round?'

'Perhaps. But in this case it's true. If anything happened to us, you'd want someone like us to watch out for Mary, wouldn't you?' He stepped out of his trousers and folded them over the back of his chair.

'And William, though they're good kids. They've never given us a moment's worry,' she added, stepping out of her underwear and wondering whether it would be too unromantic to clean her teeth. Her breath smelt of orangey Grand Marnier and lemony wine, with a smoky coffee overlay.

'Precisely my point,' he said, hopping from foot to foot as he pulled off his socks. 'We pulled Anastasia back. Now we're the ones who need to look after her – if she needs looking after. And I just think she may, that's all. She's strong. But she's not that strong. And anyway, there are limits.'

'And the resurrected Army of Christ the Infant is well beyond anyone's limits. OK, I get your drift.' She decided to risk it and sat down on the bed, surprised to find herself a little unsteady.

'So we need to get upriver as fast as we can, at least as far as the orphanage, which – if you remember – is named for the last two people who ran it. Both slaughtered and one eaten by the last incarnation of the Army of Christ while Anastasia was forced to look on!' He stepped out of his underwear and looked across at the bed because his pyjamas were under the pillow. The pillow that Robin was lying on, in fact, looking like a naked blonde Maja waiting for Goya to paint her.

'It's that bloody Galahad complex again, isn't it?' purred Robin indulgently. 'You really should have left that in the last millennium, my love.'

'Galahad complex?' asked Richard speculatively.

'Galahad. Knight in shining armour. See a maiden. Assume she's in distress. Get your lance up and off you charge . . .' She settled her hips and wondered whether to go for the Rokeby Venus pose.

'Well, I wouldn't put it quite like that . . .'

'I would. And if you're getting your lance up, then I'm first in the queue.'

He laughed. 'You always will be. Especially lying around looking like that.'

'You'd better believe it. But there is a problem . . .' She pouted.

'Do tell,' he demanded, crossing towards the bed.

'Galahad had no maiden fair. No one to get his lance up over. I'd rather you were someone else.'

'Lancelot, perhaps?' he asked, one knee on the duvet beside her.

'Oh, yes. *Lance a lot!* That'll do me fine!'

'I can see where this is heading.' He straddled her easily. 'Are you Elaine or Guinevere?'

'Both! So you'll have to be pretty active, sir knight,' she said, reaching up for him.

'Well, let's see what we can do . . .' He leaned down towards her.

Later, on the verge of sleep, with Robin snoring contentedly beside him, Richard suddenly had a darker thought arising from their little love game. For Lancelot was not just Sir Lancelot. He was – and this suddenly struck Richard as oddly sinister – Lancelot *du Lac*.

Nightmare

Anastasia Asov struggled against the hands that held her helpless. The clapping and the stamping were overwhelming. Ngoboi, the great raffia-cloaked, ebony-masked, seven-foot-high god of the jungle's darkest places, whirled and stamped in front of her. Two of his acolytes capered around him, tending to the restless strands of his costume. Apart from Sister Faith, the nun round whom the god was circling like a shark, Anastasia was the only woman there. It was death for a woman to look on Ngoboi – and Anastasia knew she was as good as dead. As dead as poor Sister Faith was doomed to be.

The Army of Christ the Infant were ranked around the orphanage's central compound. Those holding guns were stamping in rhythm. Those carrying matchets in their belts were clapping. Their eyes were burning with a mixture of religious awe, murder-lust and cocaine. The boys in Anastasia's charge were all held captive as petrified spectators behind them. The girls were locked away in the dormitory ready to be raped and slaughtered. And, many of them, butchered and eaten.

As though etched in silver and jet in the light of a full moon, the army's terrifying leader was sprawled at his ease on a chair taken out of the chapel. The priest's chair – for which the poor man would have no further use. Silver-lensed Ray-Bans sat wrapped round his head below the beret and above the ridged horrors of his cheeks, lined with massive Poro secret society initiation scars. Like those on his naked chest that gleamed between the flaps of his gaping shirt. Two hulking lieutenants also in dark glasses stood behind him, one at either shoulder. All three of them, like Ngoboi, held heavy, steel-bladed matchets more than a metre long.

The heat, like the noise and the terror, was overpowering. Anastasia's body was running with perspiration as thick and hot as blood. Her ears rang and her head throbbed. She felt like someone watching the approach of a tornado she could never escape. Sister Faith knelt at the heart of it, at the centre of Ngoboi's whirling dance, in the middle of the compound, the still point of the spinning world, until the leader's Ray-Bans moved fractionally up and down and their movement was echoed horrifically by Ngoboi's matchet. Up and down went the matchet into the body of the woman kneeling at his feet.

The mouth between the scarred cheeks below the silvered Ray-Bans split into a huge grin. Anastasia saw that the khat-stained teeth between them were sharpened to needle points, like crocodiles' teeth. And she realized she was no longer dripping sweat – she was covered in blood. Bathed in the hot, sweet-smelling, iron-tasting thickness of it. Drenched with it. Drowning in it.

Ngoboi's hand came down on her shoulder. 'Miss Anastasia,' he said, in a soft, female voice. 'Wake up, Miss Anastasia, you're dreaming.'

But the mad god's coke-wide black eyes still stared at her, white-rimmed and bloodshot, from out of the rough-hewn horror of the ebony mask. The mouth still moved – and now it, too, had those terrible, brown-stained, crocodile teeth, sharpened to tear at human flesh. And the hand on her shoulder still held that red running, gently steaming matchet. 'Miss Anastasia,' said Ngoboi, more forcefully. 'Wake up. Please! You're having another nightmare.'

Anastasia opened her eyes. Blinked. Began to focus. Ngoboi's face slowly became that of newly-arrived Sister Georginah: ebony dark – emphasized by the perfect white of her headdress, illumined by the silver moonlight streaming through the thin-curtained window, but otherwise the opposite of the jungle god's. Wide, gentle brown eyes, soft lips, square white teeth, a frown of sisterly concern. A silver crucifix instead of a steel matchet in her fist. The hands that held her so relentlessly resolved themselves into tangled bed sheets wrapped around her like a straitjacket strapped round a lunatic. And these in turn explained the sweat-inducing heat. The orphanage's meagre funds did not run to air-conditioning. Or ceiling fans. Anastasia realized with something akin to horror that, because she had gone to bed naked, she had no idea how much of her was on show between the bindings of the sheets. 'Thank you, Sister,' she said gently. 'I'll be fine now.'

'Can I get you something? Some water perhaps?' Sister Georginah was a sweet, naive creature, with absolutely no social sensitivity at all.

'No. Thank you.' Anastasia wondered whether to struggle into a sitting position; whether to start untangling her body from the sheets. But she didn't know Sister Georginah well enough to start doing a striptease in front of her.

'Perhaps you would like to pray,' suggested the young nun anxiously. 'We can pray together, here and now if you would like. Your dream must have been very horrible. You were screaming and crying most terribly. And you talked of matters that were simply *devilish.*'

'Perhaps I'll pray later,' said Anastasia, and she half meant it. 'But if you could leave me now, I just want to catch my breath.'

'Of course.' The sister nodded, straightened, half-bowed and stepped back, as though taking leave of a queen. But now that the crisis was over she clearly had the opportunity to use her eyes in a way she hadn't when she'd rushed in to wake the dreaming woman. 'Miss Anastasia! What is that? That *thing* on your . . .'

For an instant the nightmare threatened to return. What *thing* could the horrified nun possibly mean? Was she still spattered with Sister Faith's blood? Had Ngoboi scarred her in some way? Then Anastasia understood. 'It's a tattoo,' she said. Her fingers explored her naked belly and found a strip of cloth mercifully across her loins. 'A big cat. I've a gorilla on my back. Result of a misspent youth. Remind me to show you sometime.'

Sister Georginah turned and fled. *Mission accomplished,* thought Anastasia wryly. But she'd have to do some serious apologizing and fence-mending later. She pulled herself out of bed and unwrapped the sheet from round herself. It was wet. And her long, lean body was still running with moisture. She padded across to the window, towelling herself with the wet cotton. She stopped. Threw the sheet back on the wreckage of her bed. Stretched her stiff muscles, reached up and peeped out past the edge of the curtain. Her room faced due south across the river, and she could see that the moon was setting between the trees of the delta low in the west down towards Granville Harbour just as the sun was preparing to heave itself up over Mount Karisoke far away in the east.

On the far side of the river the wild jungle reared, huge and black-hearted. Timeless. Unvarying. Cold and terrifying. The exact, precise opposite of the waxing and waning lights on either side. The place where Ngoboi lived. With a shiver she looked back upriver towards the rising sun. It would soon be time to get up anyway, she decided.

She needed a shower. Some food. And yes, maybe some spiritual comfort. She might do a lot worse than spending a few minutes in the little chapel clearing the satanic figures of Ngoboi and Odem out of her mind. And the pictures of Sister Faith and Father Antoine, both of whom the Army of Christ had killed in front of her. The whole nightmare, she reckoned, had probably stemmed from her Skype contact with Robin last night, passing on what she understood of poor old Richard's concerns. Their anxiety for her was a burden she bore cheerfully enough, like any overprotected young adult treated as though they were still a child, though Robin was more like a big sister than a mother. And as for Richard! Well, that was another matter entirely . . . But still and all, she thought, it was better to have someone worry too much about you than to have nobody caring at all. What was it that had spooked Richard so badly, though? Nothing scared Richard, in her experience. Nothing. Ever. She had heard nothing on the grapevine. The jungle drums remained silent and, surely, if there was any real danger out there, an echo of it would have come out of the dark places, like a rumble of distant thunder. Wouldn't it? With her mind still full of questions, Anastasia crossed the room again, grabbed her robe and towel from the back of the door, kicked her sandals into the light, watching in case anything unpleasant scuttled out of them, stepped into them, carelessly treading down the heels, then shrugged the dressing-gown on and went off to have her shower.

As she slopped down the short corridor that took her out of the adult quarters and into the female showers, she tried to replace thoughts of the night with plans for the day – an enterprise she was helped with by the fact that the showers were walled with reeds rather than tile. And that the red-clay sluice, as usual, harboured a harmless grey house snake which she shooed away with a negligent toe before it got a nasty, soapy surprise. The shower was really just a bucket full of water that could be tilted by pulling a rope and whose outpouring was broken up by a rudimentary shower head so that it became a brief, tepid monsoon rather than a solid waterfall.

She emerged, refreshed. Her mind, like her body, cleansed of the night. With her robe tight at her slim waist and her towel round her surprisingly broad shoulders, she returned to her room, towelled the short shock of her black hair dry and began to dress. In indulgently expensive panties and a bra that was hardly needed, she crossed to her modest desk and checked the old-fashioned paper diary she kept there. Today looked fairly typical. Long on paperwork and short on appointments. So she pulled on a cotton blouse and tucked it into denim shorts before stepping back into her brokeback sandals and – as she was now officially dressed – pulling the backs erect again and buckling them up properly.

She finished her morning's work at 11.30 a.m. and had an early lunch with the other orphanage staff. She listened to the reports from the teachers, the maintenance staff and the sisters, noting that Sister Georginah kept her eyes shyly downcast when speaking to her; then, like everyone else in the place, she returned to her room between 12 p.m. and 3 p.m. This time she slept without nightmares and arose, vibrant and refreshed. And it was just as well. At 4 p.m. she met the senior girls in the largest classroom of the orphanage school. The girls were led by a tall young woman called Ado and a young man called Esan – the only male in the room. Both Ado and Esan were technically too old to be kept at the orphanage and both should really have been sent downriver with others of their age to the Ishmael Bible Seminary and then the Benin La Bas University in Granville Harbour to complete their education. But these young people were different. Esan – which meant 'Nine' in Yoruba – was an ex-soldier in the Army of Christ. He had no knowledge of his actual name. General Moses Nlong had called him Esan because he had been nine years old when he was accepted into the army by killing and eating others of his family. The ritual was less brutally point-less than it seemed. Esan had, by that one terrible act, put himself forever outside his family, clan and tribe. Beyond the reach of any of his tribal deities or the jungle gods – except for Ngoboi, whom the army's brutal leader used to keep disci-pline and motivation high amongst his troops. Especially the young ones. Particularly when cocaine was in short supply. For all the boys had been introduced into the Poro secret jungle societies. They all believed in the powers of the jungle spirits.

But Esan had changed sides. Come back into the fold. Used his Poro jungle training to do good instead of evil. He and Ado, also trained in female Sande jungle lore as a child, had helped Anastasia and Celine survive their last confrontation with the marauding army and Anastasia was doing her best to make certain that they would help her and her charges survive in the future. Later on Ado and Esan would take the girls through elementary weapons training and jungle lore. Anastasia would join in. And they would have a five-mile jog through the safe secondary jungle and out on to the farmland on this side of the river before returning for dinner. It was a simple daily routine which – if nothing else – kept the girls fit and confident. And kept the boys – and the local farmers, farmhands, families and occasional passers-by – all highly amused.

But this afternoon's session began, as many of these did, with a simple history lesson. 'Such armies as The Lord's Resistance Army, M23 and the Army of Christ the Infant will take the boys and keep them alive,' said Anastasia, not for the first time – driving home a message the girls dared never forget. 'Their life in the army will be hard. But it will be life.' She looked around the room, meeting each pair of wide brown eyes there. 'But they rape and kill the girls. I have seen it and I know. Like Ado. Like Esan. Should any girl along the river meet such men, they will be dead or a sex slave used by all, all the time . . . Until they are no more use. And then they will be dead.' She looked around the rows of wide-eyed girls – aged from ten to fifteen – sitting silently in front of her. '*But not you!*' she shouted. 'You are not slaves and fodder for animals like the Army of Christ the Infant! *Here is who you are,*' said Anastasia.

72 Peter Tonkin

And Esan pulled a slide up on to the laptop which shone up on to the whiteboard. It showed an old photograph of a line of soldiers. All armed. All black. All women. Beneath the photograph there was writing in English, which Anastasia translated into Matadi for them: '*"There they are, 4,000 warriors, the 4,000 black virgins of Dahomey, the monarch's bodyguard, motionless in their war garments, with gun and knife in hand, ready to leap forward at the master's signal. Old or young, ugly or beautiful, they are wonderful to look at. They are as well built as the male warriors and their attitude is just as disciplined and correct, lined up as though against a rope."* That was written by a man called Chauduin, who was held captive by them and lived to tell the tale in a book about his life.'

She gestured. Esan pulled up another picture. A detailed, water-coloured drawing. This time of a single woman. Tall. In full uniform. Well armed, with a matchet at her waist, a musket in her right hand and the severed head of an enemy still dripping in her left. 'Her name was Seh-Dong. She was a leader of the Dahomey Amazons,' Anastasia explained. 'The writing beneath comes from another book, this time by a man called Djivo. It says the Dahomey Amazons believed that, *"We are men, not women. Those coming back from war without having conquered must die. If we beat a retreat our life is at the king's mercy. Whatever town is to be attacked we must overcome it or we bury ourselves in its ruins. Our chief is the king of kings. As long as he lives we have nothing to fear. Our chief has given birth to us again. We are his wives, his daughters, his soldiers. War is our sport and pastime, it clothes and feeds us".*'

She looked down at the girls sitting, enraptured, in front of her. 'Remember,' she said gently. 'You are not victims. You are not slaves. You are not food for any men in any army.' She gestured at the picture of Seh-Dong on the whiteboard, with her musket, her matchet and the severed head in her hand. '*This* is who you are.'

'This is who we are,' chanted the girls in unison. '*This is who we are.*'

Spetsnaz

It took the rest of the week and several more trips to Granville Harbour International airport before Max and Felix's contingent were ready for the off. Even though all of the experts in mining, engineering, chemicals and civilian transport were already there, together with the Kamov chopper and everything else that had gone into the first, abortive expedition to Lac Dudo. A lot more large Russians arrived, but none was quite as huge as Ivan. And none proved as difficult to get through customs. After a while, they blurred into one big, bald, muscular mass for Richard. But, like Ivan, they were all impressively special ops. Like Ivan, in fact, all were Spetsnaz.

Ivan took Richard and Robin under his wing when they were in the Zubr *Volgograd*, which so swiftly became his territory even though Caleb Maina was its captain. He did this for reasons that were not immediately obvious to either of them – though they, too, adopted the overpoweringly cheery young man. For Ivan knew his special forces. And he knew the men who were slowly filling up the soldier spaces on Caleb's Zubr *Volgograd*, by reputation if not in person. But they all, oddly enough, seemed to know him and he became their natural leader long before Richard worked out that this had little to do with his rank as senior lieutenant – *Stárshiy Leytenánt*, as Kebila had called him – and more to do with his right to wear a *Krapoviy* or red beret.

So that, one morning late in the second week, Ivan took Richard and Robin down to *Volgograd*'s main area, which was every bit as large as *Stalingrad*'s. While the morning was still cool, all the men who had come through the airport during the last ten days were engaged in fearsome exercises. Silent, apart from the odd grunt of effort. Focused. Honing themselves to a level Richard – who understood only too well that he was not special in quite their way – had never dreamed of attaining. Preparing themselves for eventualities he hoped with all his heart to avoid. He exchanged glances with Robin who shrugged, mouthed, '*Boys!*' and rolled her eyes.

But Ivan clearly had a purpose in mind. A point to prove. And the little talk he gave his two guests as the three of them walked through the echoing enormity of the place was his way of proving it. 'You see those six there,' Ivan began. 'Army types. Military intelligence GRU regulars. Steady as rocks. Like those ones over there, the VDV airborne. They're elite soldiers, like the Paras and the Green Berets. There's a good solid squad of a dozen army men in all. They've been to Chechnya – right across the Caucasus, North and South Ossetia, and lived to tell the tale. That's taken some doing, I can tell you. If the going gets tough and you can't find me, you stick by them. They'll never let you down.' No sooner had he finished speaking than the men he was talking about stopped their individual routines, split into pairs and started practising dazzlingly quick fight moves.

Ivan seemed hardly to notice. 'But that little squad over there,' he continued, directing Robin's attention with a huge hand on her shoulder as light as a feather, as irresistible as gravity. 'Different kettle of fish. FSB. Anti-terrorists – Alpha group and Vympel. They've been to Chechnya too, but more likely with intelligence rather than on the front line – though they work both sides, like your SAS. They're here because they're expert on how units like the Army of Christ are structured. How they arm and feed themselves. Where they get their financing, drugs, bullets. And how to go about stopping them. In the field. In their supply lines. In their heartlands. Eradicating them. Dead. Buried. It was Vympel and Alpha group, you may remember, who closed down the siege in the Beslan School back in 2004, though none of these guys were directly involved in that. Some of their fathers may have been involved in the storming of the Supreme Soviet building back in 1993, though. This is the new breed, however. And don't believe all you read about how the special forces started falling to pieces after perestroika.'

Robin could believe him. While the regular army men were still working one-on-one, these guys had started three-on-one and nobody appeared to be pulling any punches.

'Will you be joining any of this, Ivan?' she asked as a man the size of a single-decker bus went sailing through the air to crash on to the deck like a falling tree – only to bounce erect, laughing.

'I've done my stint,' he chuckled. 'And I'm down for weapons later.'

'Weapons?' she teased. 'That doesn't sound too tough.'

'We do it stark naked and blindfold, under water. And we don't get to breathe till we've field-stripped and reassembled our weapon. Even if we get our what-nots tangled in our cocking mechanisms.'

'And if you don't do it in time?' she asked, fascinated. Not least, thought Richard, by the mental picture.

'You don't breathe and you get sent home. Sometimes in a box. But I wanted to show you that last group over there, you see them? Police, or rather *Politzia*: Vityaz and RUS. The Vityaz have the same areas of expertise as the Vympel but their intelligence work is more internal. If the Beslan siege had been organized by the late Vyacheslav Ivankov's *Moskva brigada* Mafiya kidnappers, say, instead of Shamil Basayev's separatist Riyadus-Salikhin Battalion, then it would have been Vityaz and not the Vympel who went in.

'Those guys doing the knife fighting – the ones with the real knives beside them, they're the RUS. They're Politzia too, but they're here because they travel. I've talked to a couple of them in depth and they've been all over the world. Negotiating, being trained; training. They're the real Africa hands. They've actually been on the ground out here. Libya, DRC, Ethiopia, Angola, Mozambique. They know the place. They know the jungle. They'll be training the others up as they go. And the OMON police special units guys there, they're the transport section. Military transport.'

'Spetsnaz. What does that actually mean, nowadays?' asked Richard, finding even his usually encyclopaedic knowledge taxed beyond its limit.

'In many ways it means that they've all had similar training, and that's about it. The edges are beginning to blur these days, I must admit. And that's before you start to address the fact that many of these chaps are like me – they've come

out of service and gone into the private sector as guns for
hire anyway. The army men, the GRU chaps over there, will
have been trained to a high degree of expertise in weapons
handling, rappelling, explosives, marksmanship, counter-
terrorism, how to survive the most brutal beatings, hand-to-
hand combat, climbing, diving and underwater combat,
long-range marksmanship, emergency medical procedures
and demolition. The VDV get all that plus extra parachute
work. Some of them, the regiment forty-five men, get boat
training too. Most of the rest will have had some, if not all,
of it. And they will all have received training in how to fight
with everything from knives to shovels – as well as with
their bare fists, of course.'

'They all look pretty experienced,' persisted Robin. 'What
sort of combat experience will they have had?'

'They'll have been involved in situations like the Chechen
problems, the 2008 South Ossetia war which kind of rolled
over into East Prigorodny, the civil war in Tajikistan, the war
in Abkhazia. Dagestan. Georgia. The insurgency in the North
Caucasus. Fighting Al-Qaeda in Syria back in 2012. The FSB
and Politzia men will have been involved in situations like the
Beslan School siege that I mentioned: Alpha group and
Vympel. More recently, there have been a string of internal
terrorist outrages for them to deal with – or to clear up after.
The Moscow market bombing, the Nazran bombing and the
Nevsky Express bombing, the Moscow Metro bombings,
the Stavropol concert bombing, and of course the Domodedovo
International Airport bombing. More recently still, there was
the Dnipropetrovsk bombing in Ukraine, and the Makhachkala
incident in Dagestan. Anyone dealing with anything more
recent than that's probably still in uniform.'

As he finished speaking, he glanced at his watch. '*Tishina!*'
he ordered.

There was instant silence. Stasis. Robin got the strange
notion that even if the man the size of a bus had still been
flying through the air he would simply have stopped there and
hovered until Ivan's next order. It was unnerving.

'*Obed!*' he said. '*Poshli!*'

'Time for lunch,' Richard translated cheerfully, as the small army of large Russians trooped off, in step, as though marching to war rather than to the showers and the mess.

'Time for us to be off, then, said Robin. 'I know all about Russian lunches. Even the salads are enormous.'

'And considering what's going on afterwards,' added Richard, 'there's just too much temptation all round.'

Ivan laughed. 'It is probably best,' he said. 'It will be a working lunch in any case. Felix and Uncle Max are keen to get under way. If you want an interesting afternoon, I suggest you go across to *Stalingrad* and watch Captain Zhukov taking Colonel Kebila and *his* special forces aboard.'

He leaned down between Richard and Robin with a huge grin and a boyish wink. 'But I think you will find that Kebila's special forces are nothing compared to my special forces.'

Tension

There was tension between the Zubrs right from the start. It was inevitable. When Richard remarked upon it to Robin, asking if she noticed it, she looked at him as though he was slow-witted. 'Of course there'll be tension; competition!' she said. 'They may be Russian and African, but they're still *men!*'

And Richard had to admit that she had a point. He had seen it often enough before. And in teams of women as much as in crews of men, to be fair. On one hand, it could hone everyone to performance standards that were almost Olympic. Or on the other it could lead to the kind of aggressive rivalry that led to punch-ups in pubs near football stadiums.

Certainly, Ivan had made it clear that the Spetsnaz men looked down on the local soldiers. And a brief talk that afternoon as Colonel Kebila saw his special forces team aboard *Stalingrad* made it plain that the punctilious officer was equally unimpressed with the Russians. 'Thugs and bully boys,' he dismissively referred to Ivan's men. 'Body-builders. We need ballet dancers.'

'What do you mean?' asked Richard.

'I mean they are preparing for the wrong sort of war,' shrugged Kebila.

'They seem to be preparing for every sort of war they can,' countered Richard warily.

'Except for the correct one. They are going into a situation they have never experienced. Even their so-called *Rus* contingent, the ones who are supposed to have advised various armies in Africa. They have never been in anything like they will find upriver. And as for the rest of them, this is not like Chechnya – it is like Mount Karisoke. It is not Beslan. It is Benin La Bas!'

Richard and Robin looked at each other, wondering where the colonel got his information. 'So your men have an edge of local knowledge?' asked Robin. Richard returned to the here and now, hoping that Kebila did not hear the undertone of *is that all?* that he himself seemed to discern within the question.

But perhaps he did. 'It is more than you think,' answered the soilder stiffly. 'Although they live and train in the city now, these are men of the jungle. Like their fathers, grandfathers and ancestors through the generations, though the focus is not from father to son, as some of your Western traditions are. As the Russian traditions are. You will find none of my people called the equivalent of Ivan Lavrentovich Yagula – because his father is Lavrenty Mikhailovich Yagula and *his* father was Mikhail Ivanovich Yagula! Such traditions tend to exist so that possessions can be passed from one generation to the next, and my people, the Matadi, do not operate like that. The jungle is what we know. Although we make little of the fact. Especially in the face of ignorance and lack of understanding among our Western associates. These men are all Poro. Now, that has its negative aspects, I realize. But they were all initiated at some stage into – what shall we call them? The *mysteries* of the jungle. Those – and there are many – who were raised in the shanty town under the old regime, will have been taken away from their families at a relatively early age and brought up by Poro masters in the forests of the delta. If you remember, when you first came to our country, it was only a step or two from the shanties to the jungles.'

'So most of your men were raised wild? A bit like Mowgli in the *Jungle Book?*' asked Robin ironically.

She had seen the only negative side of these tribal traditions. The deadly use that ruthless men like General Nlong and Colonel Odem made of the Poro gods like Ngoboi. She had talked to both Anastasia and Celine, who had seen women's hearts ripped still beating from their chests and fed to men with sharpened teeth. Seen the bodies of nuns literally butchered – to be cooked and served to the starving army.

But Richard had also talked to Anastasia and Celine about Esan and Ado – the boy member of a Poro society and the girl member of Sande society. He knew that Ado and Esan had stayed with Celine and Anastasia, guiding them, helping them, tending them – so he knew how the youngsters' knowledge of the wild places had actually kept the two older women alive. Without the kind of jungle lore Kebila was talking about, no one would have survived to tell the tale of Moses Nlong's atrocities. No one would have been able to organize resistance, and – eventually – rescue.

So, next morning, when Ivan asked him in turn about Kebila's comments, Richard didn't waste time asking where the Russian got his information, he simply tried to give a balanced account of what he believed the situation to be. 'Kebila's point is simple. Your men know a hell of a lot about fighting, but they haven't been briefed on fighting in the sort of terrain you'll face.'

'And his men have, of course.' Ivan's sandy eyebrow rose quizzically.

'Since childhood. In the tribal traditions of this place, young boys are taken from their families at a young age and put into groups with older boys and men. They are then taught everything that their teachers know about the jungle – practical, pharmacological and spiritual. Where the trails are. If there are no trails, how to make them. What the calls and cries of all the jungle creatures are and which animal, bird or whatever made them. How to track them, trap them, cook and eat them.'

'I thought there were almost no animals there. I thought they'd all been slaughtered for bush meat.'

'Most of them have – but these guys are still trained in what they used to sound like. How they used to behave. How to prepare them. It's an enormous body of lore and knowledge. And they're taught about the plants – which ones kill and which ones heal. God knows, there are one hell of a lot of plants up there, ranging in size from a couple of millimetres to a hundred metres high. It's the kingdom of the plants.' He stopped, drew breath, and met Ivan's highly amused gaze. 'And, less positively from our Western perspective, perhaps, they're taught about a range of jungle gods and spirits which govern the laws that bind families, tribes and societies together. In the final analysis, that's why General Nlong and Colonel Odem and their kind make the kids who join their armies do such barbaric things – they want to make sure the kids have broken such fundamental Poro laws that their families and tribes are forever closed to them. Otherwise, of course, they'd just vanish into the jungle first chance they get. So they have no alternative but to stay with the Army of Christ the Infant or whoever. They simply have nowhere else to go.'

'Rape and eat a stranger might be stretching it – but basic-ally OK. Rape and eat your sister and it's a really big no-no. Something along those lines?'

'Something along those lines,' said Richard, suddenly worried about how seriously Ivan was taking this.

'Gods and spirits.' Ivan smirked. 'Primitive superstitions!'

'They're a useful way of laying down the basic ground rules,' Richard persisted. *'If you go there or do this then Ngoboi will get you* and so forth. Keeps the Poro kids in line just as effectively as it does with the kids in the Army of Christ. Same as it does with kids all over the world. Do this and the bogeyman will get you. Break that and you'll have seven years' bad luck . . . Watch that black cat doesn't cross your path . . . Don't walk under that ladder . . . The sea's awash with super-stition. Never mind the jungle.'

'Point taken,' admitted Ivan. 'Spit on wood . . . Never carry an empty bucket . . . Never move house after dark . . . Never put an empty bottle on the table . . . Never give knives as a present . . . Never give a single girl a corner seat . . .'

'But there's more,' interrupted Richard. 'On the one hand, some of the rituals like circumcision are a bit dangerous if not done carefully; on the other hand that's true of an enor-mous number of religions and societies. It seems to me that some of the more unique rituals associated with the Poro gods do have a positive side – even if they seem a bit barbaric. They teach the kids endurance, individual strength and self-reliance as well as mutual trust. They make them more of a unit. The natural drugs, the dancing, the rites of passage, the visiting of the spirit plane when they're exhausted, stoned and awash with adrenaline – it is all brutal but effective team-building. And I bet your men are doing something equivalent now – testing each other in increasingly dangerous and painful ways, seeing who they can count on when their life's on the line.' Richard didn't mention such concepts as stripping weapons while sitting naked underwater. He didn't need to. Ivan nodded, a good deal of his thoughtlessly patronizing expression vanishing.

'Even at the end of the ritual, when the kids get covered in scars across their cheeks and chest, they're supposed to represent the claws of the gods dragging them back into the real world and up into manhood. The bigger the scars, the harder the gods had to pull, the greater a warrior they think you'll become. But in many cases the cuts originally made are relatively shallow – then the huge scars are built up by having herbs and so forth rubbed in them. But the point is clear. The rituals build calmness under extremes of pressure and tolerance to extremes of pain.'

'Hmmm . . .' said Ivan.

Richard thought back to the men Robin and he had seen training aboard *Volgograd*. 'Even the scars are a bit like the tattoos some of your men have all over them.'

'OK,' said Ivan with a slightly guarded laugh. 'But your point is – *Kebila's* point is – that because most of his men have gone through this, they know the jungle – the battleground – better than my men ever will.'

'And each other. Most of them have not only been through it, they've been through it together. And *themselves* come to that – how much pain they can take. They know the jungle, the situation, the enemy and each other inside out, in a way not even the strongest and best trained of your guys ever will.'

'Until we've been up there. I'm a quick learner.'

'Until you've been up there,' said Richard quietly, 'and come back out alive and in one piece.'

'Hmmm . . .' said Ivan again. Then he apparently changed the subject slightly. 'This Ngoboi. The leader of their gods. What does he look like?'

'Google him,' said Richard shortly and suspiciously. 'He's on the Web. Better make it *Ngoboi Poro* that you type in. There are videos and everything.'

'You're kidding, right?'

'Nope.'

*   *   *

Over dinner back at the hotel that night Robin and he discussed the tension between the two groups of men and then retired. Fortunately, neither of them was romantically inclined, because no sooner had they switched off the light and settled down side by side than the phone rang. 'Wow!' said Robin. 'That could have been a bit inconvenient.'

'We wouldn't have *had* to answer it,' Richard replied, lifting the handset. 'We've ignored the bloody thing often enough before. Yes?'

'Usually with disastrous consequences,' whispered Robin.

'Captain Mariner? It's Andre Wanago here, sir. Major Kebila wonders whether you could join him at the harbour. He has sent a car.'

Richard looked at his Rolex. 'Kebila's sent a car for us. Wants us at the harbour.'

'At this time of night?' demanded Robin loudly, clearly deciding whether or not to be outraged.

'At this very moment, if possible,' said Andre, who had clearly heard her through the phone.

'Sounds important,' said Richard. 'I'll be there, Andre. Five minutes.' He hung up. 'You want to come?'

'Yes,' answered Robin shortly.

'At this time of night?' he mimicked, stepping into his underwear.

'At the very worst, it'll be better than lying here wondering what mischief you've got yourself involved in!' she snapped, rolling out from under the silk sheet and reaching for her panties.

Within ten minutes they were dressed and down. The car awaiting them was a Jeep and the driver was familiar to both of them. 'What's up, Sergeant Tchaba?' asked Richard as he settled into the rear bench seat beside Robin.

'Bad thing!' the sergeant grunted with unusual rudeness as he engaged the gear and drove away at top speed.

When Sergeant Tchaba eased the Jeep to a halt at the dock-side, Richard was shocked by how bad things actually seemed to be. Beneath the flat sodium-yellow glare of the dockside security lighting, the better part of one hundred men stood in two tense groups on the dock, facing each other down. It seemed as though both sets of soldiers were crowded at the sides of their respective hovercraft and only the greatest efforts of their commanders were keeping them from going at each other like rabid animals. It was certainly instantly clear why Kebila had not risked phoning Richard directly and had simply sent Tchaba in the Jeep. The dapper colonel was, seemingly, single-handedly holding back his usually highly disciplined troops, almost leaning against the front row, arms spread like a policemen in front of a crowd of football hooligans. Richard saw Ivan standing opposite him, in much the same position. The air between them crackled with tension and the threat of immediate violence. It was only when they got a little closer that Richard could see Captains Zhukov and Maina with their respective ships' security teams backing the commanders and just about keeping the peace. Like the Earp brothers in Tombstone.

On the ground between the outraged soldiers lay what looked like a big pile of straw. Richard recognized it immediately. 'Oh my God,' he said.

Robin, who had not been privy to his talk with Ivan earlier, was a little slower on the uptake. But not by much. 'Is that what I think it is?' she asked as they hurried forward, side by side.

'Looks like it,' said Richard shortly. 'Looks like someone's shot Ngoboi.'

Confrontation

'Colonel!' called Richard in English as he strode across the concrete towards the fallen god. 'Senior Lieutenant . . . Has either of you called Mr Asov?'

'I did,' called back Ivan. 'He and Mr Makarov are on their way.'

'Then I would suggest to your men, Senior Lieutenant,' bellowed Richard in his rough, workaday Russian, certain that every man behind Ivan could hear him loud and clear, 'that if they wish to continue working for Bashnev/Sevmash and have any hope of a ticket home that they had better get back aboard.' His voice seemed to echo off the flanks of the massive hovercraft as they crouched side by side on the slipway, making a kind of steel-walled valley in which the two mobs confronting each other seemed trapped like gladiators in the Coliseum.

'But that's Pavel Zaytsev!' called an anonymous Russian voice.

The whole scrum of Russians surged forward, until Ivan bellowed, '*Vernis!* Get back!' And Caleb Maina's men cocked their weapons with a crisp precision which reminded Richard all too forcefully that many of them were local and – in spirit at least – on the side of Kebila's troops. Just as the men backing Kebila were from Zhukov's crew. And Russian to a man. And, now he thought of it, Caleb Maina, the man commanding the armed guards holding the Russians back was a cousin to Laurent Kebila, whose men they were threatening. And, as Kebila had already explained, that relationship here could be closer than that between brothers or father and son in the West. *Christ!* This was getting complicated!

'*Tishina!*' bellowed Richard in his foretop voice, rapidly running out of patience. 'Shut up! If it's Pavel Zaytsev, what in Hell's name is he doing dressed as an African god?' He was beside the fallen man now, kneeling at the edge of a puddle of blood that looked black in the yellow light. He pressed his fingers to a stubbled throat as rough as coarse sandpaper and checked gently but in vain for the throb of a pulse.

'You know the answer to that,' whispered Robin in her most withering voice, like a devil at his shoulder. 'It was a *boys' game*. They were teasing each other. Big brave Pavel there wanted to see if he could scare the poor benighted locals. Dress up as their ju-ju leader and do a magic dance. And if they've only blown his balls off then he's lucky!'

'He's not lucky,' spat Richard. 'He's dead.'

'Oh! Christ! I . . .'

'*Vernis!*' bellowed Richard, pulling himself to his feet. 'Shut up!'

He was probably talking to Ivan's men. But Robin wondered . . .

Then he repeated, 'If you're all still out here instead of back in your quarters aboard *Volgograd* when Mr Asov and Mr Makarov arrive, then you're finished. *Nee da dyeloni!* Totally fucked. Sacked without pay and left to find your own way home. I've seen it happen. They did it to a couple of body-guards called Paznak and Voroshilov. God knows what happened to them. They're probably out there in the jungle somewhere trying to hitch a lift to Moscow from a passing panther!'

'Hey,' called another anonymous Russian voice. 'I know them! I know about them! Paznak and Voroshilov really are *nee da dyeloni*. The Angličan is telling the truth.'

'Of course he is!' bellowed Ivan. 'And you do not want to be in the *govno* like them! Remember it was Zaytsev and his mates who started this.'

'Zaytsev's a *zalupa*!' called another voice. 'They're all mastur-bators. This whole thing is *pizdets*. I'm going back to my bunk.'

'Yeah,' called another. 'He asked for it. He got it. He's a RUS *Makaroniki* anyway. *Yobanyi karas!*'

'Right,' called a third rough voice. 'Typical *Politsiye mudak*!'

Suddenly the pressure on Ivan was lessening. It looked to Richard like the men Ivan had pointed out as being army men – the GRU – were giving up on the situation. Though, under the lemony glare, it was hard to tell one bald skull from another.

The pressure on Kebila began to slacken too as his men all began to stream away, round the corner, and in through the gaping front of *Stalingrad.*

Then suddenly both sets of men were moving slowly and angrily back up the sloping slipways, into the gaping hovercraft and back to their bunks.

So that when Max arrived, slightly the worse for wear, breathing metaphorical fire and brimstone liberally mixed with actual vodka fumes, and with Felix icily at his side, there was nothing to be seen except a circle of men and women with a fallen god lying in a big black puddle of blood at their heart.

'What's all the fuss about?' demanded Max angrily.

'RUS Sergeant Pavel Zaytsev,' answered Ivan, nodding down at the bundle of straw and raffia lying on the ground.

'Why's he in that get-up?' demanded Felix, who had less experience of Benin La Bas than the others.

'He's dressed as the local god Ngoboi,' explained Robin tersely. 'He did it to wind up Colonel Kebila's men. To see how superstitious they were, how easily frightened. But he screwed up somehow and they shot him. He's dead.'

'He was Africa trained,' said Ivan. 'One of the experts who was going to instruct the others on local conditions. He should have known better.'

'He should have known better all round,' said Kebila with masterly understatement, and a great deal of sheer *sangfroid*, for he was clearly enraged that this had happened. 'He should have known better than to put on the costume in the first place. He certainly should have known better than to come out here alone . . .'

'Ngoboi always has at least two attendants,' supplied Richard to Ivan.

'And he should have known the dance,' Kebila concluded.

'Right,' said Robin pointedly. 'There's no use putting on the get-up if you don't know the right moves.'

Max looked down at the unfortunate soldier. He was also furious and not a little drunk. But he was no fool. 'How much damage has this done?' he demanded of the two leaders. 'Will the men be at each others' throats now?'

'My men won't be too happy that the Russians have

committed a sacrilege like this,' said Kebila. 'It's not as bad as defacing the Qur'an is to Moslems. But it's close enough. All in all, it'll have strengthened my command internally, though. It's made Corporal Oshodi a local hero.' He looked up. It really wasn't necessary to explain that Oshodi had fired the fatal shot. 'Even the hard-line Poro men who wouldn't, unlike him, even dream of shooting Ngoboi think he's done a good job with a blasphemy like this. At least, that's how it looks at the moment.'

'My men will have to do some team-building,' said Ivan bitterly. 'Or rather, I'll have to do it with them. Maybe right back to the start. They're not happy with Kebila's men for killing one of their own, no matter how stupidly he was behaving. But that doesn't mean they're unified. Quite the reverse, I'm afraid. Everyone'll have a down on the Politzia – not that they didn't in the first place. They'll be down on the RUS for certain – on the assumption that it was Zaytsev's mates that dreamed this up with him – and probably the Vityaz as well because they and the RUS hang around together. Though I don't know which way the FSB will jump – they tend to side with the Politzia against the GRU under normal circumstances. And the army men think the internal services – Politsia and FSB – are a bit of a joke. The whole command could come to pieces. It'll require some very delicate handling.'

'Well, you have to handle it – delicately or not – and you'll have to do it on the run,' snapped Felix. 'We've no intention of hanging about here while you mollycoddle a bunch of prima donnas.'

'Ballet dancers,' whispered Kebila with a sneer. And Richard really, truly hoped that no one else heard or understood the colonel.

'Box him up and send him back,' decided Max brutally, his narrow, bloodshot eyes still on the late Sergeant Zaytsev. 'If you find any of his cronies was involved, do the same for them.' He looked down at the bundle on the ground. 'He's lucky he's dead,' he decided at last. 'If he'd caused all this trouble and was still breathing, I'd have throttled the stupid *durak* with my own bare hands.' And he obviously meant it.

*　　*　　*

'That was a point well made,' said Richard as he and Robin sat in the Granville Lodge Hotel's twenty-four-hour bistro, nursing cups of coffee and waiting for the adrenaline to work its way out of their systems.

'What point?' asked Robin guardedly.

'If you put on the costume you need to know the dance . . .' Some time ago Richard had planned to disguise himself as Ngoboi, hoping to perform a rescue. Only the fact that he didn't know the complex ritual steps of the god's magic dance stopped him. Someone else had put the disguise on instead. Richard had gone in after them a little later. In a Russian T80 Main Battle tank.

Robin nodded. 'It's part of a wider point, though, isn't it?' she said. 'Ivan's boys need proper intelligence. In-depth briefing from someone who really knows what he's talking about.'

'Someone who isn't part of the situation. Someone they'll listen to.'

'It can't be Kebila or Caleb Maina. They're tainted in Russian eyes.'

'Who else do we know, then? Who else can we suggest?' mused Richard.

'What was the name of the man who commanded the squad that went in alongside you and the tank when I managed to talk you out of dressing up as Ngoboi and going in undercover the last time we crossed swords with the Army of Christ?' asked Robin.

'By the grace of God you did . . .' Richard nodded.

'Hmmm. But what was his name, Richard? What was his name?'

'Huge guy. Really good commander. Steady as a rock. Moro? No . . . Draco? That's not it. But a top-flight soldier all the same – just the man we need to keep the peace between the two warring factions if we can get him. I know,' said Richard insouciantly, 'let's go to bed and think on it. Maybe something'll come up in the night . . .'

Robin tilted her head a little sideways. The corners of her grey eyes crinkled into a knowing smile. 'You're still full of it, aren't you, sailor?'

'Adrenaline?' he asked innocently. 'I certainly am! How about you?'

'Fizzing,' she admitted. 'And this coffee hasn't helped at all. How on earth are we ever going to get to sleep?'

'I'm sure we'll think of something. Let's go.'

Richard and Robin attended a brief planning meeting at eleven the next morning; the earliest a clearly hungover Max could manage. 'I've sent the lot of them back,' he snarled. 'Those damned RUS clowns were more trouble than they were worth.'

'And that confrontation has shown us that it would be better to move the men for the time being,' added Felix. 'What's left of Ivan's group would be better aboard *Stalingrad* with the Russian captain and crew while Kebila has agreed to move his men on to Caleb Maina's *Volgograd*. But that still doesn't solve the problem of losing a dozen or so RUS men.'

'And to make matters worse,' snarled Max, switching the dyspeptic beam of his red-rimmed gaze to Ivan, 'you were relying on those RUS masturbators to get your men ready for the jungle. Now what are you going to do?'

'As a matter of fact,' inserted Richard smoothly, 'Robin and I came up with something after we got back last night . . .'

Mako

'You want me to go easy?' whispered Ivan. But only Richard and Mako heard him.

'No need,' answered Mako, like distant thunder. 'Give it your best shot.'

Both men were squared off, facing each other in the centre of *Stalingrad*'s massive storage bay. They were both stripped to the waist. And, as well as Richard and – more distantly – Robin, Max and Felix, they were surrounded by what remained of Ivan's Spetsnaz command.

Mako was even bigger than Richard remembered him. His shaven head looked like a black bowling ball. The muscles of his upper torso seemed to have been carved in anthracite. And, of the two men, he was by far the more massive. Even his neck, short as it was, seemed thicker than Ivan's thigh. Richard thought he heard the word *'Gorilla'* – the same in Russian and English – but the tone was, if anything, awestruck.

Mako stood like a mountain – like Karisoke itself – and waited. He seemed calm. Relaxed. Neither fazed nor bothered by his position or his opponent. He oozed a quiet confidence that Richard, for one, would not have felt for a moment had their places been reversed.

Then, an instant before Ivan attacked, in that micron of time when his eyes dilated, his breath hissed in and his muscles tensed, the decision made, Mako struck. He moved incredibly swiftly. Ivan, mentally committed if not quite physically so, was too late to adapt his move and when the two bodies crashed together, he was the one who span away, barely able to keep his feet. There was no science to that first encounter – no hand-, arm- or foot-work. No chops, punches or kicks. Mako's charge simply slammed them hard against each other like a pair of charging bulls. The sound of the impact echoed around the massive space, extended by a kind of gasp from the Spetsnaz men.

Ivan danced back a little unsteadily. Mako seemed to settle into himself again, statue-still – except that he shook out his arms, easing and relaxing the massive muscles, opening and closing his fists. Richard noticed with some surprise that Mako was wearing a ring; what looked like a plain gold band on his wedding finger. Richard had always assumed the man was married to the service. And even if he wasn't, the glittering circle seemed somehow out of place. Out of character.

Ivan came in again at once. He had taken less than a step before Mako erupted into motion. But this time the Russian had been feinting and the massive African was met by the sole of a left boot that would have flattened his already battered nose if he hadn't caught it in those enormous fists and twisted it viciously. Ivan kicked his other leg high at once, using Mako's grip as a fulcrum, and swung his right boot at the black cranium. Mako saw it coming and looked down. His head sank between his shoulders like a turtle's into its shell. The bull-thick black neck seemed to vanish. The boot skidded off the top of the bald dome and Mako let go, leaping back as Ivan landed lightly and span into position once again.

'Hey,' rumbled Mako in an amused, friendly voice which carried effortlessly to the farthest corner of the place. And in fluent, if American accented, Russian. 'You give ballet lessons, Senior Lieutenant?'

The laugh that went round the audience was one of genuine amusement – and suddenly there was an air of excited expectation.

Mako threw himself forward and battle royal was joined.

An hour later, Richard, Robin, Max and Felix were in *Stalingrad*'s otherwise deserted mess, gathered round a table, drinking coffee, when Kebila, Mako and Ivan came in. Kebila was, as always, in his perfectly pressed colonel's uniform, complete with cap and swagger-stick – both of which were tucked firmly under his arm. His cap badge, like his pips and collar-tabs, brightly proclaimed his rank, nationality and allegiance.

Both of the others were dressed in fatigue cargo pants and sleeveless green vests. Neither was wearing any badges of rank but both wore berets. Ivan's was deep red and Mako's sage green. The cap badge on the front of Ivan's consisted of gold leaves, red star and hammer and sickle. It was the old-fashioned GRU Spetsnaz badge on a beret awarded to only the fittest, toughest half-dozen men in the whole Spetsnaz organization each year. Richard had made it his business to find out about that beret. Mako's badge was less easy to see but it looked like a dagger shaft going into a green shield. American Special Forces. *That* kind of green beret. The pair of them were well matched.

'Sandhurst . . .' Mako was saying in his abyssal growl. 'Like I keep saying to Kebila, Sandhurst's for parade ground men. Now, while I was at West Point . . .'

And suddenly Richard understood Mako's ring. Wedding finger, left hand. Plain band outermost. Stone and embossing innermost. On the finger that was traditionally joined to the heart. The ring worn with the seal and stone closest to the heart. It was Mako's West Point graduation ring.

'Well?' snapped Max impatiently, cutting through Richard's thoughts.

The three soldiers stopped talking. Stopped walking. Came to attention – or, in Mako's case, something like it. 'Perfect choice from my point of view,' answered Ivan easily. 'Except that he kicked my ass. Colonel Mako will fit right in. And I believe the men will listen to him.'

'Mako?' Max rapped.

'No trouble, sir. I can brief these guys. If they don't listen then I'll kick ass till they do. The men seem to have taken a shine to me, though, so it shouldn't be necessary. Especially as the senior lieutenant here let me kick *his* ass a little to boost my standing with his troops.'

'Kebila?' asked Max, visibly relaxing.

'I'm not sure that popularity with the men is the highest requirement for an instructor, sir. But if that's the way the colonel and senior lieutenant want to proceed then that's fine. The president has already given his authority for the transfer of Colonel Mako's duties, as suggested by Captain Mariner. So it only remains to establish how quickly Colonel Mako can get his kit and whatever he needs to begin briefing Senior Lieutenant Yagula's men aboard.'

'Couple of hours,' rumbled Mako.

'Then I believe we can brief the captains and their crews with a view to departing immediately after the men have been fed their midday meal. On *Volgograd*, that will be at fourteen hundred hours.' He looked at Ivan.

'Fourteen hundred's fine,' said the Russian easily. 'We'll just have to settle for a light *obed*.'

'Fourteen hundred,' said Richard half an hour later. 'That's not much time. Can you both make that?'

Richard, Robin, Max and Felix were in the hotel's bistro, finishing a light and early lunch. Taken, Richard noted, without the traditional bottle or two of vodka. 'I can make it,' promised Max. 'I've got the hotel staff to start moving my stuff aboard *Stalingrad*. I assume you'll be going on to *Stalingrad* too, now there's more room.'

'We will,' confirmed Richard. 'But what about you, Felix? Are you coming aboard *Stalingrad*?'

'No,' said Felix roundly. 'I'm staying here. There are still some important details to be ironed out. The contracts between President Chaka's government and Bashnev/Sevmash for the deployment of the Zubrs is not yet satisfactory and we also have to firm up details about oil concessions and whether we can return our placer systems to the delta – or even get involved in the promising situations with regard to gold and diamonds upcountry. Not to mention, of course, dotting the 'i's and crossing the 't's about Lac Dudo and all that coltan.'

'I smell a rat,' muttered Robin in their room half an hour later still. 'That stuff Felix was talking about is only relevant under one set of circumstances.'

'Yes,' agreed Richard. 'If Julius Chaka retains the presidency. However, if Celine replaces her father in the Oval Office, then Felix will have wasted his time, effort and money. And he'll look like a fool.'

'Felix won't like any of that – particularly not the last bit. Not at all.'

'I agree. Look, if you trust me to get the kit packed and

aboard, I think you ought to make a little visit to the offices of the loyal opposition. It was part of your job description anyway.'

'That's just what I was thinking, my love. And of course I trust you to pack,' answered Robin. 'But I am certainly coming upriver so you just remember where we're going and how much privacy we'll get. Don't get too adventurous with my underwear.'

'Right,' said Richard, crestfallen. 'See you aboard *Stalingrad* at four bells. And don't be late.'

In a lingering memory of the dark days of President Liye Banda, the offices of the opposition party were in the centre of Granville Harbour, immediately opposite the forbidding fortress of the central police station. Robin wondered how Celine Chaka felt each time she came in to work past the sinister building where she had spent so much time in the cells – and a certain amount of it in the brutal regime's torture chambers.

But she was far too sensitive to ask. Instead, when Celine rose from behind her desk, offering a hand and a smile, Robin forgot all about her friend's past, preferring to focus on the present and the future.

'Robin!' said Celine, coming round the desk, hand held out, to enfold her friend in an embrace. 'How lovely!'

Lovely was the word Robin would have used to describe Celine. Tall and reed slim, black hair pulled back from her high forehead in the local style. Dark almond eyes. Full, smiling lips. The traditional costume emphasized the depth of her chest, the breadth of her hips and the length of her thighs. There were very few women whose figure Robin envied. Celine was one of them.

'I thought you ought to know at once, Celine,' announced Robin, 'that things are about to get dirty.'

'Really? How so?' Celine was gently amused, both by Robin's forthrightness and by her genuine outrage.

'Felix Makarov!' spat Robin, as though the syllables explained everything.

'What's he up to now?' probed Celine, still amused rather than concerned.

'The rest of us are just about to head upriver, but Felix is staying behind. He has one or two more details he wants to firm up with your father.'

'I see,' said Celine. Her tone made it clear that she did.

'He knows any agreement he makes with your father will have to be renegotiated with you if you win. So in between discussions, he'll be doing his damndest to make sure that you *don't* win!'

'He'll have to join a long line, Robin,' Celine admitted, shaking her head.

'Felix doesn't *join lines*, Celine. He takes action. And heaven alone knows what he's dreamed up!'

'But this is becoming a civilized country, Robin. There is the rule of law. There is security!'

'And that's another thing. Do you suppose it's just a simple coincidence that your father chooses now – of all times – to send his chief of security upriver when there's no one here in Granville Harbour to watch your back?'

Celine gave her bell-like laugh. 'But Robin,' she said. 'I believe it was your Richard who caused Laurent Kebila to be reassigned!'

'It was. But that doesn't stop it being politically expedient.'

'I know that. And I'm prepared for a vigorous campaign. No holds barred. But still, Robin, we're not talking about Amin, Mobutu, Bokassa or Liye Banda here. We're talking about my father!'

'It's not your father I'm worried about. It's Felix. You could cost him millions if you win – and a lot of time and face starting all over again. I think he'll be quite happy to act behind your father's back and deny all knowledge later.'

Celine frowned. 'How far do you think he'd go?'

'In this situation, as far as it takes to keep your father in office.'

'In the face of the police and of the army?' Celine was incredulous.

'Two of whose most important commanders are now caught up in this business upriver . . .'

'Two?' asked Celine, the last of the amusement draining out of her lovely face. 'I know about Laurent Kebila, but . . .'

'Colonel Mako, his opposite number in the regular army. The man who would need to keep peace on the streets if the police couldn't hold the line. Once again, Richard came up with a vague idea and the president leaped at it. Conveniently. A bit too conveniently, maybe . . .'

'But,' said Celine, frowning, 'if Felix Makarov went too far – fomented civil unrest or did anything requiring the kind of reaction you seem to be talking about, then my father would never forgive him. And he'd have done himself no good at all.'

'If I know Felix – and I do – then I'd say that's a risk he's willing to take.'

Amazon

Celine and Robin were still deep in conversation when a discreet knock at the office door announced Celine's secretary. 'Remember, Mademoiselle Chaka, the House sits at two this afternoon.' The secretary frowned officiously.

'Very well, Yekemi, thank you. Call my car and driver now, please.'

The door had closed behind the young woman before the full significance of her words hit Robin. 'Oh, bloody hell,' she said. '*Two!* What's the time *now*?' She answered herself, looking down at her watch. 'One forty-five. Damn and bloody blast! Celine, how long does it take to get to the docks from here?'

'Ten minutes. Why?'

'They're sailing at two. Four bells. And they won't want to wait. Hell and damnation, I'm going to miss the boat! Richard will be livid!'

'Don't panic, my dear,' advised Celine diplomatically. 'Come down with me now. I'll drop you off on my way to the House.'

'But then *you'll* be late!' cried Robin.

'Don't be concerned,' soothed Celine. 'There's always a lot of procedure before they get down to debating anything important. But we'll still be lucky to make the docks in time. We must hurry. Come along. The car will be outside the door by the time we get there.'

As she exited the front door with Celine at her side, Robin hesitated. She hadn't really thought Celine's offer through. Now she found herself confronted by an official limousine flying the flag of Benin La Bas, beside which stood a chauffeur in old-fashioned uniform complete with cap and riding boots.

'All right,' allowed Robin, climbing in beside Celine in the back, speaking as soon as the directions to the docks had been detailed and the limo pulled away. 'Perhaps I was worrying too much.'

But even as Robin spoke, Celine's car was overtaken by the motorcade transporting Patience Aganga, the minister of the outer delta, which swept past them and turned right towards the parliament building. For a moment, Robin found herself looking across a surprisingly small distance at an unmistakably familiar profile.

'It's started already,' she warned. 'That was Felix Makarov. Going to attend your debate as a guest of the minister, by the look of things! Now don't tell me *that's* not sinister!'

The docks were still bustling when Celine's motorcade pulled up – much to Robin's relief. But they weren't so busy that Richard failed to notice when, how and with whom she finally arrived. 'Now that's what I call thumbing a lift,' he teased as he greeted his flustered wife. 'You get the message across?'

'I'm not the only one at it. Felix is too,' she answered tartly, striding beside him up the sloping slipway into the echoing activity of the hovercraft's central loading bay. 'And chance drove home the message loud and clear.'

'Really? Do tell!' Richard draped a suspiciously loving – possessive – arm over her shoulder as he led her through the busy soldiers. As they walked up the bustling loading bay towards the first internal companionway, Robin found herself almost dazzled by the swarming industry of Ivan's recently re-quartered command. There were squads of men performing final checks on canvas-covered trucks and their contents. Others were securing a range of weaponry from field artillery to handguns and making sure they were safe. Still others were overseeing the final positioning of a pair of T80 Russian main battle tanks, the grey fumes of their exhaust filling the hot stillness of the contained atmosphere like smoke. The heat was stultifying and Ivan had given permission for his men to work without their shirts.

And it suddenly struck her that she was the only woman aboard. The only woman, indeed, in the whole expedition. She didn't know whether to feel overwhelmed or excited by all

the testosterone around her. And – just for the briefest moment
– she wondered whether Richard had risked packing something
really sexy for her to wear. As though aware of her thoughts,
Richard hurried her upwards, away from the muscular
distractions. He guided her past their accommodation, allowing
her little more than a glance into a cramped cabin meant to
accommodate a recently departed RUS, with a bed just big
enough to pass for a small double. Then they were off upwards
again until finally he walked her forward and she found herself
in a strange, almost circular command bridge amid a bustle
of officers getting ready to set sail.

As Richard and Robin arrived, Captain Zhukov came on to
the bridge. 'She's pretty impressive, don't you think?' rumbled
the big, white-haired captain from behind his walrus
moustache.

'I know her better than Robin,' Richard said. 'I was showing
her around.'

'Well, Captain Mariner,' said Zhukov to Robin with pleasant,
old-world courtesy. 'Please just stay where you are and watch
as we get under way. It is a sight you will tell your grandchil-
dren about, I assure you!'

'He means in the future,' whispered Richard. 'In the far,
distant future.'

'All ready?' Zhukov asked his lieutenant.

'All ready, Captain,' answered the young man punctiliously.
'Forward and aft doors closed. Everything aboard secure. All
personnel in their assigned places. All crew ready and waiting.'
As if to support him in his report, the whole great frame of
the hovercraft began to throb as the main motors came on line.

Zhukov turned to Robin. 'We do not *cast* off, you see. We
lift off! Inflate the skirts.'

Robin felt for a disorientating moment as though she was
in an elevator car rising towards the first floor. As the deck
beneath her levelled and settled, vibrating with suppressed
power, Max came bustling on to the bridge. The instant he
arrived he seemed to take charge.

'Full ahead, Captain Zhukov,' he ordered officiously, and
the silver bear of a commander nodded.

'*Pulniv piot,*' he said quietly – or something approximating to that; Robin's Russian was a little rusty and the captain's accent was unfamiliar. The helmsman's hands pushed the throttles forward, however, so the message had got through well enough. The message was also immediately transferred to the engine room, the power to the three huge turbines behind the bridge house cranked up to maximum. With the whole of her massive hull vibrating gently, *Stalingrad* lifted up her skirts and flew.

Anastasia was not consciously thinking about Ivan, but he was never far from her mind at this time of day. In the first cool of the evening she, Ado and Esan were leading the girls in a route march much like the ones Ivan described in the days when they had been in regular contact. Except that there was no route – they went where Anastasia chose on the spur of the moment. And they did not march – they jogged. Further, in an addition to a routine already deeply foreign to the tribal societies of the west coast, they carried makeshift backpacks. Most of the weight of the backpacks consisted of drinking water, so each time they stopped to rehydrate their burden became lighter. It was a system Anastasia had designed and she found it worked well. The girls were fit, lean and strong. Metamorphosing from a group of frightened schoolchildren into a fighting force. Her Dahomey Amazons reborn.

Running was a familiar tribal custom further south and east, she knew. No one would have looked twice at a Masai or a Zulu running across the veldt. But here the girls were followed by cheers, whistles and hoots from Matadi, Yoruba and Kikuyu farmers whose traditions were rooted in fields and forests. Only the boys from the orphanage, out working in the fields with the farmers, looked on silently. And, if the truth be told, a little jealously.

Anastasia and her girls were dressed in clothing suited to their efforts – and again this broke with tribal traditions. Instead of the modest traditional costume of *buba* and *iro*, such as Celine, in fact, was wearing in the parliament building away downriver, they were dressed in loose trousers and vests. The trousers were light, baggy and modest. The vests were high-necked and sleeved to the elbow. When the girls set out, they could have been going to church. The trouble was, of course, that a lot of the water they used to rehydrate their bodies came out again, almost instantly, as perspiration. And, try as she might, Anastasia could not overcome the fact that after a couple of miles the trousers moulded themselves to straining buttocks and pumping thighs, while the vests effectively became as revealing as layers of body paint.

This evening, in an attempt to spare the girls' blushes, Anastasia led them through the cultivated fields first, with the sun setting warmly on their backs, then she swung right off the beaten track and down southwards towards the river. Here, although the soil was fertile, the jungle was thickest. As the sun sank into the tops of the trees far down the delta itself, and the moon began to rise behind her left shoulder across the wide expanse of the river, she led the girls back towards the orphanage, past the township clustered around it and the enhanced landing and docking facilities that had so recently been built there. But it was more than the gathering cool of the evening that made her skin rise into goosebumps, her nipples clench to firm points beneath the soaking cling of her green vest. Suddenly Ado and Esan were at either shoulder.

'Someone's watching us,' whispered Esan.

'I feel it,' gasped Anastasia.

'I don't like it,' hissed Ado.

Anastasia could see her point. Everyone who watched them usually was open – and noisy – about it. This was something else. This was someone watching them in secret from somewhere in the nearby jungle. Her mind suddenly flooded with fears about the news that had arrived from several quarters – not least from Robin on Skype – that the Army of Christ was back.

Automatically, Anastasia picked up the pace, looking around carefully – hopefully without giving her suspicions away to whoever was spying on her and her girls. Let it not be Odem, she prayed. We are not ready for the Army of Christ! A worm of self-doubt gnawed at her, whispering, *We will never be ready for the Army of Christ*. But all she could see was the jungle through whose edge they were running. The slope down to the river on her left. The river, occasionally visible through the trees and the undergrowth. The darkness of the gathering shadows in between.

Without conscious thought, she began to push right, up a slight incline, towards the brightness of the first fields – empty now as everyone had trooped back to town for their evening meals. But even deserted fields would be better than the shadows, she thought. A little breeze sprang up, running down towards the coast. It was a furnace-hot wind, locally called Karisoke's Breath, which often blew just after sunset. Today it made the branches overhead heave and sway, filling the jungle with sinister hissing whispers. And, abruptly, there in her imagination, stepping straight out of her nightmares came Ngoboi.

Ngoboi danced in the gathering darkness at the edge of her vision – never clear when she looked directly at him. But as she ran uphill, fighting to get her little command out of the sinister, watching jungle, he swirled and capered before her. She could see the flash of his raffia skirts as they twirled out of sight behind bushes and trees. She could hear the beat of his dancing feet in the pounding of her heart. The deadly magic of his devilish song in the blood rushing through her ears and in the wind rustling through the trees.

Anastasia and her girls were running full-tilt and very near at the edge of panic, when she burst out of the jungle by the river's edge and plunged on to the new slipway. The ghostly, taunting presence of Ngoboi was replaced by the unexpected bustle of two huge hovercraft unloading what looked like hundreds of soldiers, their transport and their kit. Anastasia did not hesitate. As though the reality of what lay before her was just the product of another feverish dream, she pounded relentlessly into the middle of it. Until suddenly somebody tall and unbelievably familiar straightened and turned to confront her. It might as well have been Ngoboi for all the credence her reeling brain was willing to give what her staring eyes could see.

'*Privyet, Nastia,*' Ivan said in that familiar voice, in those familiar terms that took her back to her childhood before the nightmares began. 'Hi, Nastia.'

'*Vernis!*' she spat. 'Get back!' And she began to add, '*Ya nenaviju tebya!*' I hate you!' But somehow it came out as '*Ya lublu tebya!*' – the exact opposite – instead. Then, like the heroine of the romantic fiction that she so despised, she fainted dead away.

If it had been a romance, Ivan would have caught her and carried her tenderly to safety in his strong but gentle arms. It was not. So she went down like a pile of bricks at his feet. Had the slipway been made of concrete, she would have done herself serious damage. But it was just a rough-hewn slope of red riverbank.

So it was, as Robin observed to Richard later, the mud and not the man that saved her.

Mission

'Ivan! My God, what have you done to her?' cried Robin, simply horrified.

At first glance it looked as though Anastasia had been shot in the head. The side of her face and the T-shirt that clung to her like a coat of paint were liberally splattered with a thick red mess. Her short hair hung in mud-thick, red rats' tails. Her mouth gaped and her eyelids flickered, showing nothing but white between the trembling lashes.

'Nothing!' snarled the Russian angrily. 'The silly little *zaychek* keeled over the moment she saw me. This is red mud, not blood. But I couldn't think of anywhere else to bring her, except to you.' He held her out a little helplessly, like a child with a broken toy. There was more than anger in his eyes. There was pain and confusion. And Robin suddenly started feeling sorry for him.

She looked across her cabin at the bed which was only just large enough to accommodate Richard and herself. It was made up with a pristine, perfectly starched white cotton sheet. She closed her eyes, closed the case she had just put on it and swung it on to the floor. 'Put her down here, Ivan,' she said wearily. 'Then go and get a medic. And Richard. In the meantime, leave her to me.'

No sooner had Ivan closed the door behind himself when the Russian girl's eyes opened. 'Was that Ivan Lavrentovitch?' she asked Robin, her voice soft and croaky. 'Or was I dreaming?'

'Ivan as ever was,' said Robin bracingly. 'Though you look a bit of a nightmare, young lady. Did he hit you or something?'

'I fainted.' Her rasping voice was somewhere between wonderment and outrage. 'I took one look at the big ox and keeled over. It was like I was in a romantic novel. Anna Karenina! Emma Bovary! Pathetic!'

'Are you sure he didn't hit you? You look dreadful.'

'The only thing that hit me was the ground. And I was lucky it was mud instead of concrete. I went down so fast, anything really solid would probably have impacted like Anna Karenina's bloody train!'

Richard announced his presence at that moment, pushing his head round the door. His arrival was a relief to Robin, who was beginning to find the literary references a little testing. But at least she knew that Anna Karenina threw herself under a train near the end of Tolstoy's novel.

'Ivan's gone looking for the medic,' said Richard. Then he registered the two pairs of eyes looking less than charitably towards him. 'How are you feeling?' he asked Anastasia solicitously.

'I'm in shock and in pain and in need of a huge vodka and a long shower. In that order,' Anastasia announced, sounding for once very much like her father.

'But this is a dry ship!' Richard said, almost outraged.

'Is my *otets* aboard?' demanded Anastasia.

'Well, yes . . . Max has a cabin just up the corridor. As it happens . . .'

'Then it's not dry. Go get me some paternal vodka.' She changed from a wounded harridan to an injured kitten in a twinkling. '*Please*, Richard . . .'

'All right. But I know when I'm being ruthlessly manipulated . . .'

Richard arrived at Max's cabin to find that Ivan had beaten him to it. The Russians were in the middle of a heated debate which under most social circumstances would have been private. But Ivan hadn't closed the door and Max hadn't told him to. Richard hesitated uncharacteristically for a moment, testing his Russian to the utmost both in terms of vocabulary and understanding. For although the last couple of Ivan's words came loud and clear, Max's reply was anything but.

'You know very well what the problem is!' Ivan was saying. 'Simian Artillery. Or, more particularly, the lead singer, Boris *whatshisname*!'

'He left his brains on the ceiling. That's all there is to him!'

slurred Max angrily. 'He was lucky we didn't just stake him out and pile his guts on his chest so he could watch himself die in the old way . . .'

Richard thought that this was probably more information than he strictly required – especially as his Russian was not really up to the task of translating Max's slurred voice with absolute accuracy. His understanding of what his business partner had just said would probably not stand up in court, for instance. 'Excuse me,' he asked, feeling as English as Bertie Wooster – and suspecting that Bertie was asking a thoroughly redundant question. 'Have you any vodka handy, Max?'

'Richard! Is that you? Yes, I have vodka. Naturally I have vodka. Russian vodka. But who do you want it for, my poor, teetotal friend?'

He knew how the truth would play out. *It's for your daughter* would be answered by *I have no daughter!* Like dialogue from a Victorian melodrama. So he lied. 'It's for Robin. You know she likes a good solid belt of alcohol every now and then, Max. Well, tonight's the night . . .'

Max gave a grunt of ribald amusement. *'Tonight's the night*, eh?' he said. 'Then only the best will do.' He reached down into a case on the far side of his bed and pulled out a bottle of Stolichnaya *Elit.* 'Tell her it's with my love,' he said, handing it over. 'No. With *your love*, eh?'

'You can rely on it,' said Richard, taking the bottle and finding himself awestruck by the fact that it was so cold his hand nearly stuck to it.

When he got back to the cabin, he found the women in a conversation about Anastasia's childhood and her relationship with both the Ivans who had filled her young life. The conversation stopped when he entered, however. He crossed to the tiny en-suite shower room, reached over to the basin and lifted out a tooth glass. 'Your father says it's the best,' he said, pouring a single measure and passing it over to her. And failing to mention that Max meant it for Robin, not the disinherited Anastasia.

'Did he?' she said. 'Then I'll need to have enough so I can taste it.' She held out her hand for the bottle, and when Richard passed it over she filled the glass to the brim, then tossed it back in three great swallows. She rested both the glass and the bottle on the red wreck of the bed, one on either side of her hips, eyes closed. Her whole body rigid. Then she took one great, shuddering breath. 'So,' she said. 'Bring me up to date before I drag myself off to the orphanage showers.'

'I thought you knew that Colonel Kebila was going to use this area for his first base,' said Richard with a glance across to Robin, who had been the Skypemistress of the trip so far and therefore the head of communications. 'He plans to set up camp here – using any of the orphanage facilities you can share, and then send out patrols to secure the farmland and protect the farmers in the cooperatives as necessary – while tracking and catching Odem and his Army of Christ.'

'He thinks they're on this side of the river?' she asked, frowning.

'They could be, he thinks.'

'He could be right. I had the feeling I was being watched just before I bumped into Ivan. Esan, Ado and I were pretty certain someone was spying on us from the jungle on the bank just a little way from here.'

'Then Kebila may have arrived just in time,' said Richard. 'If whoever was watching you was a point man for the Army of Christ, this lot will scare him away. Even if it was Odem himself, he'll think twice about taking on Colonel Kebila and his command. But I'd better pass on your intelligence to him just in case. Unless you want to report to him yourself.'

'Looking like this? I think not, Richard.' The vodka was mellowing her. He could almost see the strain draining out of her long, slim body.

'I'll talk to him then. Better safe than sorry,' decided Richard, thinking of the way Mako had struck at Ivan just in that second before the big Russian was ready. That might be a stratagem that could appeal to Odem if his army was close at hand, given that it was probably as well equipped as Ivan's men were. 'But he's bound to want to check with you, Ado and Esan.'

'I'd better get moving then,' said Anastasia. She swung her legs off the bed. 'Unless,' she said, 'I can shower here and borrow a towel and a change of clothes from you, Robin.'

'Well, of course,' said Robin without thinking. Then she saw the implications of her generosity. She shot a slightly hunted look at her suitcase and the wisps of silk and lace that were bulging out of its ill-closed side.

'Fear not,' said Anastasia. 'I won't steal any frillies. Just lend me a shirt and some jeans and I'll go commando.'

Richard was deep in conversation with Kebila in his makeshift office – the captain's day room – when Anastasia arrived. She had brought Ivan with her, and Kebila nodded at the huge man companionably enough as he joined the conference as of right. Richard found himself marvelling at how fast the couple seemed to have mended fences – to the extent that they had achieved a sort of armed truce, at any rate – and speculated as to whether vodka had played any part in their reconciliation.

'Thank you for coming so swiftly,' said Kebila, rising and gesturing Anastasia to a seat. 'What Captain Mariner tells me you experienced may be of the greatest importance. I have sent a man to the orphanage to ask Esan and Ado to join us. I expect your stories to match what Captain Mariner has told me and when they do, I will use this information as the basis of my strategy.'

When Esan and Ado arrived mere moments later, they confirmed that someone had been secretly watching them from the jungle close to where they were completing their route march. On this side of the river, therefore. And no – they had never experienced this feeling before, they explained to Richard, who got the question in a moment or so before Ivan. And, no – no one local had ever spied on them. It was not in the nature of the local farmers or the townspeople, all of whom called and whistled when the Amazons ran by, they explained to Ivan, who nodded and said that Russians were the same. Open. Honest.

Sexist, thought Richard. Antediluvian.

So, by the time the six of them had finished their conference, Kebila's mind was made up. It was his mission to set up camp here and then to seek and destroy the Army of Christ. But the army, it seemed, had come to him. Chance had given him the opportunity of completing his mission more quickly than he could ever have dreamed. All he had to do was get enough of his men ashore and he could send out the first patrols tonight.

'I can call for air support from dawn,' he said. 'I can have planes within half an hour, attack helicopters within one hour and troop transports within two, if I need more boots on the ground.' He looked at Richard and Ivan. 'We have the Chegdu Jian sevens which can get up there at twice the speed of sound. They are armed with a range of weaponry effective against troops and light armour on the ground. We have the Hip and Hind attack helicopters with gattlings and hellfires. And the Eurocopter Super Puma transports. All armed, fuelled and ready to go!' He rubbed his hands in anticipation. 'With any luck, we could have settled things with Odem within a day or two.'

'And in the meantime,' said Ivan quietly, 'while you're looking after our main worry here, we can take the second Zubr and head straight upstream in the morning. You could have your mission finished within days. And, if Odem and his army are down here fighting with you, then there's nothing between us and Lac Dudo – so we could get our mission completed in record time as well!'

Decline

But it wasn't quite as easy as that. In spite of the care with which the plans had been drawn back in Granville Harbour, there was no way Kebila was able to move his entire command ashore swiftly enough to get his camp set up overnight. No more than Ivan and Mako could move the Russians out of their cramped quarters to fill the spaces left by Kebila's troops. On the other hand, Richard and Robin had come packed and dressed for bush work, even if some of Robin's underwear was more suited to bedroom work, and even though at least two items had already come ashore with Anastasia. Richard's main interest in the long term might be the lake, but Robin's more immediate concern – and therefore his own – was for the safety of Anastasia, her colleagues and the orphans they were guarding against the Army of Christ.

The Mariners' kit followed Robin's shirt and jeans off the hovercraft pretty quickly, therefore, and they were moved into the orphanage's cramped but comfortable guest room, to which the clothing was returned almost immediately as Anastasia dressed in her own attire. No sooner had Robin settled in than she was off, making the acquaintance of the orphanage staff and as many of the children as she could find on whom to practise her increasingly fluent Matadi. Richard only caught one distant view of her, already at the refectory's high table, talking animatedly between mouthfuls of modest supper.

The truth of the matter, thought Richard as he strode through the ordered chaos in the orphanage's great square playground, was that it was going to take another full day at least to get the rest of Kebila's men as well sorted out as Robin and he were. It was fortunate that the expanse of the orphanage's central area opened on to fallow fields which allowed Kebila's men to set up camp in the very area that might be most exposed to sneak attack. But erecting the tents and getting the men fed and organized was slow work, even if the Russians were catered for by the teams aboard the hovercraft.

And the situation was exacerbated by the fact that Kebila was as good as his word, thought Richard, as he went past the inner perimeter, chewing on the last of a *Kyinkyinga* – a meat and vegetable kebab dusted with peanut powder then wrapped in flat bread – which he had grabbed in passing when it became clear that he and Robin were not going to share their usual dinner *a deux*. The first squad of men who had come into the open area at the heart of the orphanage in the early darkness did not stop to help set up camp. They were fed first – and then focused on unpacking arms and equipment and preparing to go out into the jungle immediately. Anastasia, Ado and Esan agreed to guide them to the point where they had felt themselves being secretly observed. And, for no reason other than that he was on hand and at a loose end, Richard decided that he would go with them as well.

The patrol was led by one of Kebila's most trusted men, Sergeant Tchaba. Tchaba knew and respected Anastasia, Ado and Esan. He knew Richard also – and so was willing to take him along. But the sergeant blamed Richard for the fact that he had a false foot – though, to be fair, Richard had done no more than borrow the sergeant's lucky boots at an unlucky time – and their relationship was one of professional respect rather than mutual admiration, therefore.

'You can come, Captain Mariner,' growled Tchaba. 'But you stay low, remain quiet and do what I tell you. And you don't get a gun.'

'That's fine, Sergeant,' said Richard equably. 'If anything violent happens I'll get my head down and keep out of your way.'

'It's all right, Richard,' whispered Anastasia. 'Ado, Esan and I will look after you.' The three of them held up the guns they had come into the compound carrying. Richard recognized them. He had given them to Anastasia some time ago in the face of the earlier attack by the murderous Army of Christ the Infant, under the now deceased General Moses Nlong. It was Anastasia's shot, indeed, which had dispatched the general in the end.

'Ado and Esan, you know where we're going and you know

the jungle better than the rest of us. You take point,' rasped
Tchaba. He handed each member of the patrol night-vision
goggles and checked everyone's weapon. 'These goggles are
dual function,' he explained quietly as he did so. 'Setting one
– here – is enhanced light. It works by picking up what light
there is in the environment – and there is almost always some
– and amplifying it. Setting two is simple infrared. It picks
up and enhances heat. Setting one gives you wide vision in
green. Setting two gives you specific ranges of vision in red.
We use setting one for general work. Setting two if we suspect
heat sources nearby. It's particularly useful for tracking
enemies in the jungle. Or any animals large enough to pose
a threat. OK?' They all nodded, though the sergeant had
obviously only been briefing the newcomers rather than his
experienced squad. They put on the goggles. They tried both
settings. They gave a general thumbs-up for *Ready*. 'Lead on,
Ado,' said Tchaba at last.

Anastasia fell in beside Richard and they all headed off into
the darkness. The goggles took a bit of getting used to, as did
the requirement for absolute silence. But the hand signals were
pretty standard and the vocabulary limited. Stop. Go. Right.
Left. Down. Up. That just about covered it, thought Richard.
Other than that, there was just the discomfort of the goggles
on his face and the way they seemed to channel the perspiration down his cheeks like tears. Anastasia's proximity had a
strange effect upon him. As they crept into the weird, night-
vision world, in the heart of the tight phalanx of glowing
figures, he began to replay that odd conversation he had overheard as he approached Max's room in search of restorative
vodka for the warlike woman at his side.

'*You know very well what the problem is!*' Ivan's words
echoed. 'Simian Artillery. *Or, more particularly, the lead
singer, Boris whatshisname!*'

'*He left his brains on the ceiling,*' Max had answered almost
incoherently. '*That's all there is to him! He was lucky we
didn't just stake him out and pile his guts on his chest so he
could watch himself die in the old way . . .*'

It was the phrase, '*He left his brains on the ceiling . . .*' It
seemed to Richard that there was a problem with the grammar

there. A conundrum that took him back to the half-forgotten Latin lessons of his schooldays. For Russian, like Latin, had a range of cases from which words acquired subtleties of meaning as well as of ending and pronunciation. The main grammatical cases through which nouns declined were Nominative, Accusative, Genitive and Dative. In Latin as well as in Russian, they all had the same basic functions. Nominative for the subject of a sentence. Accusative for the object.

'The *nominative* cat sat on the *accusative* mat,' he had learned to chant while he still wore short trousers. Genitive to show possession: 'The *genitive* cat's bottom was on the mat,' his Latin teacher used to joke.

But this Russian grammar lesson was anything but funny. *He* – the Russian '*oh*', was in the Nominative. It was the subject of the sentence. *He left his brains.* That was the start of the problem. 'His brains . . .' '*Yuvan mosk . . .*'Somehow the second *his* '*yuvan*' had become moved into the Genitive. And Richard's understanding of the Genitive case in Russian was that it described the possession of someone other than the subject of the sentence. So the *he* and the *his* could not refer to the same person, as they could in English. There had to be two people in that sentence. And, now he came to think of it, Russian was a reflexive language. Shouldn't it be *his own* brains?

So, parsing the sentence like his Latin master had taught him to do, the meaning seemed to be something that the belli-cose Julius Caesar or the equally gory Homer would have approved of: Man One had left Man Two's brains on the ceiling. Man Two, the possessor of the brains, seemed to be Boris.

Was it, therefore, possible that the '*he*' who was the subject of the strange first sentence wasn't Boris at all – the possessor of the brains on the ceiling – but someone else? A murderer, in fact, that both Max and Ivan knew had *caused* Boris's brains to be placed on the ceiling. An assassin who had shot the unfortunate singer through the head.

But was all this semantic supposition an irrelevancy? An indulgence? A simple waste of time and mental effort? Perhaps it was – except for the damage the whole incident had done to Anastasia, who in the end had blamed herself for the deaths of her brother and her lover. Who had, indeed, discovered both corpses. No wonder she had gone off the rails. But, in Boris's case at least, had she been *pushed* off the rails? By Ivan and her father?

For the next section of the patrol, therefore, Richard followed the greeny-black shapes around him silently but automatically, his mind wandering in and out of immediacy into increasingly lurid speculation. Like Anastasia, he had always assumed that Simian Artillery's lead singer had chosen to end his own life. But now he wasn't quite so certain. There were one or two questions he would like to ask. To ask Ivan, certainly. To ask Max, if he could get him in the right frame of mind. Perhaps even to ask Anastasia herself . . .

Richard's thoughts were interrupted when Ado held up her hand forcefully and the whole patrol came to a silent stop. She motioned *forward* with one finger and Esan joined her. Then she motioned again with a second finger and Sergeant Tchaba limped soundlessly up beside them. For a moment or two they all remained even more motionless than the wind-stirred trees whose restless rustling had more than covered the sounds of their careful movements so far. Then there was a more general direction to move forward.

Tchaba signalled them all to raise their night-vision goggles, then he produced a torch which he shone around with a carefully shaded beam. Richard saw at once that Ado had discovered a carefully prepared bivouac – one that had been used on more than one occasion by the look of things, by more than one secret observer. Not so much a point man as a forward outpost. And if whoever had made and used the bivouac was with the Army of Christ the Infant, then that made it an extremely sinister discovery.

The torch went out at once. The night goggles came down over their eyes once more. Everyone stayed still until their vision readjusted and the green world reassumed its ghostly forms around them. Then Tchaba gave a series of silent signals and his patrol fanned out – except for Anastasia and Richard. Richard saw the sergeant's point. Gifted amateur he might be – competent soldier he was not. And where he went, Anastasia went; where he stayed, she stayed. They both hunkered down silently, side by side, until Richard's knees started complaining, then he knelt on the soft, cool ground. But Richard was never one to waste his time. He looked around the bivouac with his night goggles in position one, straining to discern anything unusual in the green maze beneath his knees. Then he switched over to the infrared.

At once the picture changed – and more than simply in its colour. Anastasia burned at his side like a molten figurine beginning to sink into the cold, dark ground. Cool trees soared, slightly warmer than the ground, the heat of the afternoon still being transmitted through their trunks by faintly glowing sap. Sun-warmed leaves became things of gold and red in the kind of autumn even New England could only dream of. Almost dazzled, Richard looked down at the cool darkness of the ground again. The warmth of the patrol's footprints was fading in parallel pairs out into the gently glowing bush. One set showed only one print and Richard had a ridiculous image of someone hopping away towards the river – until he remembered Sergeant Tchaba's prosthetic foot.

But then, nearer at hand there was something else; proof that they were near the place from where Anastasia had thought her girls were being spied on. The floor of the jungle had been disturbed. It was a different colour to the surrounding area. Someone had been digging here. Richard also began to burrow with his fingers and it was only when they touched something hairy and prickly that he jerked back, suddenly fearful of spiders and scorpions. After a moment, when nothing moved, he reached back into the hole and pulled out the thing he had discovered. It was a fetish. A ju-ju. A magic manikin, like a voodoo doll from Haiti. It was crudely made but he recognized it – it was Ngoboi, deity of the dark places. The Poro god he associated most closely with the Army of Christ the Infant.

Therapy

Colonel Kebila frowned silently at the manikin of Ngoboi standing on the briefing table of his newly erected tent. Richard and Anastasia stood with Sergeant Tchaba, waiting to hear his thoughts. The night wind that had stirred the jungle at the river's edge flapped the canvas walls. The bustle outside was quietening down sufficiently for Richard to hear the steady tread of the inner and outer security guards. Always out of synch – one nearby and the other further away.

'This certainly makes our suppositions look stronger,' said Kebila at last. 'What are your thoughts, Captain?'

'It was a spy point, all right,' said Richard decisively. 'Someone has been keeping a close eye on the orphanage. No matter who they were, that has to be of concern. But as things stand, I would suggest that manikin proved it was the Army of Christ. They were either waiting for Odem to come up with his forces, or they were advising him to wait. But he won't wait long. Odem has scores to settle here. It was where he was defeated and nearly killed. Where his own personal Ngoboi was faced down and shown to be a fake. If he wishes to use magic to re-establish his power then the orphanage is the place his ju-ju proved to be the weakest – and it is here he must come to restore his reputation.'

Richard looked around the earnest faces in the tent, then carried on. 'But of course when he left here, wounded and defeated, the orphanage was a lonely and unprotected place at the edge of the jungle. Now his spies are telling him it's at the edge of a township. Facilities have improved. Communications upgraded. He will likely have more of a fight on his hands if he comes in half-cocked. But on the other hand, there's much more that's worth taking, apart from the restoration of his reputation and power. And his revenge on Anastasia and the rest. So he hesitates – maybe tools up, looks for reinforcements.

'But before he can move, we arrive. That really puts the cat among the pigeons. The spy point is deserted; his men must have pulled back. They'll only have done that on his orders. Because now he *really* needs to think. It was one Zubr that did for him last time. *Stalingrad*, in fact. Now there are two. That's got to make him stop and consider his options. At the very least he has to find out why the Zubrs are here and who – what – they brought with them.'

'But, as you say, he's in a bind . . .' purred Kebila.

'Between a rock and a hard place,' agreed Richard. 'What sort of a general claims Ngoboi is his personal god – and then daren't test him out? I'd double the guards, Colonel. And consider putting out one or two forward posts in the farmland; perhaps even in the jungle to keep an eye on the river. Even with us in place he has to hit the orphanage somehow. Sometime. Soon. If he's even got half a chance then he'll have to come to us before we go after him.'

'And we don't know how he's armed this time,' added Anastasia. 'Last time it was technicals with heavy duty Russian machine guns. If he's come across the river now then he must have boats as well this time around. If he's got mortars or missiles into the bargain, a couple of Zubrs might just look like fish in a barrel to him – just sitting there waiting for his guys to use as target practice.'

'Right,' said Kebila. 'Sergeant Tchaba, double the guards and set up a river watch, then come back here for a further briefing. And Captain, tell Senior Lieutenant Yagula and Colonel Mako I want to see them. And Mr Asov as well.'

Anastasia followed him. Her presence seemed to slow him down. Something in his subconscious probably prompted him to ease back on the quick march. Which, given the way their conversation went, was apt enough. Probably even Freudian. As they both seemed to be heading in the general direction of Ivan and Max – even if she was going to stop at the orphanage before he got to the Zubrs – his earlier thoughts abruptly came flooding back to him. 'Anastasia,' he asked, his voice only just rising above the eerie moaning of the night wind in the tent-rigging all around them. 'Can you tell me anything about how Boris died?'

'My Boris? Boris Chirkoff? Boris from Simian Artillery?' she asked, surprisingly equably. 'Why do you want to know?'

'It was something I heard your father and Ivan discussing,' he said. 'I wondered what actually went on that night. Don't tell me if it's too upsetting.'

'No, I can handle it. You and Robin paid the psychiatrist's bills that got me over it, after all. And your very expensive shrink said it would do me good to talk it all through – especially with people I respect. What do you want to know?'

'I don't know.' He shrugged. 'Just talk it through.'

'OK. It'll be just like another visit to the shrink. Perhaps it'll do me some good. Especially as I've been having nightmares lately – about Ngoboi and Boris. I guess it's because my father's in the country. And now Ivan . . . Well, we were all in the hotel. Simian Artillery and I don't know how many girls. All of the guys had a steady girl, except Fydor Novotkin on the lead guitar. I think he had the hots for me. But I was with Boris, you know? So, we were all in this hotel. The Petrovka just near Red Square. Simian Artillery had given a concert there on the stage in front of the Kremlin. It was a disaster. They got booed off and then they all got bottled. Fydor was terrible that night. But oddly enough, he was the only one the bottles didn't hit, though he was usually a brilliant guitar and a good leader. He held the band together for six months or so afterwards. After Boris . . . But then he vanished and it all just fell apart. I heard he'd come into some money but I was too far gone to care by then.

'I'd never seen Boris so down as he was that night. It was the last concert they gave with him in the lead – though Fydor took over, as I say. We went back to the Petrovka. We had adjoining suites there. A couple of crates of Russian Standard were already waiting in Boris's room and Fydor had been slipped some really high-grade coke and passed it to Boris so we all started to party. Things get a little hazy after that. The only one of us anywhere near sober was Fydor. He was pretty cut up about screwing up his solos, I guess. Boris was there to begin with. He was so depressed. He just wanted to get drunk and high. He did that a lot towards the end. I had to fight off Fydor but he went off himself after a while and left me alone. We all just crashed.'

Richard's footsteps had slowed almost to a standstill. They were three-quarters of the way across the playground, heading down towards the Zubrs, past the main buildings. There was a light in the window of the room he and Robin were sharing but he was caught up in the story. 'Any idea when Boris went and got the gun?' he asked.

'No.' She answered matter-of-factly, her story practised. He got the impression that she was hardly even listening to herself any more. But he was. He was listening more and more closely. 'I have no idea. But there were always guns: Simian Artillery by name and nature. Fydor was our gunsmith – we called him the AKman instead of the axeman. I was so drugged up I didn't even hear the shots. I just remember waking up suddenly, certain that there was something terribly wrong. There was someone beating on the door and screaming like hell. Which was strange, because we never locked the door. Not after Boris nearly killed poor Fydor playing Russian Roulette. I mean, who's going to break in on a well-armed, spaced-out heavy metal rock band, right? But I do remember people beating the door down at the Petrovka that night. Anyway, there was this smell . . . Gunsmoke. Blood. Whatever. A stink like you wouldn't believe! I didn't answer the door. I went into the bathroom because I was feeling pretty rough. And there he was. He was sitting on the toilet wearing only his jeans. No shirt. No shoes or socks. He had the AK under his chin. He was holding the barrel with both hands. To steady it, I guess. He'd put a towel there too. So he wouldn't miss. Even at that range. He must have been *wasted*. And there he was, like, *frozen* there. The top of his head was gone. His brains were all over the ceiling and the wall. His face wasn't on straight. But at least his eyes were closed.'

'If he was holding the barrel under his chin,' asked Richard knowing that he could not be the first to raise the point, 'then how had he pulled the trigger? An AK is a long gun. It'd be a hard trick . . .'

'With his toe,' she answered simply, sadly. '*Simian* Artillery. Apes with guns. He had this trick onstage. His trademark. He used to play the guitar with his toes. Like a gorilla would. Pulling the trigger must have been a breeze.'

'I see, said Richard. 'But even so, there seems to have been a lot of damage. Brains on the ceiling, you said . . .'

'Yeah. Tile. The whole place was white tile. And the blood was really bright red. Like jam. Raspberry *varenye*. And *borscht.* The ceiling tiles were all over the floor, too, mixed in with bits of his skull. You couldn't tell what you were walking on but it all went crunch. I took one look, one step, sat down and started throwing up. I was still there when they broke the door down and came through, though they said that Fydor had pulled himself together by that time and he was holding me. And that was apt, as it turned out. I went with Fydor after that – for a while at least, till he got tired of me and turned me over to the others. The federal prosecutor later told me I was lucky Fydor did that: held me back – I hadn't damaged the crime scene. Killing yourself is still a crime in Russia, though people find new ways to do it every day.'

Richard opened his mouth again. Shut it.

But she had heard it all, and knew the answers to the questions before they were even asked. 'It was really lucky that the Petrovka is a loft hotel – he'd have killed anyone upstairs if there had been a room above. Then it would have been murder too, I guess. But he just fucked up the roof instead. Boris set the selector to automatic before he pulled the trigger with his toe. I don't know how long he held it down for, but the bullets came out at six hundred rounds a minute, went four hundred metres or so straight up. Through his brain. Through his skull. Through the tiles. Through the roof. At seven hundred metres per second. Poor Boris. You don't get any deader than that.'

They parted at the door into the orphanage's accommodation wing. 'You going to be OK?' asked Richard, consumed with guilt. 'It could be a long night.'

'Yeah. They all are, Richard. I'll get through it one way or another. I always do. And – don't worry, it's not the start of a slippery slope – I've the rest of my father's bottle of Stoli to fall back on if the going gets too tough.'

Richard walked slowly down to the Zubrs as the howling of the tent lines faded and the hissing of the black river gathered, going over what she had told him in his mind, trying to work out why on earth there hadn't been more of an investigation. Working it through and through.

Until the penny dropped.

Akunin

Anastasia's father was nowhere to be found. Mako was helping Ivan organize the move of more Russians from one hovercraft to the other, but Richard found Ivan without too much trouble in the bustle. Ivan saw the danger of a waterborne missile attack against a couple of beached Zubrs packed with men and so he handed over to a lieutenant and joined Richard. But as they walked back across the compound, Richard was still fixated on everything he had learned about Boris Chirkoff's death. So he had no hesitation in asking, 'What do you know about the death of Boris Chirkoff?'

'Who?' asked Ivan innocently enough. *Boris whatshisname* echoed in Richard's memory. That was what Ivan had called the unfortunate victim when talking to Max: Boris whatshisname.

'Anastasia's Boris,' he answered.

'It was suicide.' Ivan's tone was dismissive. 'Epic and noteworthy, fair enough. Big enough to hit the headlines, even in Moscow. I mean, an AK under the chin. Brains all over the ceiling . . . That's all I remember. Killed himself.'

'You don't really believe that, though, do you?' probed Richard, going for confrontation. 'You think Max had him killed – God knows he had reason enough, according to his own ideals and with his son dead and daughter seduced. Someone may have made it look like suicide, or enough like suicide to satisfy a perfunctory investigation. But there were too many little details wrong for that to ring true. You know that. You've always known that.'

Ivan stopped, turned and looked down at Richard. His gaze was level and calculating. The black water chuckled against the slope of the shore. The wind moaned distantly in the tent ropes. 'Who says so?' he asked.

'I do,' answered Richard. 'Offhand I'd say it went something like this. A section of the crowd at that last concert in Red Square had been bribed to barrack the performance and throw bottles, though apparently Fydor Novotkin's playing gave them a good excuse. Fydor was the lead guitarist. There's more about Fydor later. Simian Artillery were booed offstage. Their reputation was ruined. Then someone put several cases of Russian Standard up in their suite. That's, what, two hundred roubles a bottle? So right there, someone invested seven and a half thousand roubles in getting the band and their hangers-on drunk. And someone slipped Fydor a really sizeable baggie of good-grade cocaine which he duly passed on to the already miserable Boris Chirkoff. Street value? No idea. But again, not cheap. And the free drink and drugs just laid them all out. Money well spent. But my point is – it cost a lot of money. They were put to sleep on purpose. Price no object.

'Next, Anastasia said they never locked the door to their suite so it would have been easy for someone to sneak in. The band and their girls would never have noticed. But the door was locked when the hotel staff arrived after Boris's death. I'd guess whoever killed Boris did that. To give himself a little breathing space. One way or another.'

'One way or another?' queried Ivan. They were passing the orphanage accommodation buildings now. Ivan glanced at the lit windows and Richard wondered whether he had found out which one belonged to Anastasia's bedroom.

Richard lowered his voice, but his tone remained urgent, his words clear. 'Either someone crept in and did it, then locked up on the way out. Or someone who was already there did it and locked it from the inside to give himself a little more breathing space before anyone else arrived.'

'Someone who was already there?' Richard had Ivan's attention back now. The Russian's voice also dropped secretively. But his tone carried his words over the moaning ropes and the restlessness of the sleepy men. 'Like who?'

'As the police say – *look for motive, opportunity and benefit*. Max had motive and he benefited by way of revenge. He had no direct opportunity but he almost certainly hired someone who had.'

'*As the police say* . . . Like they do in books, TV and films you mean . . .' Ivan's tone carried a sneer now. 'Christ, it's like talking to Boris Akunin!'

'Who?' Richard was genuinely lost for a moment, and not only by the abrupt change in Ivan's tone.

'He writes detective novels. Historical ones. On old, dead subjects.' There was a definite edge to Ivan's voice. Hostility. But it wasn't an outright threat. Yet.

'And apart from Max,' persisted Richard, raising his voice again as they neared the tents – the flapping sides and doors adding to the general restlessness, 'the other man who fits the bill of course is Fydor. Fydor Novotkin, the AKman. What was his motive? He had at least three – all well known. Boris nearly killed him during a game of Russian roulette. He wanted revenge. He wanted to lead the band. He wanted Anastasia. He wanted all three really badly. And to top it off, he probably got a good deal of money from Max into the bargain.

'Did he have opportunity? He certainly did. Opportunity in spades – especially as he was apparently the only halfway sober one there that night. He was the guy who screwed up the performance – but didn't get hit by any bottles. He was the guy with the cocaine but he handed it to Boris – and Anastasia doesn't remember him snorting all that much. And he was the guy in charge of the guns. To top it all, that unexpectedly locked door just makes it look more like an inside job than a visiting hit man. Locking the door gave him just the few moments he needed to get everything straight. And Fydor benefited, didn't he? He got the band, he got the girl. And later, when he decided to give both of them up, he suddenly came into a fortune and vanished.'

Ivan stopped in the middle of the compound. He turned and looked down at Richard. The wind suddenly dropped and everything went quiet apart from the relentless tramping of the sentries marching along their patrol patterns. 'It's lucky you weren't the one in charge of the investigation by the sound of things, Richard! You'd really have stirred things up!' Ivan's tone was ironic. But was there a hint of threat there? Had Richard rushed in where angels might fear to tread? Further in and more foolishly than even he had calculated?

'Yes, indeed,' he persisted at once. *In for a penny – in for a pound.* 'And now that you bring that up, we've arrived at the cherry on the cake, haven't we, Ivan? Because who was in charge of the investigation? Why, the *federal prosecutor,* of course. He took a personal interest, I'm sure. He made sure all the 'i's were dotted and all the 't's were crossed before he filed it away and forgot about it, just like Max would have wanted. The federal prosecutor. Lavrenty Mikhailovich Yagula. Max's secret partner and Felix's *eminence grise*. Your father!'

Ivan said nothing in answer to that; nothing at all. And Richard had nothing more to say either. Which was just as well, for they had reached the door of Kebila's tent.

Kebila's briefing of Ivan was short and to the point – then it was repeated as Mako arrived, and the pair of them went off to find Max, make certain he was safe, then to make sure that their men were on the alert, in case of a possible surprise attack from the river – and to mount extra guards on the Zubrs to supplement the extra sentries posted along the bankside. Richard left Kebila's tent as silently as he had arrived there, with the Russian senior lieutenant and the massive colonel. But he parted company with them at the same point Anastasia had left him, preferring to go into the orphanage's accommodation rather than continue listening to their technical conversation about fields of fire and reciprocal night actions.

He crept along a dark corridor past a door he was sure belonged to Anastasia's room, then opened his own. He found Robin lying on the bed they were to share, clad in her lightest nightgown, with the sheets thrown over the bed foot to lie piled on the wooden floor. In the hot yellow flame of a smoking oil lantern, the little room was stultifying. There was no air conditioning and no fan. The window was shut and the curtains drawn. There were supposed to be no malarial mosquitoes in the area – but there weren't any mosquito nets either and fair-skinned, notoriously bite-prone Robin wasn't about to take the risk. She had a mosquito coil burning in the corner just to make sure, so as well as being stultifying, the room was suffocating. 'Good,' she said. 'Lock the door now you're here. I'm wearing far too much!'

'My God!' he whispered as she stripped off entirely. 'For once in my life I'm afraid I'm just too hot to fool around!'

'So am I,' she snapped. 'Besides,' she added, lowering her voice, 'the walls are extremely thin. And we're surrounded by *nuns*!'

'Oh, that does it!' he agreed, also stripping off as swiftly as humanly possible, already awash with perspiration. 'Consider me a *monk*!'

'If not a eunuch,' she whispered as his pants came down. 'Thank heavens not a eunuch. But where have you been? And what have you been up to?'

Richard lay gingerly on the bed beside her. They both shuffled further apart – in the exact reverse of their normal night-time movements. The bed, however, groaned salaciously. Trying not to think what the nuns must be imagining, he leaned over and blew out the lamp. As the air filled with fragrance from the cooling wick, he whispered, 'It's too hot to sleep as well, isn't it?'

'Damn right!' she answered. 'So tell me all.'

'OK. Right. Remember when Ivan brought Anastasia to our cabin?'

'Looking like she'd just been shot in the head? Of course I remember!'

'And she asked me to go to Max and get some vodka?'

'Stoli *Elit*. Yes, I remember. She still has the bottle, the lucky girl . . .'

'Yes, she does. If you get desperate you can bang on the wall and ask her for some. Well, at the door, I overheard Max and Ivan talking. And what I thought they said was . . .'

Half an hour later Richard had detailed the whole story, how he had worked it out and who he had told about it. Halfway through, Robin's hand crept into his and clenched it tightly. And more tightly as the story proceeded.

'So,' said Robin when he had finished, 'let me just get this clear in my mind. You told Ivan that you believed Max had this Boris person murdered because Boris's drugs had killed his son and heir, and Boris had seduced Anastasia away from him. He did this by arranging the group's big Moscow concert to be a failure. By supplying drinks and drugs in the expectation that the kids would all get so totally blasted they'd have no idea what was going on. By bribing this Fydor creature – who had a grudge against Boris as well as a strong desire to get hold of his band and his girlfriend – to kill him. That Fydor pulled all of this off, got the group, the girl and the money, in the end. And then the whole thing was swept under the carpet by Ivan's father the federal prosecutor in return for becoming a silent partner in Bashnev/Sevmash.'

'That's about the size of it as far as I can figure,' said Richard.

Robin lay silent for a moment. Then, 'And you put this all to Ivan?' she said incredulously. 'I mean, you actually went through it with him step by step?'

'Pretty much.' Richard nodded, banging his head against the wall that divided their room from Anastasia's. 'Seemed like a smart move at the time.'

'He'll take it straight to Max. And what then?'

'Well. Then I was going to suggest to Max that if the secret was out in any case, but it was only hearsay and suspicion, and no one – least of all the federal prosecutor – was going to do anything about it . . .'

'Yes, *what then?*'

'Then shouldn't he tell Anastasia what really happened? She's been blaming herself all these years. Borderline suicidal. And none of it was her fault after all.'

'You were going to suggest that, huh?' she said, her voice suddenly throaty. As though she was on the verge of tears.

'I was going to tell him either he should lay it all out for her, or I would.'

'You'd do that? You'd run that risk for her?'

'Well, wouldn't you?'

'Come here, you bloody man. Come here and kiss me!' She took the hand she had been holding and placed it squarely on her stomach.

'Now, I thought you said it was far too hot for that sort of thing,' he whispered, beginning to roll lazily towards her.

'It was. It is. But I don't care.' She arched up off the mattress towards him. The bed groaned suggestively beneath them.

'The nuns,' he teased. 'What about the nuns?' His hand slid down.

'Sod the nuns,' she said huskily, sliding her arms like snakes around his neck and lacing her fingers into the short hair at the back of his head. 'They can get their own men. Now kiss me. *Please* . . .'

And that was exactly where their conversation had reached when the shooting and the screaming started.

Commando

At the first echoing report, Richard leaped off the bed. Even in the pitch black of an unfamiliar room he reached unerringly for his clothes and stepped into his trousers at once, zipping up and cinching his belt as he felt around on the floorboards with his toes, searching for his boots. For a moment, he regretted returning the night-vision goggles to Tchaba. He could really have used them now. But then there was the flare of a match behind him as Robin prepared to light the lamp. The shadows danced weirdly across the floor but he was able to see his boots with his underwear beside them before darkness returned, accompanied by some rather unladylike language. And, more distantly, a second fusillade of shots. He reached down, grabbed the boots and sat on the edge of the bed to pull them on. Then he crossed to the door, pulling on his shirt as he went. There was no time for anything else. If ever there was a moment to go commando, he thought wryly, this was it.

As Richard ran down the dimly lit corridor, a nun in dishabille jerked back into her bedroom two doors down, and he remembered he was still half naked. He glanced through Anastasia's open door as he sprinted past. Her room seemed empty. Her bed was undisturbed. An almost full bottle of Stoli *Elit* stood on a bedside table. Then he was at the door into the compound. Like the bedroom door, this was open. It seemed Anastasia was moving even faster than he was. But when he stepped out into the vast, noisy midnight, she was nowhere to be seen. He paused, his mind racing. He needed to orientate himself.

Another burst of firing echoed across the orphanage. In the nearby town, there were lights coming on in the windows. Under the rattle of fire, he could now hear the revving of engines. And out here he could discriminate between the thudding of heavier machine guns and the rattle of assault rifles.

The fields must be full of technicals – flatbed Toyota Hilux four by fours with machine guns mounted on the back. Everything from Shipunov gattlings to Bofors forty-millimetre light anti-aircraft guns. African armoured divisions.

Kebila would be sending the T80 main battle tanks against them and hoping they didn't have too many tank-killing rockets. In the last engagement Richard had been involved with the Army of Christ had used Milan anti-tank missiles. If they had many more of those, the T80s would be in trouble. Then the penny dropped. The screaming he had heard could well have been the sound made by the treads of the tanks moving forward. He looked down at the hard earth of the compound and there indeed were the telltale caterpillar tracks.

These thoughts and impressions were all-but instantaneous. Richard was convinced the attack across the fields at Kebila's most heavily guarded positions would be a feint in any case. In a heartbeat he was in motion again, sprinting down towards the Zubrs. Since he had split away from Ivan and Mako, there had been a change in their disposition – a welcome one. The hovercraft were no longer facing upslope and inland. Sometime during his conversation with Robin, the skirts had been inflated and the Zubrs had been turned right round. Now they crouched with their great trios of turbofans facing inwards, their rear access ramps down, and their bows – not to mention all the weaponry mounted upon them – facing out into the river. Even so, they were sitting ducks. Richard sprinted towards the nearest one, just in time to meet half of the Spetsnaz men coming out at the run. Ivan was leading them. He had a field radio on the side of his head and was clearly updating Captain Zhukov on what was happening on the ground. Like Tchaba's patrol, they were all wearing night-vision goggles.

'Tell Zhukov he's got to get moving,' said Richard, joining Ivan. 'If they have boats they'll be coming downriver with all the missiles in their armoury!'

'I agree,' snapped Ivan. 'You hear, Captain? We're clear. Close up and inflate. Get moving as fast as you can.'

'In the meantime,' Richard panted, 'we need to protect his flank if we can. What do your men have on them?'

'Assault rifles. Grenade launchers. The stuff you saw.'

'What's the heaviest you have?'

Both men were shouting now, as *Stalingrad*'s rear ramp screamed up into position and the huge black skirts began to inflate as it did so. 'We have a couple of RPG twenty-eight MANPADS – the RMG variants,' Ivan bellowed.

Richard paused for an instant, calculating. Man-portable air defence systems were all very well but unless they could be guided they were of limited use against waterborne targets. The RMG variant, however, was designed to go anti-personnel and anti-tank as well as anti-aircraft. It would do very well indeed. 'Just what the doctor ordered,' he decided, in action once more. 'Hopefully not the *witch* doctor – as you could find yourselves shooting at Ngoboi himself. Now, we need to locate our positions down by the shore, right at the edge of the jungle there, where we can set up a decent field of fire upriver. I'd suggest you get Mako's men to back us up as quickly as possible. And if they have any MANPADS, they should bring them along with them. Until *Stalingrad* and *Volgograd* are up and out, with their weapons zeroed and readied with their countermeasures on line, we're all the protection they have.'

While the two men were talking and Ivan was relaying relevant sections to Captains Zhukov and Maina – and to Colonel Mako – Richard hurried them down to the edge of the river. On their left the jungle gathered itself into a thickening, almost triangular heave of blackness. But at the edge of the bank itself there was a low cliff, for they were at the back of a meander. And, as though extending the tall jungle on the crest of the bank, a jumble of freshwater mangroves reached out for twelve metres or more. Against the breadth of the slow, black water, the outreach of the mangroves looked minuscule. But on a more human scale, they were as wide as one half of a dual carriageway road.

There was still no moon, but the stars were hanging low and fat in the indigo velvet sky, giving a surprising amount of pearlescent light. Enough to show that the broad reach of the river was clear of everything except for some floating islands of water hyacinth. Richard shook his head, hardly able to believe it was little more than four hours since he was following Sergeant Tchaba wearing the night-vision goggles.

Having taken Richard's points on board, Ivan now assumed command and plunged into the cover of the trees, staying as close to the bank itself as possible, looking for secure positions where he could place small groups of men armed with MANPADS to cover the river and protect the Zubrs from waterborne attacks. Almost immediately Richard began to fall behind, increasingly blinded by the shadows. He moved more and more slowly and carefully, deeply regretting the loss of his night-vision goggles. And, because he was not a member of Ivan's team, he didn't have the communications earpiece either.

But then again, perhaps it was because he was blind and not distracted that he heard the whispering grumble of outboards running on almost silent first. He crouched, forgetting that he was going commando, and almost made a eunuch of himself after all. He looked around through streaming eyes, but the tail-end of Ivan's men were vanishing into the black forest shadows. He looked downstream towards the distant brightness of the slipway where the Zubrs were beginning to stir like sleepy dinosaurs. This was the moment of greatest danger. If Ivan was still looking for secure emplacements and calculating fields of fire, then whatever Richard could hear might well slip past him.

Richard crouched there, turning his head from side to side as though his ears could work like sonar dishes and locate the precise source of the sound. Was it coming from nearby or further away? Richard knew how a Zodiac – a sixteen-seater rigid-hulled inflatable boat or RIB – could slip along a tunnel of clear water under the overhang of mangroves. Odem would know about such things. Ivan wouldn't. On the other hand, the floating islands of water hyacinth would also furnish excellent cover. Richard wiped his eyes, trying to calculate whether the hyacinth was tall enough to offer realistic cover. Ivan would probably work out that the floating plants were a potential danger. But Richard was still worried about the tunnel beneath the mangroves. That was the sort of thing Mako would be briefing them about in the future – which was no use if they needed to know about it now.

Richard moved down to the very edge of the river bank and lay on his belly, easing himself out as far as he could, using the mangroves to support him. But he stood no real chance of penetrating the roof of the tunnel that lay so tantalizingly close. Still, the position he managed to achieve allowed him to listen to the sounds whispering along the channel immediately below the tangle of stems. And it was here that the quiet grumbling of the outboards seemed to be coming from. Burning with frustration, he pulled himself up and scrabbled back until he was kneeling on solid ground.

Abruptly, he was surrounded by legs dressed in cargo pants. Monstrous three-eyed faces stared down at him like something out of a science fiction movie. Then a huge black hand reached down, lifting the three-pointed headset free. 'Hi, Captain Mariner,' rumbled Mako. 'What's happening?' As briefly as he could, Richard explained. But even as he did so, the nearest of the water hyacinth rafts erupted into flame as one of Ivan's men sent a missile out at it.

'Under the mangroves, hunh?' growled Mako, paying no attention to the spectacular distraction and hunkering down beside Richard. He produced a long, articulated stick with a mini camera on the end of it. 'Look in this.' He handed Richard what looked like an iPad. He flicked a switch. Richard saw a light-enhanced version of what the camera on the end of the stick could see. With no further comment, Mako pushed the stick down through the mangroves, turning the camera round until Richard could see a tunnel of woven branches. And there – disturbingly close within it – a narrow boat packed with men in a range of bush uniforms. In the bow, crouching low, but unmistakable in his raffia costume and mask, was the god of the dark places, Ngoboi.

'They're there!' spat Richard. 'Ngoboi . . .'

But as he did so, the second raft of water hyacinth seemed to simply vanish and a sizeable Zodiac inflatable appeared. This too was full of men. And, set up on the bow in place of the evil deity, was a tripod. 'Night glasses!' rapped Richard, and one of Mako's men handed him a pair. He slammed them to his eyes and fixed his gaze on the bow of the Zodiac. He focused until he could see a sleek-looking missile sitting on the tripod, with a guidance system rigged beside it. 'If they launch that it'll do quite a bit of damage. Are you in contact with Ivan?'

'Separate systems. Vladimir! Bring up the RPG! The rest of you fall back. He needs twenty metres clearance to be safe!'

'Warn Zhukov then,' hissed Richard. 'He can try to get his countermeasures on line while Vladimir sets up.' Mako saw the wisdom in that. Just as everyone else saw the wisdom in his orders and cleared twenty metres behind the kneeling soldier.

It was the fact that the men in the Zodiac were equally careful that saved them, thought Richard a few moments later. The inflatable was suddenly rocking wildly as the Army of Christ men cleared out from the missile's exhaust path. The laser guidance system was thrown off. The operator hesitated.

Ivan must have seen something then, because one of his MANPADS came streaking out of the jungle half a kilometre further upstream, just at the very moment that Vladimir loosed off his RPG. The men on the Zodiac saw the rocket-propelled grenades heading their way and threw themselves into the water. But the man with the launcher fired it anyway then all three weapons came together in one unholy meeting. Thirty kilograms of TNT equivalent all went up together with a flash that blew the Zodiac and its crew to atoms.

But no sooner was that threat neutralized than Richard was on his stomach again, probing through the mangroves with Mako's camera stick, his eyes focused on the square of the hand-held screen in front of him. The sinister, mangrove-walled tunnel was empty. The men he had seen had vanished.

Ngoboi was gone.

Immanuel

Richard sat back on his haunches, his mind racing. Where could they have gone?

He turned to Mako. 'Colonel, can you see anything moving out on the water, just beyond the edge of the vegetation?' Mako eased into a better position, swivelled his alien, almost insect-like head, and focused the night-vision goggles on the outer edge of the mangroves.

'Nothing,' he rumbled.

Richard hissed with frustration, looking back into the vast blackness of the jungle behind him. You could hide an army in there, if you could avoid the night-vision goggles, he thought bitterly. Ngoboi had come ashore. And there was only one likely target important enough to tempt the angry god. 'Colonel,' he grated, handing back the camera stick and the handset, 'we've got to get back to the orphanage as quickly as we can.' He paused, his mind whirling. 'Except for one patrol. Leave a patrol here to search along the bankside. There's a way down to the river through the mangroves and the undergrowth. It'll be hidden – camouflaged. But it'll be there. And there'll almost certainly be a boat tied up and someone guarding it.' Then he turned and began to work his way back.

Mako stayed crouched in position for a few more moments, giving orders and passing others along, then he rose, motioned to his men and followed Richard. He caught up after a while, his movements speeded by the night-vision goggles, and he fell in at Richard's shoulder. 'What's your thinking on this?' he rumbled, almost silently.

'Odem has to hit you before you get settled and ready. Before Kebila can call up air support and anything else he has planned for the morning. But he really has only one target at this moment: Anastasia. If Ngoboi doesn't feed her heart to Odem, then he's not half the god he's supposed to be. And as an instrument of terror and control, he's a busted flush. So he's sent his technicals in across the fields and his Zodiacs down along the river – but they're something of a distraction. He's sneaking a little commando unit undercover to grab Anastasia and anyone else he can get hold of. The more hearts the better.'

'This Ngoboi sounds like a hungry son of a bitch to me,' rumbled Mako.

'And then some. Given his head, he's insatiable. And that's the point. With Ngoboi behind him Odem's in total control. No one knows who's next on Ngoboi's list – except for Odem himself, of course. It's a guarantee of sheer, naked power, for as long as the army believe in the magic.'

'Getting his little team in is one thing,' rumbled Mako, returning to the logistics of the situation. 'Getting them out again is another – especially if he wants to take prisoners with him.'

'He'll have thought of that. We keep underestimating him. Odem's no fool. Quite the opposite, in fact.'

Richard's conclusion seemed more than fully borne out as the pair of them led Mako's Russian contingent out into the orphanage's central compound. What had been a bustling encampment was now a deserted ghost town of flapping tents and moaning guy-ropes. The slipways were empty, *Stalingrad* and *Volgograd* out on the wide black water, their searchlights probing the shadows on the stream and along the banks. The tanks, troops and transports were all out in the fields chasing Odem's technicals. Or, at Richard's request, in the jungle along the riverside, watching out for waterborne attacks.

Apart from the restlessness of the wind in the tents, the whole place was eerily silent. The buildings of the orphanage were all in darkness and apparently deserted. That made Richard's blood run cold – in spite of the fact that the wind must be thirty Celsius or warmer. Apart from Anastasia and Robin there should be several nuns, a priest, an imam and a couple of helpers. And the better part of a hundred kids – not counting the twenty or so that made up the army of Amazons that Anastasia, Esan and Ado were apparently training up. That was a lot of people to be sitting silently in the darkness in the middle of a fire fight. He motioned to Mako, and the whole contingent stopped and hunkered down in the shadow of the largest of the tents – the unit refectory tent. 'Pass the word for any Vympel, Alpha and OMON men,' he whispered, peeping round the square canvas side at the dark, silent buildings.

Half-a-dozen burly Russians answered by moving silently forward.

'Any of you know about Beslan?' he asked in his lumpy Russian. They all nodded. That figured, he thought. They were all probably too young to have been involved in the notorious school siege of September 2004 themselves, but stories like that get passed down units like family lore. They were the ones likely to have any experience of what this could turn into, he thought grimly. At the very least they'd know what not to do.

'Zubarov,' one of them introduced himself, taking the lead. 'We know. We lost seven of the Alpha team and nine Vympel at Beslan. And nearly four hundred hostages, shot, blown up, burned and buried. We're not looking at another Beslan here, are we?' He shuddered.

'We almost certainly have between ten and a dozen hostiles in charge of the orphanage,' whispered Richard. 'Possibly a hundred and thirty hostages. They haven't had time to rig explosives and there's no central holding area unless they get them all into the orphanage's refectory building. The enemy's main objective is to get several of them out and away. It'll only become a hostage situation if there's a stand-off.'

'So our best bet is to stand back,' said Zubarov. 'Move away, keep a watch and hope they haven't seen us. This tent makes good cover, thank God.'

'Let them think they're getting away with it,' said Richard. 'Then hit them when they come out with whoever they kidnap. That'll do as a game plan for now. But . . .'

'But?' whispered Mako and Zubarov together.

'They're being led by a god and a commander, both of whom have to make a statement here. They want to eat the hearts of whoever they take. And probably the rest of them into the bargain. They may not want to leave anyone else alive in the meantime.'

'That could complicate things,' said Mako. '*Immanuel*. God with us . . .'

The theological discussion was interrupted by an inhuman howl. A long, tortured scream that seemed to echo from the dark depths of the orphanage.

'That's it,' said Richard. 'Let's go . . .'

The whole of Mako's command tensed, ready to move forward *en mass*.

'*Richard!*' hissed a familiar voice from close at hand. 'Richard! *Wait!*'

'*Anastasia?*' gasped Richard, thunderstruck. The whisper was coming through the canvas wall immediately beside him. He eased himself out of his crouch position and moved to the flap. As he did so, Zubarov pulled off his night-vision goggles and handed them up to him, so that when Richard peered through the tent flap into the troop's eating area, he could see quite clearly, even if everything was a submarine green. And what he saw brought him up short. For Odem wasn't the only military commander he kept underestimating.

The tent was filled with everyone missing from the orphanage. The priest and nuns were all seated with groups of frightened children around them. And the whole lot sat safely under the guns of Anastasia's Amazons. As Richard entered, twenty rifle barrels swung towards him. He held his hands up. Anastasia and Robin stepped forward, flanked by Ado and Esan. 'Has he gone?' breathed Anastasia. 'I heard him scream and I heard you whispering.'

'I don't know,' rumbled Richard. 'But if you're all safe in here then there's nothing stopping us going to have a look . . .' He stepped out of the tent and crouched beside Mako. 'The kids are all safe in there under guard,' he hissed. 'There's nothing stopping us taking a close look at the orphanage.'

'I'll take Sergeant Zubarov and the men you called forward,' Mako decided. 'You wait here with the others. *Guard the guards*, to paraphrase Juvenal. Anastasia's guards and the nuns and orphans they are guarding.'

Zubarov held out his hand for his goggles and the Beslan men were gone the instant Richard handed them back. Richard gestured to the rest of the Russians and they fell into a protective cordon round the mess tent, facing out, weapons at the ready. After a moment, Robin stepped silently out and stood at his shoulder. 'From what I've seen,' she said, her lips and breath hot against Richard's ear, 'the best this lot can hope for is to keep poor old Ngoboi safe from Anastasia and her Amazons.'

But the wry little exchange was hardly over before the lights in the orphanage building came on and Mako's unmistakable *basso profundo* voice called in English, 'Captain Mariner. Ask Miss Asov to come here, would you?' The three of them headed towards the bright building at a trot and walked in through the doorway Richard had run out of a couple of hours earlier, still shrugging on his shirt. This time the doorway was half blocked by a three-quarter-size figure of Ngoboi. The mask and raffia costume had been hung on the wooden slats of a bed roughly lashed together into a sticklike manikin. But the thing still seemed to ooze an eerie sense of threat. Especially as the restless river wind made it seem to dance. 'Take it out,' ordered Anastasia at once. 'It is a Poro curse. If any of the children see it they will be afraid to come in here.'

'I know what it is,' rumbled Mako like a distant thunderstorm. 'I am Thoma myself. Thoma is the third of the great societies of our country. But I cannot allow this to stand. Nor this.' He gestured Anastasia to follow him and led the way down the corridor as Zubarov and one of the others took the makeshift Ngoboi out into the darkness and away.

Anastasia's bedroom was a mess. But not a random one. Her walls had been daubed with bright red splotches of blood. The floor was covered in strange patterns and complicated footprints as though a wild dance had taken place in here. Her bed was covered in blood – but the blood had been used to draw the rough shape of a splayed body. Where the eyes would have been, two long black stone daggers had been thrust into the pillow. Where the throat would have been was a thick red line of blood. Where the thighs would have joined, a huge ebony phallus had been thrust into the bedding with enough force to rupture the mattress. And where the heart would have been there was a gaping, blood-rimmed hole.

'Christ, girl,' said Robin, horror-struck. 'Ngoboi certainly seems to have some sick plans for you.'

Anastasia looked down. She snapped the safety off her assault rifle. 'And I have plans for him, the *ebanatyi pidaraz*,' she swore. She turned on her heel and stormed out into the night, with Richard and Robin at each shoulder. The whole camp was bathed in security lighting now. The two hovercraft still prowled along the nearest river reach, searchlights on full-beam and weapons at the ready. The battle in the farmland seemed to have stopped.

Then, out of the darkness where the tongue of shadowy jungle licked up against the eastern end of the compound, Ivan and his men came in at a steady trot, pulling off their goggles as they came into the light. They were carrying four makeshift stretchers, on which lay the corpses of the little patrol Mako had left looking for the route Ngoboi had taken to and from his boat. The dead men had been laid out reverently enough, but none of them had been covered. Eight dead eyes stared up at the starry sky, the foreheads above them skinned from eyebrow to hairline. Eight hands lay on still stomachs, all their fingers gone. Four mouths gaped silently, their teeth red and their tongues torn out. Each of the four corpses had a hole in his chest, apparently reaching from front to back, where his heart had seemingly been simply ripped out of his body. And each of them had a broad-bladed spear thrust up under his chin to come out a foot or so above the crown of his head.

As chance would have it, Ivan and the corpse bearers came face-to-face with Anastasia first, and the huge Russian stopped, shocked at having confronted his childhood friend with so much bloody brutality. Ignorant, as yet, of how much horror she had already had to face this evening. But then he stepped back, his open gaze clouding with confusion, at the simple rage in her expression. At the tenseness of the finger curled around the trigger of the assault rife that pointed at him with the same steely directness as her usually soft brown eyes.

'*You!*' she spat. 'You and I have something to discuss, Ivan Yagula!'

'What . . .' he said, simply nonplussed.

Richard closed his eyes wearily as it all fell into place,

remembering the unruffled bed and untouched bottle of vodka he had seen as he ran past Anastasia's door, pulling his shirt on amid the screaming and the gunfire. She hadn't been anywhere near her bed or her booze. She had been listening at the paper-thin wall separating her room from theirs while he told Robin what he had found out about the end of Simian Artillery.

'About how Boris Chirkoff really died,' Anastasia snarled now, stepping forward as Ivan stepped guiltily back. 'About who paid for him to be murdered. And who actually killed him. And who let me live *in hell* for ten years and more believing he had shot himself and it was all my fault, you *bastard . . .*'

Confrontations

'Who cares what Anastasia knows or thinks she knows,' snarled Max. 'The stupid little *shluha vokzal'naja* isn't going to tell anyone who matters. Not in this godforsaken hole anyway. And even if she gets back to Moscow and starts making trouble, who's going to take her word over that of her father, her godfather and the federal prosecutor? And remember, your father isn't just the federal prosecutor for the Moscow office any longer. He's just about the most senior law officer in the country! She opens her mouth anywhere north of Armenia and she'll rot in Butyrka prison waiting for a trial that'll never come!' He grabbed the bottle of *Stoli* Elit and gulped down a mouthful without bothering with a glass, then slammed it down on his bedside table with enough force to make the black pearls he kept in a bowl there dance and rattle.

Ivan looked at him, leaning his full weight against the closed cabin door – only too well aware that much of this trouble had arisen from conversations half overheard by people who were never meant to share the secrets.

'In any case, if what you tell me is true,' continued Max brutally, 'this Ngoboi will take care of her long before I have to ask any favours from your father or the prison governor.' He reached for the vodka again.

'That's why I've moved her aboard,' said Ivan quietly. 'To protect her. That's why I've agreed to talk to her.' He took a step towards Max's bunk, stopping just before he could tower over his adopted father. He had come here to reason, not intimidate. And, besides, Uncle Max was drunker than he had ever seen him before. Perhaps there was some feeling for his wayward daughter behind all the vodka-fuelled bluster. 'But I still think we ought to put all this bullshit aside, Uncle Max, and agree how much of the truth I'm going to tell her when we finally go *tête à tête* – or head to head as she'd rather have it.'

'Tell her what you like, boy. *Têtê à têtê*, face-to-face, head to head or *mano a mano*. We're off upriver in the morning. The little *sooka*'s staying here. And with any luck Ngoboi will have sorted everything out for us before we even get these *huesos* home.' He used the bottle to gesture towards the pile of pearls overflowing from the big glass bowl. Then he swung savagely back towards Ivan. 'Though he'll be lucky to find enough of a heart to eat!'

'Why do you hate her?' asked Ivan. 'She's your daughter, after all.'

'Don't you understand anything?' snarled Max, drunk enough to open up. A living example of the old Latin saying. *In vodka veritas.* 'She has cost me everything! All my hopes and dreams. Every plan I made, every idea I had about my Ivan's future, about how my tall, strong son would take over Bashnev/Sevmash and rule it alongside you, with Anastasia at your side cementing our families, passing the inheritance down, father to son in the old way. Lavrenty Mikhailovich, Felix Makarov and I had it all planned. You were even to be married in Saint Basil's! Either there or the Church of the Spilled Blood in Saint Petersburg! Then honeymoon aboard my yacht. Nearly a billion dollars' worth! In those days she was called the *Anastasia. In those days!* And that's all gone! *Why?* Because she killed my Ivan. Then she destroyed herself. That destroyed her mother, God rest her. Then she destroyed my plans. Then she destroyed *me*! Me! Who was going to build a business dynasty to rival Abramovich, Lisin, Ivan *Grozny*, Peter the Great! I can never forgive the damage she's done to me. If there was anyone left alive I thought the little *sooka* loved, I'd destroy them too, just to see her suffer!'

'She heard?' snarled Robin. 'She heard *it all*?'

'She must have,' said Richard. 'I didn't realize the walls were *that* thin!'

'And she had no idea?' grated Robin.

'Apparently not!' he snapped, his countenance darkening again. 'As you heard her say, she thought it was suicide – and she's been blaming herself for the whole mess ever since. Until this evening.'

'But the shock of it, Richard! The shock! I must go to her!'
Robin surged up off the bed in their cramped new quarters
aboard *Volgograd*, as though she would go to the girl at once
wearing only her nightgown.

'You can't!' Richard raised his hands to restrain her. 'She's
been moved on to *Stalingrad* for safety. In the same way we've
been put here aboard *Volgograd*. And the sentries are so jumpy
after what happened to that patrol, you'd get shot for sure if
you even thought of crossing from one to the other. If you
went like that they'd probably think you were a ghost in any
case!'

'Aboard *Stalingrad* with those . . . *men*!' Robin sat, quivering with outrage.

'She wants to be there, Robin.' Richard secured his pyjama
cord, reached for his top – and thought better of it. Even
though *Volgograd* was air-conditioned, the cabin was still hot.
'That's where Ivan is. She wants to have a heart-to heart with
Ivan.'

'It's where her father is too. That murderous little shit,
Max!'

'She doesn't want to talk to Max. And it's mutual from
what I can make out.' Richard shrugged and padded over
towards the bed.

'That's the point, isn't it?' snarled Robin. 'We're not talking
about what *Max* wants! He's done his worst. And damn near
destroyed his daughter. It's what *she* wants now that's important. It's what *Anastasia* wants!'

'Well, I'll tell you what Anastasia wants!' rumbled Richard,
picking up on more of Robin's outrage but spinning it from
a different angle as he strode towards the bed once more. 'She
wants to take that wooden obscenity Ngoboi left in her bedroom
and, when she finds him, she wants to stick it where the sun
doesn't shine! That'd make him dance a whole new set of
steps.'

Robin choked on a laugh. It was a combination of his adroit
change of subject and pace combined with the lingering outrage
on his usually open face that amused her. And even her amusement caught her off guard, for she was still simmering with
rage. But of course, she wasn't enraged at her Richard, she

thought more gently. And he hadn't meant to overhear Max or be overheard by Max's errant daughter. None of this utter mess was his fault really. But of course he felt responsible when he was nothing of the sort. Just the same as poor Anastasia had done, she thought. Until earlier this evening.

'So,' she said, her voice mellowing, 'what are we going to do about it?'

'On the one hand,' he decided, stretching out beside her on the sheet – and snuggling up against her because the bed was so small – 'we want to let things well alone. Let her and Ivan work out whatever it is they are going to work out between themselves. No matter what happened in the past, they're all grown up now. He's a big boy and she's a big girl. But even so . . .'

'Even so?' she prompted, snuggling back against him – with little option as he had her wedged against the cabin wall.

'Even so, I'm not too keen to rush upriver in the morning and leave her to hope that Kebila catches Odem before Odem lets Ngoboi loose on her. Especially as Ngoboi managed to waltz in here and out again tonight, pausing only to put the frighteners on everybody and slaughter four top-flight ex-Spetsnaz mercenaries. Especially as it's probably Odem in the Ngoboi suit anyway – and he's got a hell of a lot of anger to take out on her. Hence the sexual threat, I suppose – as well as the magic and the heart-eating.' He hesitated. Reached for the light and snapped it off. 'No. I'm not about to let her face that on her own – or with her scary-looking army of nuns and Amazons. And in the meantime . . .'

'In the meantime what?' she asked, arching slightly as his hand found the hem of her nightgown and slid gently upward.

'Just where were we before the screaming and the shooting started . . .'

'Look,' said Ivan, a great deal more forcefully than he meant to. 'If I could undo any of this I would, believe me.'

'If *you* could!' spat Anastasia. '*Ohooiet*', Ivan, where would you *start*?'

'I'd start with that dumbass *eblan* Boris and the bad drugs he gave you that night!' he snarled. 'I'd stop you sharing them

with your brother and then none of this would have happened!'
He strode forward, towering over her in a way he had not
done to her father.

But she was not sprawled on a bed. She was sober. And
she was every bit as angry as Max had been. 'Too late, you
moron!' she shouted, squaring up to him in the way she
always had. 'Too fucking late! One step behind as always!
You needed to start with that *svoloch'* bastard Fydor Novotkin!
He was the one who gave my brother the drugs. It was always
Fydor who supplied the drugs!'

Ivan stepped back. 'I didn't know that,' he admitted, nonplussed.

'Of course you didn't, dumbass!' she snarled, coming
towards him like a terrier harrying a bear. 'It wasn't your
scene. You were a goody-goody military boy! How would you
know a thing like that? Think about it! We might have grown
up together but you were my brother's friend rather than mine.
I don't think I was ever anything other than a kind of a pet
to the pair of you. And when you came back from military
school in your smart little uniform, what was I to you then?
Some kind of porcelain princess! You told me that you loved
me but it was all bullshit, wasn't it? Something arranged
between our fathers! You never saw me as a real woman. As
an equal. As your wife! I was just something out of Tolstoy,
Tchaikovsky or Checkov – the idiot Dushecha, probably! I
don't think you really saw me at all until after my brother
died. It wasn't until I met real men like Boris and Fydor that
I got treated like a proper woman!'

'Well, both Boris and Fydor certainly treated you like a
proper woman later on!' spat Ivan, striding towards her again,
his rage reawakening.

'You bet they fucking did!' she hissed, relishing the shock
and hurt in his eyes; using the brutal words like clubs to beat
him with. 'And Fydor got me every fucking way he could. In
ways not even you and that sick satyric slob of a father of
mine could imagine. Though Fydor had to drug me out of my
head first! And then again and again *and again* . . .' Each
repetition got louder and more forceful until she was literally
spitting in his face. 'But I tell you what, Ivan Lavrentovitch,
my hulking great Ivan *Grozny* – I came through. I fucking

survived! And no thanks to you! Or to Maxim Kirilovitch Asov, billionaire businessman, corporate magician, top-rate cocksmith – fucking trainwreck of a parent! And now, I hear, the man who likely had my boyfriend killed. Who allowed me to sink into a pit of guilt and self-loathing because of it. Who could have pulled me out just by telling me the truth. *The truth*. Nothing more than that! And who let me sink and drown instead! *And you let him, Ivan!* You could have helped me and you didn't lift one finger. Not one finger, you bastard!'

'But I didn't realize you were . . . I didn't know Fydor . . . I've always . . . I still love you, Anastasia Maximovitch . . .'

'Don't you call me that! Don't you *dare* . . .' She hit him then, pounded her fists on his chest and reached up towards his face with clawed fingers.

But he caught her wrists in his massive hands and held her still, surprisingly gently, looking down into her overflowing eyes, unable to work out what was rage in them, what was confusion and what was simple, agonizing hurt. 'Anastasia! I'll do anything to make it up to you!' he said. 'Tell me what to do.'

'*Kill Max!*' she spat.

'I can't, Anastasia!' He released her and stood back. But the fight was gone out of her. Her hands fell to her sides and she looked up at him with her shoulders slumped. 'This isn't some Greek tragedy!' he whispered, only half convinced. Wondering if she could see the horror of what she had just said.

'Then you can't do anything for me, Ivan!' She turned away and crossed the room, putting the bed between them like the wall of a fortress. 'You let me down in the past. Oh, *Christ*, how you let me down! You might as well keep right on doing it in the future .'

'Anastasia . . .' He came forward until the sharp side of the bed frame struck against his shins hard enough to bruise them. '*Nastia* . . .' Then he stopped, helpless.

She turned back, her face a wilderness and her eyes empty, hopeless. 'I'd have come for you, Ivan. If things had been the other way round, I'd have come for you no matter what. I swear it on my life!' She pulled her hand down her face and Anastasia the Amazon Queen was back. 'Now get the fuck out of my bedroom and leave me alone!'

Cats

R ichard strode across the makeshift landing field towards the nearest Aerospacial Super Puma helicopter, thoughtlessly swatting a mosquito that had settled on his forearm. Somewhere in the back of his mind he admitted that maybe Robin's anti-insect campaign might not be such a waste of time after all. And he wondered vaguely what other jungle scourges might be returning to the river and its margins if the mosquitoes were making a comeback. But the thoughts were subsumed beneath an overwhelming tide of breathtakingly vivid sensation. He was chewing on the last of a breakfast sandwich prepared with flatbread and highly spiced *bush bacon* – made, he was relieved to hear, from dried beef – washed down with strong black coffee. The flavours on his tongue were suddenly drowned by the stench of exhaust from the choppers idling on the flat grass field; the rumble of their motors and the thrumming of their rotors drowning out the morning bustle of the camp he was just leaving behind him. Workaday bustle augmented by the arming of the squads of locals destined to board the choppers and the detailing of those Russians getting ready to board the Zubrs. Ahead of him, the square bulk of the nearest sand and sage-coloured Super Puma's fuselage was dwarfed by the simple enormity of the morning.

The sun was rising over Karisoke into a huge blue sky, cloudless except for the traces of pink and grey smoke that marked the mouth of the volcano, whose jungle-clad peak was still so distant that it lay below the farthest turquoise horizon where blue sky and green canopy seemed to bleed into each other like colours running on a wet watercolour. On his right, the forest massed along the river's edge in ranks of vegetation tall enough to disguise the fact that *Stalingrad* and *Volgograd* were already out on the water beyond the mangroves, preparing to depart, their course set for the invisible volcano and the black lake halfway up its side, while Kebila and his men stayed in the camp, preparing to go after Odem on foot. On his left, the fields of the farming cooperatives were already full of figures assessing the damage done by Odem's technicals last night in the first light of day. The whole place – the whole country, indeed – seemed to be bustling with vigour and excitement. And no one more so than Richard and the tall, slim, vibrant woman at his side. Though, to be fair, Richard allowed, much of the energy that seemed to be sparking out of Anastasia Asov might well be latent rage as much as latent electricity.

Anastasia was pouring all of her considerable force – wrath, outrage, frustration – into the strength with which she was checking her assault rifle. She had stripped and reassembled it on the breakfast table as she had talked over her immediate plans with Richard. Or talked them *to* Richard – who had hardly got a word in. The Russians around them were at first amused but eventually impressed by the dexterity with which her fingers worked on the weapon while her eyes were on her companion, her lips busy and her mind so clearly elsewhere.

The only interruption to her impassioned speech had come when Sergeant Zubarov appeared. He was looking for a couple of men who hadn't reported for breakfast duty: Brodski and Livitov. Not part of the Beslan veteran brigade from last night, apparently, but a couple of Ivan's patrol. And there was some debate whether, after the confusion of the attacks and Ngoboi's almost supernatural infiltration, they had even been seen in their bunks. But, what with the move from one Zubr to another and the reassignment of quarters, not to mention the midnight adventures, hardly anyone had slept in their assigned quarters last night. After a while he went off to report to Ivan with a shrug, assured that they'd turn up soon – as soon as they smelt the bacon, in all likelihood. Richard caught a look on Anastasia's face at the mention of her old friend, which made him glad that Ivan hadn't come looking for the men himself.

Now she opened and closed the breech, ensuring it was empty, before flicking on the safety, all with almost brutal strength. 'He won't be out there,' she said to Richard, raising her voice to a snarl as they neared the Puma. 'Kebila can follow the tracks as long as he likes but they won't lead him to Odem. He's too canny for that.'

'Then why are you coming?' Richard shouted, stooping under the rotors.

'To see for myself. To make absolutely double sure. In case there's a double bluff. In case I'm wrong.'

'Wrong?' he bellowed as they neared the slide-door. 'You? *Wrong?*'

'I've spent most of the last ten years being wrong,' she spat. 'Wrong about almost everything I believed in. Everyone I thought I was sure of . . .'

That shut him up. They climbed into the chopper silently, side by side.

Kebila was waiting for them, and had reserved the two seats closest to his own. Richard was unsure whether this was as a courtesy or so that he could keep a close eye on them. The latter seemed most likely, he thought as he saw Sergeant Tchaba occupying the next available place to his own. He glanced up the cabin as he prepared to fold himself into his seat. There were fifteen of Kebila's finest, all armed to the teeth, their faces set in ebony masks, many of them bearing the scars of Poro initiation. He had to wonder, as he sat and tightened his seat belt, how many of them would be willing to follow their orders to shoot on sight if the target was Ngoboi.

Well, if Anastasia was right, they wouldn't find out on this trip, he decided. But, on the other hand, if for once in her life she was wrong . . . He stopped the thought there, as the helicopter seemed to leap into the air, sidetracked into assessing her new-found lack of confidence in herself. He had talked it over with Robin last night in the sleepy haze after their love-making – the effect that all of the revelations would be likely to have on Anastasia.

Richard's thoughts were simply stopped at this point by the view out of the window beyond Sergeant Tchaba at his shoulder. The fields, full of tiny figures and toy trucks, gave on to the thickening wall of forest and secondary jungle which in turn reached out in mangroves along the edge of the great river. And the great River Gir spread wide, a huge, steady red-brown flow. And there, like water beetles creeping up it were *Stalingrad* and *Volgograd*, heading for the land of the big trees, where they would be dwarfed to near insignificance

– let alone the arrogant overreaching specks of men inside them. He shivered.

And as he did so, the helicopter angled its square body to the left and swooped away from the river, heading inland and downwards until the tracks of Odem's technicals were plainly visible either as sets of parallel scars across green pastures or white-flattened roadways through ruined crops.

'They're turning in towards the river and the jungle,' observed Anastasia. The cabin had canted slightly over to the right and if there had been a magnetic compass handy it would have been reading south-east as the tracks and the wide riverine jungle inevitably closed with each other. But then, striking north/south, shockingly rule straight amid all the natural curves of the land so far, there was an ancient concrete-sided irrigation ditch. The tracks converged on a fissure in the side which looked to be of recent origin, pulling the red mud down on to the flat, dry concrete bed of the thing, weaving past and over each other into a red mud braid, and then they faded into invisibility as the man-made channel disappeared into the jungle overgrowth.

Kebila's chopper settled beside the others and the colonel led his men on to the ground with Richard and Anastasia at his side. There were three choppers in all and, after a brief meeting, Kebila decided to split his forces. The other two took off again. One to follow the drainage ditch inland to the north in case Odem's men had laid a false trail and then doubled back. The other questing straight ahead in case this was all an elaborate trick and Odem was lurking upriver, waiting to catch them unawares. Then Kebila himself led his command on foot patrol into the concrete ditch.

Richard, like all of them, found it an easy enough scramble down the dry slope of red earth impacted by the technicals' tyres into a makeshift pathway. Then, aware that he was the only one there not armed to the teeth, he fell-in just behind Kebila between Tchaba and Anastasia. There was one moment of noise without progress as everyone took their weapons off safety and made sure that a round was in the chamber. Even Kebila pulled out the Desert Eagle he usually carried in the webbing holster at his hip, slid the top back, then snapped it forward again. Then they quietened, ready to begin the patrol. Silently, the colonel gestured them onward and they all followed him.

Over Kebila's shoulder, Richard's view was of a steep-sided, arid grey-white perspective, all geometrical lines to a point perhaps three metres in height. Then brown trunks exploded upwards into bright bursts of greenery – branch, twig and leaf – like rockets filling the sky on Guy Fawkes' night. The wind stirred fitfully, coming from all directions, bringing river odours and forest smells; the essence of prairie and of building site, drainage and sewer stench. As they walked into the shadow of the jungle itself, the overhang of the trees concentrated the sounds as though they were entering a tunnel. It seemed to Richard that even his eyes began to fail him. The perspectives, worthy of any engineer's drawing, faded beneath those shadows. Distances became harder to judge. Richard started to wonder whether the tension was releasing something more than simple adrenaline into his bloodstream. Whether there was some strange narcotic on the stultifying air. Whether there was witchcraft here.

So it came as almost no surprise at all when Ngoboi burst out of the darkness dead ahead and came running towards them in a weird kind of slow-motion dance. Kebila stopped. Straightened. Stood, as though no more able to believe his eyes than Richard. The whole of his command froze. Richard could hear the sudden superstitious intake of breath, feel the universal *frisson* of sheer terror. The tall, raffia-covered figure came towards them as though Quasimodo, not Odem, had donned the disguise. Stooping, weaving, limping, rearing, cavorting. But running towards them with a strange, mad intensity. Ngoboi – ebony mask, raffia headpiece, raffia cloak and raffia leggings. All two metres and more of him, like something out of a nightmare.

'*Tchyo za gàlima?!* What the fuck?!' shouted Anastasia and she tore her SIG Sauer up to her shoulder, flicking off the safety. But the moment she pulled the trigger, Tchaba hit her rifle so that her shot went high. The sound of it slammed along the drainage ditch and stopped Ngoboi almost as effectively as a bullet would have done. He froze there for an instant, then began to charge forward again.

But even as he did so, a leopard hurled itself down from the high side of the drainage channel on to the back of the capering god. It was a sizeable beast, though it was only there for an instant – and its arrival and departure were so utterly unexpected. But Richard saw it land, knocking Ngoboi back and over to one side. And the instant it impacted, Ngoboi detonated. There was a massive explosion that vaporized the big cat and most of the man in the costume. Shrapnel howled out into the air, decimating the overhanging branches and leaves but mercifully not the patrol, which was standing rooted in place with shock and horror.

Though the shrapnel went up into the forest, the wall of flame-hot force rolled back down the channel, staggering and singeing everyone there, battering and deafening them as they stood.

After some uncounted time, Kebila staggered forward. Richard went with him at his shoulder. The destruction of the god had left a black star on the concrete as though a missile had exploded there. The stunned soldier reached down at the outer edge of the destruction and picked up a boot. An unexpectedly heavy boot. An army boot, Richard realized. It had a foot inside it. And, as with students at school, soldiers personalized their kit, all of which was uniform, by putting their names on it. With boots you wrote your name or number on the instep where the sole received least wear.

And, although the writing on the instep was Cyrillic Russian, Richard easily read and understood it. It identified the boot as belonging to Livitov – one of the soldiers Sergeant Zubarov had been looking for at breakfast.

Terrorist

'A suicide bomber?' gasped Robin, shocked and horrified. 'Disguised as Ngoboi? But why? What in God's name were they thinking?'

'Not suicide,' corrected Richard grimly. 'Murder. I read about it in a book on the most recent conflicts in the Middle East. The technique is to kidnap a member of someone's family, brutalize them then load them with bombs and send them home. Their family has the choice of killing them and leaving them to rot while the authorities go on the firing line to try to defuse the corpse. Or try to help them. Most people try to help them. And BOOM!'

It was late in the afternoon and the sun was westering downriver towards Granville Harbour and the ocean. The choppers had returned an hour ago and the interim had been taken up with feeding the men. Richard and Anastasia had not been alone in finding they had no appetite. Instead of eating, Richard had gone to find Robin and bring her up to date. Now the pair of them were hurrying across to Kebila's command tent as they had this conversation. Robin, of course, had hundreds of questions arising from Richard's terse report of their adventure and his equally terse explanation. But Kebila's briefing answered most of them before she managed to frame them – let alone ask them.

'It is clear that Corporal Livitov was not a suicide bomber in league with Odem and the Army of Christ,' the colonel began, looking around the frowning faces of his senior officers. 'We found enough of his head to be certain that his mouth had been taped shut. Indeed, the fate of Colonel Mako's patrol last night makes it quite possible his tongue had been cut out. From the strange way he approached us, I am certain that he had been restrained or crippled in some way, had explosives packed with shrapnel strapped to him, then put into the Ngoboi costume and left behind for us to find.'

Kebila paused and looked around the assembled faces in the tent as though expecting questions. But neither the men who had gone upcountry nor the others who had followed the drainage channel inland had anything they wanted to ask yet. 'We were doubly lucky when we did find him,' continued the colonel soberly after a while. 'The first piece of luck was that Sergeant Tchaba stopped Miss Asov shooting him. The second piece of luck – the leopard – shows us that the device Livitov was wearing had an impact detonator.'

He turned to look directly at Anastasia. 'Had your bullet struck him, he would certainly have exploded and at least two thirds of the command – starting with ourselves – would have been killed either by the explosion or by the shrapnel wrapped around it. The leopard spinning him round and knocking him back saved us. The unfortunate creature's body soaked up much of the explosive force. The shrapnel decimated the trees above us instead of tearing us to shreds. We even found some dead birds and monkeys when we began our search of the area. But I still find it hard to see how Odem could take the risk of disguising his bomber as Ngoboi . . .'

Richard held up his hand. 'I believe Odem very reasonably expected someone to shoot Corporal Livitov, believing him to be Ngoboi,' Richard said slowly and clearly in his best Matadi. 'It is the most logical conclusion. And had anyone shot him, there would have been two likely outcomes. Either *all* of the patrol would die, in which case the Ngoboi disguise was hardly relevant, for no one other than the Army of Christ would know about it. Or *most* of the patrol would die – in which case the survivors would describe how the desecration of the god brought enormous death and destruction as an immediate result. You can bet he's got more Ngoboi costumes – and the reputation of the next man wearing one would have been immeasurably enhanced.'

'He's fucking with our minds,' observed Anastasia.

'He has been all along,' replied Richard grimly.

'Let's hope he stops at our minds,' added Robin, glancing at Anastasia's pale, determined face and thinking of the obscene wooden phallus in her blood-spattered bed last night. Then she changed the subject slightly, raising her own hand and catching Kebila's eye. 'And was it only the impact of a bullet – or a leopard – that was designed to detonate the bomb? One hears so much about mobile phones being used. Bombs set off by hand, simply by dialling the right number. Or putting it in the memory and hitting *recall* . . .'

'We searched the jungle right the way down to the river itself,' countered Kebila, 'but we found no one there. Certainly no one close enough to have seen what was going on and decided when to detonate by hand . . .'

'But,' interjected Richard, 'your local mobile phone company has such a well-structured network here that phone signals can be broadcast for miles up and down the river. And I don't suppose my phone is unique in having a very effective built-in video camera.'

'I see your point, Captain Mariner,' said Kebila formally to Richard. 'Someone miles away could have been watching pictures transmitted by the phone strapped to Livitov's chest as part of the bomb. And as soon as he saw we were close enough, he would simply hit the right number, even if he was up on the shores of Lac Dudo or on the slopes of Karisoke. This has all clearly been very cleverly thought through and quite meticulously planned – not to mention being extremely well-equipped. And that fact alone immediately raises another consideration . . .' Kebila paused, clearly deep in thought.

After a moment or two, Richard continued with what he supposed the colonel's sentence would have concluded. 'That Odem, or someone close to him, has been to the terrorist training camps in Pakistan, Afghanistan, Sudan or Somalia. That they have returned not only with the knowledge and the techniques used by Al Qaeda, the Taliban, Al Shabaab, Boko Haram and the rest, but also the sort of equipment they use. That means money and – probably most worryingly of all – pretty upfront political support. And, if the evidence shown to President Chaka and the conversations I have had with him are anything to go by, that support may well be coming from just across your south-eastern border. Just on the eastern slopes of Mount Karisoke itself. Which, at the very least, also explains his access to replacement technicals and – suddenly and unexpectedly – to river boats that are large enough to transport them.'

Kebila nodded. 'It also means,' he continued, 'that we – and of course Mr Asov's men – will be facing something relatively new. A seventies-style jungle-wise bush army like Joseph Kony's Lord's Resistance Army, combined with a terrorist trained and equipped cadre, equivalent to a top-flight Al Qaeda cell, with access to and expertise in the most cutting edge of twenty-first-century hardware. We may all find that we are fighting two entirely different types of war with the same people in the same place and at the same time.'

'Everything from AKs, cocaine and Ngoboi,' nodded Richard thoughtfully, 'to IEDs, smart phones and the Internet.'

'It seems to me,' said Anastasia militantly, 'that it doesn't matter a damn whether you've got smartphones or spears, clubs or computers. Or whether you're Abubakar Shekau, Habeeb Bama, Odem, Ngoboi or Osama Bin Laden. Once the bullet goes through your head, you're dead.'

'That's true,' answered Kebila gently. 'Our problem will be getting to Odem's head. Or Ngoboi's.'

'They managed it with Joseph Kony, Habeek Bama and Osama Bin Laden. It shouldn't be beyond us!' persisted Anastasia curtly. 'We cut our way through the jungle to the Army of Christ. We cut our way through the Army of Christ to Odem and Ngoboi. And we shoot the fuckers. Job done. Simple!'

'If that was all there was to it, then it would indeed be simple,' agreed Kebila. And both Richard and Robin were relieved that his tone was not in the slightest bit patronizing. 'But you know as well as I do, Miss Asov, that it will not be anywhere near that easy. Even for the impressively skilled army of Amazons you have trained to protect your orphanage.'

'I didn't train my people just to sit here and wait for someone to come up and go *boo!* to them,' said Anastasia brusquely. 'Any more than you did. Or are doing now – I assume!'

'Quite,' said Kebila drily. 'But we are here to regroup and to plan our next foray upriver. You are not. You and your command will remain here to guard the orphanage. I will leave some of my men to stand alongside you under the command of Sergeant Tchaba, with whom I believe you will work very well. But I'm afraid you have accompanied us for the last

time. For the immediate future, at any rate,' he added as he
saw a murderously mutinous look descend on Anastasia's
face. Then he looked back at his own officers. 'And of course
we have a new priority as well. On top of finding and
neutralizing Odem and the Army of Christ, it is our clear duty
to try and rescue the other Russian, if we can. Corporal
Livitov's missing companion.'

'Brodski,' snarled Anastasia, as though the word were an
insult she was throwing in Kebila's face. 'His name is Sandor
Abramovich Brodski.' And she got up, grabbed her rifle and
turned to leave the tent.

'It might be just as well if you were to stay here,' said Robin
to Anastasia later, as Richard accompanied the two women
back to the main orphanage building. 'The camp was deserted
all morning except for the maintenance, admin and catering
staff. The Zubrs were both gone and all the Russians aboard
them. It was tense here, *creepy*. Obviously Father Emil
and the sisters were all bustling about, taking classes and
running the orphanage as usual. The ancillary staff were
cooking for the children, feeding them breakfast, lunch after
the lessons and so forth. We even had a visit from the elders
of the town to see how we were – and to catch up on the
gossip. But everyone was on edge. Your Amazons were all
like cats on hot bricks until Esan and Ado took them off.
And then, when they were gone, the rest of the children
were simply terrified . . .'

Anastasia nodded curtly. 'I know. They rely on me more
and more. Too much, I think. But it's only because of the way
the country's still being run – too much military, not enough
police. Yes, I know. Like at home in Russia still. The best way
to deal with the army and get some civil order is to put Celine
in the President's Palace. And the best way to deal with everything else they're afraid of is to bring Odem to justice and
prove Ngoboi is no more than his puppet.'

'You've thought this through, haven't you?' asked Richard
gently.

'Of course I have, Richard,' she said quietly, pronouncing
his name *Reekard* in the Russian way. 'Without Celine running

things beside me, this place is becoming as much of a prison as a home to me. I do not want to spend the rest of my life in an African Butyrka. I have been planning my escape. And it looks like getting rid of Odem is the best way to make a start.'

Mosquito

D eep in thought, Richard escorted Anastasia and Robin back to their refurbished rooms in the orphanage and then over to the orphanage refectory for dinner. And the smell of the *egusi* soup and *jolloff* rice the staff and students were just about to eat proved irresistible, reminding him that he had skipped lunch altogether. Egusi soup was in fact a thick stew of minced beef and seafood with shredded spinach in a spiced tomato sauce. It was accompanied by traditional *eba* – roasted cassava flour seasoned and boiled then rolled into balls. It was eaten from a communal bowl and looked a little like mashed potato. *Jolloff* was a fiery rice full of chicken and all sorts of peppers. Richard tucked into it all hungrily. Then he went to the communications tent and found Kebila talking to his cousin. 'Now that Odem's on the water, you'll have to keep a sharp lookout, Caleb,' Kebila was saying. 'And warn Captain Zhukov to do the same. He has explosives. The kind they put into vests for suicide bombers. In all likelihood he has a prisoner – so be wary of Russians staggering into your camp, particularly if it's Brodski.'

'Both *Stalingrad* and *Volgograd* have a full set of counter-measures in place, capable of handling anything he could throw at us,' came Caleb's reply. 'But I'll warn Mako and Ivan to keep extra watches out when we beach and set the Russians down to proceed on foot. At that point we'll decide whether to wait or return. We'll be in contact then, as planned. But I've been thinking: with Odem on the river, the orphanage's back door is pretty wide open until we get back on to your slipway there. If you're off upriver after the Army of Christ first thing tomorrow, then they'll be vulnerable to attack from the water, even if you leave Sergeant Tchaba and a pretty strong squad to back him up.'

'I've thought of that,' said Kebila. 'When I've finished

speaking to you I was going to call for a couple of fast patrol boats to get up here at full speed.'

Richard held up his hand.

'Wait, Caleb. Yes, Captain Mariner?'

'Since the passage through the ruined bridge at Citematadi downstream has been cleared,' said Richard, 'you could get something bigger than a patrol boat past it. You could get a frigate up here if you wanted. She'd have to drop anchor as there's no docking facility big enough to take her, but something like your frigate *Otobo* is as well armed as the Zubrs. And as fast as your fast patrol boats. If she could be spared from her sea duties . . .'

'Did you hear that, Caleb?' asked Kebila. 'What do you think?'

'I think Captain Sanda might never forgive you for taking his beautiful blue-water command and demoting her to brown-water duties. But apart from that, Captain Mariner is right. The river should be deep enough, *Otobo*'s draught is seven metres fully laden. And now that the main channels are clear of both water hyacinth and rubble . . .'

'Consider it done, then,' said Kebila decisively. 'Talk to you later, Caleb. Have a quiet night. Over and out.' Kebila broke contact and sat for a moment, deep in thought.

'Do you have the authority to order Captain Sanda and *Otobo* up here, Colonel?' asked Richard.

'No. But Minister Aganga does,' answered Kebila.

And she's in Felix Makarov's pocket unless I'm very much mistaken, thought Richard, remembering what Robin had told him of her last ride down to the docks with Celine Chaka. I wonder how *she'll* view Kebila's request.

But he was not to find out immediately. The minister was not available, it seemed. Kebila was given unusually short shrift. Disturbingly short shrift, considering his position, power and influence.

Undaunted, the colonel contacted Captain Sanda directly, explained the situation and asked him to get his command ready to sail. Sanda appeared to be quite willing to do so, but seemed to doubt that the minister would be as immediately compliant as the colonel assumed. The line was not of the best quality and there were undertones in the swift Matadi language that Richard could not quite grasp. Certainly, when he broke contact, Kebila was frowning thoughtfully, and Richard was really beginning to wonder what was up.

Kebila stood back from the radio transceiver and gestured to the army operator to resume his schedule of contacts. Richard sat, watching the routine, his mind busy, wondering whether to bother with the radio after all when he could contact Ivan on his Benincom cell phone almost as effectively – as long as the electrical current that the orphanage's generator produced was compatible with the phone's charger.

Both men were still there five minutes later when Robin came into the tent. 'Has either of you seen the television?' she asked. Richard swung round to look at her, pulling his mind back to the here and now. 'The news is on,' she said. 'And it looks as though things are hotting up over the presidential election. There's growing unrest in Granville Harbour, apparently. Talk of riots.'

'Riots?' asked Richard, stunned. 'What on earth about?'

'Apparently Celine gave a TV interview yesterday evening while we were playing hide and seek with Ngoboi and co. It was a pretty routine affair, to begin with, at least, but there was a discussion started by one of the other interviewees that ended up with her being trapped into suggesting that if she won the election she would try and move some of the money spent on welfare and infrastructure in Granville Harbour city into expanding the cooperatives out here. The discussion seems to have got a little heated. Manufactured confrontation – no news like bad news; that sort of thing. There seems little doubt that Celine simply meant that more efficient production in the hinterland would help feed the increasing numbers flocking to the city as prosperity there continues to grow. At least that's what she and her people are saying by way of clarification this morning . . .'

'But?' asked Richard.

'But the whole thing has been spun. It's now being presented as announcing that she will take money from ethnic Matadi tribal city folk in order to support the Kukuyu, Masai and Bantu interlopers who are stealing their jobs and prospects – as well as their traditional farmlands out here.'

'But the farmlands have been without tenants and allowed to run to seed for decades! The Kikuyu and Bantu farmers are simply the experts who are helping rebuild successful farms, cooperatives and so forth,' said Richard, frowning. 'Captain Caleb explained it all when he was taking us through the map.'

'I remember what you told me,' said Robin grimly. 'But one man's *foreign expert* is another man's *economic invader*.' Robin shrugged. 'Look how we English have reacted over the years to immigrants from Ireland, the West Indies, India and Pakistan, China, Poland . . .'

'I see your point,' rumbled Richard. 'But surely it was President Chaka himself who invited these people in—'

'No,' interrupted Kebila. 'It was a project that Celine espoused as soon as she entered parliament. She was not always the leader of the opposition. She held a minor government post for a while. Rebuilding the farms in the tribal hinterland has always been one of her most precious projects. But this interpretation of her work is something utterly new.'

Richard looked at Robin. '*Felix Makarov . . .*' he mouthed silently.

She nodded, frowning. For it was she, after all, who had begun to suspect that their other Russian business partner was more than capable of mounting a dirty tricks campaign to ensure his man – and his contracts and his promised concessions – got safely back into the presidential palace.

'But there haven't actually been any riots yet?' asked Richard.

'No, none,' Robin answered. 'Yet.'

Kebila suddenly leaned forward to his radio operator. 'Put me through to the central police station in Granville Harbour,' he ordered. 'I want to get a full and detailed update from the senior officer on duty . . .'

Richard stood up, crossed to Robin and steered her towards the tent flap with one arm around her waist. This conversation was unlikely to be one Kebila wanted to share. And it was likely to be lengthy. Therefore he decided to risk his Benincom cell phone after all.

*　　*　　*

'*Dobryy vecher Reekard,*' said Ivan before switching to English. 'How are you?' Because Richard had come through on the phone rather than the radio, the conversation started off with gossip rather than business. But that was OK with him as he stood in the dark room looking through the tight-closed window down the slope towards the broad reach of the dark river, trying to work out what were gathering shadows and what were thickening clouds of insects.

'I'm fine, thanks, Ivan,' he answered. 'I understand you're beached and jungling up some supper.'

Halfway through his sentence, Richard saw the door, reflected in the window behind the reflection of his shoulder, silently swing open. Anastasia came tiptoeing soundlessly into the room. Their eyes met as though in a mirror – his narrow and thoughtful, hers wide and almost luminous in the shadows. Richard raised his eyebrows, thinking *they really ought to do something about the walls in this place.* Anastasia shook her head, put her finger to her lips and crossed to stand beside him as Ivan talked about supper. Richard tilted the phone so she could hear him. 'That's about it. We've done a good day's travelling and now we're bedding down in the last comfortable place we can find before we head on inland tomorrow. Except . . .' There was a sound like a pistol shot. 'Except for these damned mosquitoes. I'll be sleeping aboard.'

'We've had some here too,' said Richard sympathetically. 'You think they're spreading downriver?'

'Looks like it,' said Ivan. 'Though God knows where they're coming from.'

'The jungle,' said Richard, distracted by the eavesdropper and the soft warmth of her breath on the back of his hand.

'Anyway,' persisted Ivan, blissfully unconscious that his words were being spied upon. 'It's lucky we brought our food with us. There was some talk of living off the land but it's all come to nothing, as Colonel Mako said it would. Some of the men were certain the river would contain catfish. But no luck yet. I think Zubarov has given up with his rod but he wants to go for a quick swim before we bed down. He says the river mud will help make him mosquito-proof.'

Richard chuckled a little theatrically so that Ivan would hear him over the phone. He glanced at Anastasia, raising his eyebrows again. *Want to join in?* She shook her head. *No.*

'You call about anything in particular?' asked Ivan guardedly, coming nearer to the heart of his concerns. *And hers*, thought Richard.

'Just as agreed,' he said vaguely, still looking at Anastasia's almost luminous gaze. 'To update you on today – whatever hasn't come to you already from Kebila via Caleb or Zhukov.'

'Poor old Livitov, you mean. And Brodski, whatever's happened to him. I must be slipping to lose two men like that.'

Richard made no immediate comment but after a moment, he said, 'Odem's been running rings round us all. With the help of his friend Ngoboi. What happened to Livitov is bad but not your fault.'

'But still,' said Ivan distantly. 'When I think of what they did to him. What they probably did to him before that. What might have happened if their plan had worked. To you. And Anastasia . . . How'd Anastasia take it all?'

Ivan's innocent question brought a new, intense electricity into Richard's room. 'As you'd expect,' he said blandly once more, wishing the vibrant girl beside him would either get involved or get the hell out. 'One more reason to catch them and kill them as soon as she can.' She gave a lopsided grin at that and nodded.

'Has she said anything about me?' Ivan asked.

Richard stopped, apparently to think; actually to look into her intense gaze once again. This time she shook her head more vigorously than ever. Then, 'No,' he answered truthfully, if tactlessly. 'She hasn't mentioned you at all.'

'Well, tell her . . . Tell her from me . . .'

Richard and Anastasia never discovered what Ivan wanted him to tell her, for as the unhappy Russian paused for the second time, all hell was let loose. The connection was suddenly full of shouting and swearing that grew so loud Richard pulled the cell phone even further away from his ear. He met Anastasia's eyes; her look was simply agonized. She, like he, was clearly wondering whether Ivan was at the centre of a sudden attack. She opened her mouth to call to him, but his voice came over the connection and prevented her. 'It's

Zubarov, Richard. I've got to go. He went swimming like he said he would – and they say that a crocodile got him. A *crocodile*! A huge one. A monster. Five metres or more. My god! Looks like there's more than mosquitoes coming downriver!'

Pushkin

Zubarov's death seemed to Ivan to signal the beginning of an increasingly dark and dangerous time. None of the men were certain they had seen the crocodile that took him; only the kind of disturbance on the dark surface of the benighted river that would be expected if a crocodile had taken him. But as Ivan's swift – yet thorough – enquiry established, none of the witnesses had ever actually seen a crocodile in real life. And those that had – like Mako – hadn't witnessed Zubarov's disappearance. There was no body. But a search of the water and the riverbank revealed nothing, so at last they all went to their quarters aboard and slept as best they could.

Ivan slept little, his head whirling with worries about his missing men, his increasingly drunken and difficult boss, and the mess he seemed to have made of his relationship with his boss's tempestuous daughter, for whom he was rediscovering feelings he had thought long dead.

Next morning began for Ivan and his companions with a quick service for the missing man which Max chivvied along impatiently enough to alienate the popular sergeant's friends, followed by an even quicker breakfast. Then they broke camp, went back aboard and sailed on. Ivan was aboard *Stalingrad* with Max and Captain Zhukov. He started the voyage on the bridge with them, watching as the vista through the clear-view windows darkened – quite literally – in spite of the brightening day. It seemed to Ivan that the trees they were approaching would never stop growing. It was an optical illusion, he knew, but the nearer the drop-off approached, the more massive the palisade of tree trunks seemed to rise – as if they were being thrust up from the ground beneath, closing off the sky ahead as they did so. Sky which, in any case, was darkened by increasingly thick clouds of smoke blown north on the southerly wind, thick enough to dull even the noonday sun. What looked like a wooden wall with foundations of freshwater mangroves from a couple of kilometres out actually looked more like a sheer brown cliff close-up. A cliff with a massive overhang jutting out, seemingly just below the thickening smoke. What really disturbed him was the fact that the fifty-metre-high monsters near the south bank they were sailing along were all too obviously the small relations of the hundred-metre giants further inland – their simple scale seemingly enhanced by the fact that they stood on rising ground.

It came as a relief when Max reminded him that Mako was waiting to give his final briefing on survival and warfare in this particular jungle – and he needed to attend with his men. Max himself attended some of Mako's talks, but by no means all of them. On the one hand, he considered himself the leader of the band bound up the tributary to the lake. On the other he saw no reason why he should burden himself with too many details when he was paying a great deal of money to men whose primary mission might be to get to the lake and secure it for Bashnev/Sevmash, but whose secondary mission, less than a short *vershok* behind of it, was to get Max safely up to the lake and back.

Mako's lecture was beamed from *Volgograd* via a video link in a specially prepared section of the main handling area. Ivan's men were seated there, looking expectantly at the big screen as though awaiting a re-run of *Apocalypse Now*. Mako appeared on screen almost immediately after Ivan arrived. 'This has to be just about the last of these briefings, men,' boomed the colonel. 'Though I'll deliver a final pep talk when we disembark. Remember, we got enough clear feedback from Mr Asov's original overflight in the Kamov to be certain it would be a waste of time taking the Zubrs further than the mouth of the tributary. So we go on foot from there. The river is narrow, overgrown, treacherous and increasingly precipitous. We have to prepare for a hard walk in from where we disembark.'

It was not a lecture designed to raise morale, thought Ivan as he watched and listened, his concentration absolute. Then, when it was over, he led his men in applying what Mako had talked about – prioritizing what they had to carry with them, starting with their weaponry. When they had brought it through

customs, it had seemed like biggest was best. Now it seemed
that lighter was better. Especially when they had to reckon on
carrying all the other stuff Mako had warned them they would
likely need, starting with food and water. Even the hard men
– like Ivan himself – trained to exist for days on end with
nothing but rainwater and iron rations, found it hard to calculate
what there might be to eat out there in the realm of the big
trees. As opposed to what or who might be out there wanting
to eat them.

The grim preparations were brought to a halt by the Zubrs'
arrival at the mouth of the black river they were going to
follow inland and upslope to the lake on the volcano's side.
Leaving his men to complete their arrangements, Ivan went
back up on to the bridge, where he found Max and Captain
Zhukov looking grimly across a sullen heave of black mud
as the massive Zubrs settled, side by side. On a screen
beside the grim captain, shots from Max's Kamov helicopter
showed their landing place from above – and also revealed
how swiftly the jungle closed over the black ribbon of the
river rolling down towards it. How soon a flash of grey amid
the overhanging green warned of the first set of rapids that
barred the way to the Zubrs as effectively as the Victoria Falls.

The bank they were sitting on stuck out in a long, curving
tongue, extended westwards by the flow of the black tributary
river out into the main stream. On the left, looking north, pure
black water swept out into the red of the main river like a
stain. The wide surface of the Gir was marked with a line of
oily darkness that dominated this side of it like a tarmacked
road on a broad red desert. Beyond the far band of red, the
distant bank heaved mistily. Dead ahead and near at hand, the
low rise of black slime fell away into the mouth of the tributary
itself, as wide and dark as the Moskva River flowing behind
the Grand Palace of the Kremlin. The far bank was forested
with the western fringes of the impenetrable jungle cover that
reached to the top of Karisoke then away into Congo Libre
beyond. On the left, the black river vanished into the first great
stand of nearby trees. Grey ferns rose man-high between them
but seemed to be as dwarfed as a well-trimmed steppe beneath
a Siberian Pine. As short, thought Ivan grimly, as the grass

behind the mill, where the doomed poet Lensky duelled with
Eugene Onegin; or that beneath the January snow beside the
Chyornaya Reka in St Petersberg, where Lensky's creator and
alter-ego Pushkin himself duelled with the French officer
D'Anthes. Tragically fatal duels for both Lensky and Pushkin,
of course.

Now what on earth had put all that in his mind? Ivan
wondered grimly, turning away from the depressing scene.
And then he realized. *Chyornaya Reka* meant Black River.
And from then on, no matter what the locals called the stream
connecting Lac Dudo to the great River Gir, it remained
Chyornaya Reka – the Black River, to Ivan.

'Come on, boy, stop dreaming,' growled Max. 'Time to get
moving.'

Ivan shrugged off the sense of depression that had been
threatening to overwhelm him and joined Max. Side by side
they ran down to their cabins and collected the kit they had
prepared. Or rather, Ivan collected what he had prepared. Max
collected what had been prepared for him. It looked bulky but
was relatively light. It pandered to his post-Putin macho
but was designed to give him an easy ride. Ivan's was the real
deal, all thirty kilos and more of it. As were the metre-long,
razor-sharp blades of the matchets that went on their left hips,
and the nine-millimetre Grach side arms they both strapped
on their right. Then they went on to the main area and exited
down the forward ramp.

The tongue of mud felt and smelt even worse than it looked,
though it was unexpectedly dry underfoot. The whole atmosphere seemed impossibly humid and the men were soaked
with sweat immediately. The river stank like fish left rotting.
The jungle stank, as though a couple of White Sea factory
ships had emptied their gutting holds into the place.

Mako kept his final briefing short, then he and Ivan led their
fifty men into the jungle, with Max between them, apparently
in command. Behind them, the Russians fell into their
prearranged order. Communications men next in line. Point
men ready to go forward on Mako's signal. Flank men with
matchets and side arms at the ready. Pack horses in the middle
and the afterguard warily behind. All of them creeping forward,

overcome by the sheer scale of the environment they were creeping into, moving between the massive tree trunks like ants in a cathedral.

Mako's wise eyes spotted a makeshift track at once and he led his silent men along it, happy to take the lead himself while the awestruck Russians came to terms with the reality in which they found themselves. Ivan kept up with him, but Max for once began to fall behind, weighed down by the atmosphere more effectively than he was by the load of his Bergen. It was Mako and Ivan who walked into the clearing first, therefore. It was large enough to accommodate all of the Russians and, had anyone other than these two been in charge it might well have done so. As it was, they were not quite quick enough to understand exactly what confronted them, and so a good deal of damage was done which might have been avoided had Anastasia or Richard been in charge.

On the far side of the clearing stood the tall trunk of a dead tree. Time and the overpowering growth of its super-competitive offspring had beheaded it so that branches and splinters of its original greatness lay scattered underfoot. But no one was really paying much attention to what they were walking on, because of what they were looking at.

There was a body crucified on the dead and rotting trunk. The body of a man, dressed from the waist down in camouflage and boots. From the waist up it was hard to tell precisely what he was wearing because he was covered in a crawling carapace of flies. Even his head was just a shapeless black mass at once hanging deathly still against his chest and at the same time busily swarming with insects, and a halo of them hovering just above, waiting to join the feast. Mako and Ivan walked forward, mesmerized by the horror, and by the time they thought to call a halt, the first fifteen or so of their troops were in the clearing behind them.

Then the crucified figure shuddered. The head came up, skull slamming back against the trunk behind it with enough force to dislodge the flies for an instant. And they saw that it was Livitov's missing companion, Sergeant Sandor Abramovitch Brodski.

Ivan knew then. He grabbed Max by the back of his Bergen

and jerked him sideways, twisting desperately to move the pair of them out of the clearing and fall on him at the same time. 'BOMB!' he shouted at the top of his voice, and he felt Mako also hurling sideways after him so that the pair of them landed on top of Max and the three of them were given some sort of protection by the trunk of the nearest tree.

And just in time. Brodski exploded just as Livitov had done. But he was not spun off line by an attacking leopard. The force of the explosive strapped to his chest and the shrapnel packed so carefully around it scythed precisely as it had been designed to do into the front rank of the Russians. The men carrying the portable radios were all wiped out. The leading load bearers with their heavy packs of camping equipment, food and water, soaked up the rest of the terrible power. The point men and the flank men, warned by Ivan's shout, had hurled themselves sideways into the shelter of the bush. And the rearguard automatically spread out to watch over those who were left.

Then, for an instant, there was silence, except for the echoes of the explosion which chased each other up towards Karisoke itself. And stillness, but for the blizzard of burning leaves and branches that tumbled down from a hundred feet above their heads.

Charge

Anastasia had never seen Richard take charge of a difficult situation before. Robin had, of course, but even she was still secretly impressed. Richard's campaign of decision-making began the instant that the bad news started to arrive. First, from the Central Police Station in Granville Harbour came the information that Colonel Kebila had been most fearful of. A general strike had been called in the city, and there were demonstrations promised – riots threatened. It was not simply industrial action. For the first time in living memory, it was literally tribal. Anyone who was not Matadi might find themselves a target, along with the leader of the opposition, who had invited the interlopers into the country to steal the peoples' livelihoods. Kikuyu, Bantu, Masai, Hutu and Tutsi families were warned to stay indoors. Even the Pakistani and Chinese shopkeepers, the Lebanese and Saudi merchants were warned to shut their businesses for the day. And Celine Chaka was the immediate object of the peoples' fury. Her father, the president – or rather, Minister Patience Aganga speaking on his behalf – demanded calm, deprecated the threat of violence, and warned of the financial and political damage that such actions might engender. But when all was said and done, they lived in a truly diplomatic state, she observed, where the will of the voting population was paramount, especially in this election season.

Richard, Robin and Anastasia were in the colonel's tent when the news came through from his headquarters. Robin had seen the start of a news report on R.T.B.L.B. – Radio Television Benin La Bas, Benin La Bas's state broadcaster, and had called Richard through. Then they had picked up Anastasia, explaining what they had learned from the bulletin to her as they all crossed to Kebila's tent. 'If only I knew where the Army of Christ was with any degree of certainty,' fumed the colonel as the four of them reviewed the situation and the radio operator apparently did his best to make himself invisible. 'It is clearly my place to be in Granville Harbour – but it is my mission and my duty to stop Odem before he does any more damage!' He slammed his hand on the table top in frustration, making both the radio operator and his equipment jump.

'Perhaps it would be as well,' Richard suggested, quietly, 'to continue the patrols upcountry with two of your Super Pumas, as the president himself has ordered, but hold the third in reserve to get you back to your Granville Harbour HQ as fast as possible, just in case . . .'

Even while Kebila was pondering that, Captain Sanda came through from the frigate *Otobo* and was passed by the nervous young communications man to his increasingly frustrated superior. 'Minister for the Outer Delta Aganga has given me orders to come upriver,' reported Sanda. 'Clearly she has decided that we must protect the orphanage and everyone around it. But you are already in place, Colonel, and I am frankly worried about the situation in the harbour itself.'

Richard and Robin exchanged glances as the two men finally finished their coded conversation. Anastasia watched them, narrow-eyed, then focused all her attention on Richard. 'Look, Colonel,' said Richard quietly. 'If we assume that Minister Aganga is at least partially influenced by Felix Makarov and his plans, not to say some underhanded realpolitik on the part of the president himself, then some element of her motivation might well be to remove Captain Sanda's contingent from the city – and leave the police unsupported in the face of a general strike. But if Sanda refuses to sail now, not only will he have disobeyed her orders, he will have given our suspicions away. I suggest that that would seriously curtail your room for manoeuvre. Perhaps he could come upriver as far as the township of Malebo and make some excuse to anchor there – within equally easy reach of the orphanage here and of Granville Harbour itself, depending on where the shit hits the fan first.'

Anastasia's eyebrows rose fractionally. Richard was not normally given to language like that. The fact that he would even consider using it showed how serious he thought the situation was becoming. But his resolution of it seemed cunning enough, which was what she was thinking when the shit really did hit the fan.

'Colonel Kebila?' squawked the radio.

'Kebila here,' said the colonel, easing back into the communications chair.

'Kebila, this is Mako. We have been hit by an IED. Extensive casualties . . .'

Communication broke then into a crackling whisper. Anastasia found herself on her feet, heart pounding and cheeks burning with shock. She looked at Richard but all his attention was focused fiercely on the stricken colonel. She glanced at Robin and found a calm gray gaze meeting her own. She sat again, suddenly feeling a little faint. But then the connection was restored. 'I say again, Senior Lieutenant Yagula, Mr Asov and I are unhurt, but it was a close thing. And we have lost ten men dead and wounded, not counting Sergeant Brodski, who had the device attached to him. Our communications have been severely curtailed. A good deal of the kit is gone. We are rearranging things as best we can and will be proceeding once again as soon as possible, working on the assumption that the Army of Christ is somewhere between us and our objective, Lac Dudo. We can use our mobile phones for contact, as long as the batteries last. Unless you have any other thoughts or advice.'

Anastasia had never heard the huge man sound so unsure of himself. What sort of a state must he be in? What sort of a state was Ivan in? she wondered, nausea burning the back of her throat severely enough to make her choke and cough.

'Just a moment, Colonel Mako,' said Kebila, also shaken by the suddenness of the disaster. 'Give me a second to consider the options.' Apparently without thinking, Kebila glanced across at Richard, who leaned forward decisively, his lips moving almost as fast as his brain. 'Send *Stalingrad* to patrol the south bank at once – keep Odem in the jungle. Then you'll know where he is and be free to act. *Volgograd* will have to return with the dead and wounded; however, if *Stalingrad* keeps patrolling, then not only is the north bank secure, but Mako, Ivan, Max and his men have a safe haven within call if they need it – until their cell phone batteries start weakening. Then, of course . . .'

'Then of course I can go back downriver in *Volgograd* with

Caleb Maina and his crew as well as most of my men – and Mako's wounded,' said Kebila. 'Medevac them to the Granville Harbour Hospital and get my own patrols out on the streets to keep the peace.'

'You'll have to leave some men here, though,' inserted Robin. 'Just in case.'

Anastasia felt herself frowning at Robin. Couldn't they rely on her Amazons? If only she had been with Ivan, she thought, she and her girls would have seen the danger. Would have known how to avoid disaster . . .

'Sergeant Tchaba and a really reliable squad. Augmented, perhaps,' agreed Kebila. Then he continued, 'There'll have to be a big enough squad to mount some kind of back up in the jungle as well. The Russians are all very well, but so far all they have demonstrated any real talent for is dying.' He sighed. Then he seemed to shake himself, and his expression lightened. 'But let's hope for the best. They are fit and strong. Well supplied and well armed. Colonel Mako knows the jungle, even if he is not Poro. And Senior Lieutenant Yagula seems competent enough. We'll trust them to survive. To keep Odem occupied. And we'll trust *Stalingrad* to keep the river safe. What else can we do?'

'That will answer everything for the time being, I think,' agreed Richard, then he continued with hardly a pause. 'Caleb Maina will bring *Volgograd* straight here with the wounded, take your men aboard and head downriver. You might make it to Granville Harbour before dawn with any luck. But now I think of it, the choppers might be quicker for those not needing bed-tending. Especially as there's an excellent medical facility at Malebo, and Sanda's frigate *Otobo* might be there too – and *Volgograd* might want to pull in if push comes to shove. But a chopper would get you home even faster than a Zubr, Colonel. If *Volgograd*'s here by sunset or soon after, you could sort things out, get on your chopper and be at police headquarters before midnight.'

'I'll get ready. We'll decide final details when *Volgograd* arrives.'

'In the meantime, *Otobo* can stay at Malebo, ready to support *Stalingrad* if Odem tries to break out of the jungle and cross the river – or to support you in Granville Harbour if there really are serious riots,' continued Richard, confirming Kebila's thoughts. 'Or to support Sergeant Tchaba, Anastasia and the rest of us here if anything else goes wrong.'

'Right,' said Kebila decisively. 'I'll get busy.' And he turned away from them, tacitly dismissing them.

'Are you all right?' Robin asked Anastasia. 'You went very pale there.'

'I'm fine,' snapped Anastasia. 'Thank you.'

'You can probably speak to Ivan soon, after Colonel Kebila's finished,' persisted Robin gently. 'He'll be busy by the sound of it, but they have their cell phones – until the batteries die, at any rate. I'm sure he'd make time for a quick word with you. Then you can check whether he's all right.'

Anastasia stopped, frozen with an uncontrollable reaction to Robin's innocent words. She was suddenly so full of rage that she had to let it out or simply erupt like Karisoke. '*Speak to Ivan!* Why would I want to speak to *Ivan*? Why should I even care whether that big *oslayob*'s alive or *dead*?' she shouted and stomped off, leaving Richard and Robin looking after her in simple wonder.

'Wow!' exclaimed Richard. 'Is it just me – or is that *love*?'

'Very funny!' spat Robin. 'What's an *oslayob*?'

'As I understand it, the word *oslayob* suggests someone is a very close friend indeed of various members of the equine family. And I'm not talking about teenage girls and ponies.' He shook his head and gave a lopsided grin. 'Like I said, it looks like love to me!'

But Robin wasn't so sure. All things considered, it might well be hate.

The next time Richard and Robin saw Anastasia, she was pounding out into the farmland at the head of her team of Amazons, her expression as black as thunder. Ado and Esan were at her shoulders and twenty Amazons behind them, barely looking more cheerful.

The afternoon was wearing on. *Volgograd* was due soon after sunset and Kebila had got his men ready to depart either aboard the Zubr or aboard the Super Pumas. Tchaba's augmented command of twenty experienced soldiers were finishing an early supper preparing to take over the night patrol after the rest of their companions had gone. Kebila was leaving them a good range of transport – a sixteen-seater Zodiac with extra fuel in case they needed to go on the water, a truck in case they needed to go upcountry, a chopper – engineer and pilot, fuel and spares. And an equally impressive range of arms and equipment, from MANPAD portable rocket systems to the SA80 assault rifles with the under-barrel grenade launcher he had just bought for his whole command, along with tents, a field kitchen, cooks and makeshift mess hall as well as any other supplies and support he felt they needed, for all in all they were too large a contingent to rely on the orphanage's accommodation, supplies or kitchens. But it was clear to Richard that the departing colonel did not really view Tchaba and his men as much more than a guard unit – certainly not a front-line combat unit, for all his protestations. And, in Richard's own mind at least, they were nothing like a match for Anastasia and her Dahomey Amazons.

In the face of the bustle in the camp, Richard and Robin joined the orphans for dinner once again and enjoyed a powerful fish and groundnut *maafe* – a stew accompanied with starchy, dough-like cassava *fufu* and *klouikloui* crisp fried rings of peanut butter. Halfway through the meal, Anastasia and her girls, and Ado and Esan returned, drenched in perspiration but in no better frame of mind. They dumped their packs and their weapons in a corner much to the disgust of the priest and the nuns, then they sat together hunched in a circle with their backs to most of the rest of the room, sharing a big bowl of the *fufu* which they rolled into balls and dipped in the maafe stew as they whispered.

Kebila arrived soon after to inform Richard and Robin that *Volgograd* had arrived. So the rest of the evening was a whirl of embarkation and departure. Both the Russians and Caleb's Zubr crew had battlefield-trained medics but all the wounded were too severely hurt to move. So Kebila filled his Super Pumas with his troops and whirled away, while *Volgograd* inflated her skirts again and swept downriver with the rest of the colonel's command. Richard and Robin got to bed earlier than usual. Exhausted, they went straight to sleep.

Richard woke at midnight, certain that something was going on. He reached across and felt Robin's hip. She rolled over and snored quietly. But he was certain he had heard an almost silent movement. The quietest of groans. In the pitch blackness he swung his legs out of bed and padded towards the door. It took him a moment to find it and feel his way down to the handle. Then he opened it and peered into the corridor. Silence. Stillness. The whole camp seemed at rest. He crept back to bed, and eventually fell asleep.

But he found that he wasn't surprised to find out in the morning that Anastasia, Ado, Esan and the Amazons had vanished, along with the Zodiac Kebila had left behind. And a good deal of the arms and equipment Tchaba's men had been supplied with.

Forest

'I cannot go,' said Tchaba. 'My place is here. And, besides, my foot . . .' He did not add, *you stole my lucky boots.* But he was thinking it, decided Richard.

'Then who can you send?' asked Richard. 'Who's your next best man?'

'Corporal!' called Tchaba by way of answer. The man who responded was wiry and slight. His face looked as though it had been clawed by angry leopards.

'This is Corporal Sani Abiye,' said Tchaba. 'He is the best jungle man in the regiment. If I send anyone, it will be Corporal Abiye.'

'You know you will have to send someone,' persisted Richard. 'Miss Asov is a close friend of Celine Chaka, who is perhaps the next president. She's a national heroine after killing Moses Nlong. You can be certain she's gone into the forest after the other Russians – and Odem. You have to check at the very least.'

Robin was at breakfast. The sound of the chopper warming up gave her a good idea of what was going on and the look on Richard's face as he strode between the tables told her everything else she needed to know. 'They're going after her,' she said. 'And I take it you're going with them.'

He sat down opposite her. 'Look, darling,' he said, his bright blue gaze burning into hers. 'The last time Anastasia went off the rails it was you who pulled her out. You got her up from the gutter in Moscow, into rehab and into the recovery programme. Now it's my turn. I'll stay with Corporal Abiye and his men. I won't take unnecessary risks, I promise. Then I'll watch her back if we find her and I'll bring her back out if I can. Besides,' he cajoled. '*Abiye* is Yoruba for *born to live forever*. What's the worst that can happen?'

Richard had attended every one of Mako's briefings possible and he felt confident that he was up to speed with the requirements of armaments and equipment, with the rules and expectations and the basics of jungle warfare.

Until the Super Puma lifted off and left him standing with Corporal Abiye and his ten-man squad on the scimitar-shaped tongue of black mud last visited by the Zubrs. And, presumably, by Anastasia's Zodiac RIB, though there was no sign of the inflatable vessel any more than there was of *Stalingrad*, which was presumably patrolling somewhere further upstream. Nor, as he looked around the set, scarred faces of the Poro-trained jungle experts, was there any sign of kit or survival equipment – anything much other than the guns, grenades and matchets they all carried. Except for the two beefiest, who also shouldered MANPADS man portable missile systems. Previous experience with the Benin La Bas army had made Richard expect headphones and a central comms set. But no. Abiye was clearly going to do this the traditional Poro way.

The corporal squatted on the balls of his feet with his SA80 across his knees, leaning the weight of his forearms on the weapon as he studied the tracks and footprints on the driest surface at the crest of the mud bank. He spoke rapidly, making no allowance for Richard's shaky grasp of the local language. 'The footprints all head into the forest,' he observed, his quiet voice as ravaged as his scarred cheeks. 'Two sets. Russians, heel-down with heavy backpacks and lots of equipment. Going with confidence; returning with dead and wounded. The effects of the hovercraft lift-off over the top of those. Then another set of Russians again, still overloaded but a lot less confident. On the balls of their feet – almost tiptoeing.

'Then the second set: lighter, over the top of everything else, laden on one shoulder only. Recent. Only just beginning to dry. The children, carrying their rigid inflatable boat. They'll want to have hidden it carefully, I suspect, as it is their only line of retreat. Let's see how good they are. If we find it, then they're nowhere near good enough.'

But the tracks of Anastasia's Amazons that the corporal followed so confidently at first vanished at the edge of the forest, which seemed interesting to Richard and instructive to the men he was with, because the Russians' tracks remained all too easy to follow, both before and after they had been caught by the improvised explosive device Odem had wrapped around the unfortunate Brodski. Richard remained uncharacteristically quiet as the patrol spread out to search among the trees, challenged by Abiye's observation to find the Zodiac. But it seemed to him that the Russians' tracks were the ones to follow in any case. Now that they were certain Anastasia was here, these would be the tracks she would be following herself. And after ten minutes of searching they knew that they were wasting their time looking for the Zodiac.

They hardly needed to follow the tracks through the giant ferns between the enormous tree trunks to the clearing where Odem's trap had sprung. The smell would have let them follow their noses. Corporal Abiye stopped them well back from the edge of the clearing. A few silent flicks of his hands spread them out so that the only people in anything like proximity to each other were Abiye and Richard himself. Only when he was certain his men were in position did the corporal step forward. Richard went with him – until another silent gesture halted him. But he was able to make out the killing ground clearly: the shattered stump where Brodski must have hung, still perhaps five metres high. The sphere of withering destruction that resulted in a circle of blackened debris on the ground – all of it alive with insects; some of it iridescent with beautiful blue-winged butterflies. The column of blast damage reaching up and up the towering tree trunks into the shattered branches, splintered twigs and decimated leaves hundreds of feet above. Abiye gestured again, stepping silently back. The rest of the command coalesced soundlessly out of the shadows, becoming visible only as they drew near. The corporal gave an infinitesimal gesture with his head and led them off around the bomb site, following the upward inclination of the ground beneath his feet as they began to follow the path of the black river.

They picked up the Russians' track again immediately. Richard reckoned he could have followed it himself without any special Poro training. There were clear footprints pushed into the leaf mould between the hacked banks of fern. And every now and then, in spite of what Mako no doubt would have wished, scorched patches where the men had jungled up something to eat or drink. Soon enough, Abiye was also able to point silently with the tip of his matchet to half-buried, fly-covered piles of excrement and paper where the men had relieved themselves at the side of their path.

But it was only Richard's blind faith which kept him certain that Anastasia and her Amazons were following Max's men. For where the Russians left an abundance of signs, Anastasia's command left none. Nor did Abiye's, and for much the same reason. None of them was heavily laden. Even Richard was carrying nothing more than a water bottle, a backpack, his phone and his weapons. The soldiers were dressed in uniform trousers, vests and headgear. Richard's thornproof slacks, shirt and waisted bush jacket made him feel overdressed. But he seemed to have chosen well in the matter of high-sided boots into which his trouser cuffs were tucked. On the other hand, he was the only one bareheaded – in spite of the fact that sunlight was a distant memory kept out by the thickening canopy that spread ever higher above.

They kept inland of the Russians' route along the river bank and Richard at first wondered why – but then, as the sounds of rushing waters gathered into the first series of rapids, Abiye's logic became clear – distance from the noisy water made the jungle sounds easier to hear. Not that there were many. Especially as the invisible sun so far above them rose to its overpowering zenith. Every surface was suddenly running with condensation, as though the entire jungle was sweating. In his shirt and jacket, Richard found it hard to breathe. His heat-assaulted mind began to fantasize that the amount of perspiration soaked up by his inappropriate clothes was actually weighing him down.

Abiye did not call a halt as they marched silently up the steepening hillside. He simply gestured, and his command spread like shadows into the jungle once more. Richard doggedly focused on the corporal's scrawny shoulders and sweat-soaked T-shirt vest, paying no attention to the fact that they were suddenly all but alone. A glance over his shoulder, however, assured him that the men carrying the portable missiles were still close behind, seemingly as fiercely focused on his back as he was on the corporal's.

The four of them weren't alone for long, however. The

questing men returned. Richard found himself between two noiseless soldiers. One carried a length of vine that looked like a short fat snake. He held it up and made a pantomime of putting one end to his lips. Richard took it, did so, and found his mouth filled with sweet water. He sipped judiciously until he felt his body quicken and his mind clear. The second soldier passed him a small hand of tiny red bananas. Richard peeled the fruit and ate its slightly astringent flesh, keeping his sharpening attention on the others around him doing the same, noticing that they did not drop the skins. They eased across the track they were following and broke through to the river, just at a point where its roaring dwindled. Here there was a pool in the midst of the rapids with a low waterfall above it and a rushing sluice below. Abiye gestured and the banana skins went into the water, vanishing down the sluice so that they would continue to leave the minimum of signs behind them.

The river also allowed them to relieve themselves at last. Richard was surprised to see the corporal post the first of a series of guards, then unlace his boots and strip off his trousers before stepping into the water. The expression on his face told Richard what he was doing and he was only just able to contain the urgent need to do the same until his turn came. The water was icy cold, and aided the process he was standing waist-deep in it to perform. He reached down to dash a handful of cool liquid into his face, but a gesture from Abiye stopped him. The black mud that bedded the stream contained who knew what – besides the coltan they were all here to claim. He waded back out, grabbed his clothes and crossed to the edge of the forest, overtaken by modesty – born of the fact, he thought wryly, that he alone here possessed the lily-white ass from the well-known saying. He was leaning with his right shoulder against a convenient tree, trying to pull his pants up his still-wet legs as the rest of Abiye's men courteously let him dress in something like privacy, when Anastasia started talking to him from the shadows on the far side of the trunk.

'Tell Corporal Abiye I think it's time we joined forces,' she said so quietly no one else could hear – so quietly he wondered whether her words were something he was imagining. 'We've been watching you and we don't think you'll get under foot too badly,' Anastasia continued. 'Fifteen of us and twelve of you will make a neat little unit. And we'll be able to move fast because we've already checked ahead and know which paths are safe and which are not.'

Fall

The problem was that Abiye and his men were here specifically to look for Anastasia and her girls. It was the soldiers' mission to bring them back safely now that they had found them, not to join forces and follow the Russians up the mountain and deeper into the jungle. Especially, Abiye observed, as the Russians had treated his men's beliefs with arrogant disrespect. A point of view supported by the fact that the little unit's radio operator was Corporal Oshodi, who had shot the Russian wearing Ngoboi's costume in the first place.

On the other hand, Anastasia countered, she and her command were going after Max and Ivan no matter what Abiye and his men did. The only way the corporal stood any chance of fulfilling his orders was to help her. And, Richard observed calculatedly, the best method of avenging the late Pavel Zaytsev's insult was to show his companions how much better the professional soldiers were at jungle warfare. Who better to do that than Corporals Abiye and Oshodi? That idea appealed to Abiye, but he still needed to check with base.

It was their entirely reasonable attempt to do this which established the fact that their communications were being jammed. This was not immediately obvious. At first, Corporal Oshodi simply thought his equipment was faulty. Richard pulled out his Benincom cell phone. There was no signal for that either.

'There's a cliff up ahead,' said Anastasia. 'My father's men have left ropes in place so it's easy to climb. And we've checked the place out – it's safe. Perhaps you'll be able to get a signal from the top of that.'

And so they took the first step almost in spite of themselves. Abiye led the way through the forest towards the cliff with Anastasia at one shoulder and Richard at the other. Oshodi and the others followed. Ado and Esan appeared and disappeared in the forest shadows, but there was no sign of any of Anastasia's Amazons until the soldiers reached the foot of the cliff. It must be the better part of thirty metres sheer, thought Richard, and he could see why Max's men had left ropes and equipment in place. No matter how easily they had managed to get up there, they would find it a considerable obstacle if they wanted to come back down at any speed. The first obstacle of many they would find facing them on their way up the black river to Lac Dudo.

But while he was standing there lost in thought, Ado shinned up the rope with impressive sinuous ease, then she and several others appeared at the crest, looking silently down, waiting for the men. Richard was fit and strong. The cliff face immediately in front of him was by no means as smooth as it had first appeared. He found it surprisingly easy to climb. The toes of his boots slipped securely into cracks and ledges. His shoulders and upper arms found no difficulty in hauling his lean torso aloft, while his thighs and calves powered him upwards from beneath like springs. He went hand over hand, his eyes fastened on the irregular cliff face immediately in front of him with its outcrops of vegetation, its little bushes and pendant creepers with a seeming nest of dry leaves at every sizeable juncture. He had gone about two-thirds of the way when he stopped and hung there, his mind racing. Immediately in front of his face there was a considerable bush, its leaves and branches a tangle of creepers packed with dry leaves. In this micro-jungle, there suddenly seemed to be more life than in the larger jungle all around it. A bright yellow-banded centipede the better part of thirty centimetres long suddenly erupted like a multi-legged snake. And, beside it, in the crack where the roots of the bush were lodged, a yellow scorpion scuttled into the light. Richard hung there, his mind racing, frozen – not with fear or disgust – with overwhelming memory.

His mind raced. Flies, mosquitoes. The leopard that had ironically saved them when Livitov disguised as Ngoboi had exploded in the drainage ditch. The crocodile which had taken Zubarov. It was as though he remembered seeing each one individually in Ngama's zoo all that time ago when he had been shown around it with Robin, Max and the others. Alongside gorillas, baboons, chimps, panthers, leopards, even elephants; Nile crocodiles ten metres long, dwarf crocodiles half that length – but still more than long enough. Spiders, scorpions, centipedes. Snakes of every sort from spitting cobras to reticulated pythons. What if disgraced ex-minister Bala Ngama hadn't just sold them off when he'd been removed from government, as people thought? What if he'd released them up here, still planning to open his private wildlife park and make a fortune after all? What if he was somehow repopulating this section of the jungle?

A hand fell on his shoulder and he jumped. Anastasia was hanging at his side. She raised her eyebrows: *Is there a problem?* He shook his head: *Everything's fine.* He pulled himself easily on up to the top of the cliff where Anastasia and Ado pulled him up on to his feet. Even up here, the roar of the waterfall was too loud to allow speech at less than a bellow, so he kept his suspicions to himself, and his lips remained sealed for the time being.

On they went, onward and upwards, through what Richard ruefully recognized was going to be a very long day. Literally a long day – they were climbing the west-facing slope of a steep mountain standing high above a riverine plain, racing the shadows up as the sun rolled away past the meridian and began to wester, then set away beyond Granville Harbour – and the lower slopes behind them became clothed in night while daylight lingered here. But although the brightness and the heat persisted, the signal strength got no stronger for either the cell phones nor the radio. They paused at the top of each slope, at the crest of every cliff with the river throwing itself into vacancy on their left hands and the sun beating through the overgrowth on to their shoulders and the backs of their heads. But there was no sign of a stronger signal.

During the unnaturally long afternoon they fell into an easy rhythm, an unspoken but generally agreed disposition. Point men came from both the soldiers and the Amazons, always checking ahead, paying particular attention to the lines hanging down cliff faces and occasional TR portable bridges over sheer-sided chasms, left in place by Max and the men they

were following. For places like these would be perfect for
IEDs, booby traps or ambushes if Odem and the Army of
Christ were worried about anyone following the Russians into
their lair. But there was nothing. The two teams went swiftly
and silently through the forest along the riverside, therefore,
following the trail of the Russians, pausing only to check
whether they had any signal yet; never stopping at all.

Until the most unexpected thing of all stopped them. A
corpse. But not a Russian corpse. Not on the track – or
anywhere near it. Richard saw it first, for, with his mind full
of speculation about Bala Ngama's menagerie of dangerous
animals and the possibility that they had been released into
the jungle here, he was paying extra attention to everything
in front of him. For as well as banded centipedes and yellow
scorpions he remembered all too vividly a wide range of native
snakes – venomous ones as well as constrictors. While the
others looked for IEDs, Richard tended to scan the shaggy
cliff tops for mambas, adders, vipers and cobras; always
double-checking the creepers nearest to the climbing ropes for
pythons and other constrictors. He was looking upwards, therefore, scanning the jungle overhang at the top of yet another
waterfall when he saw the body hurl itself over the edge like
someone trying to ride Niagara without a barrel. It was outlined
against the sky for a moment, seemingly frozen there, spread
like a skydiver. Then it plummeted downwards.

The body was too listless and unresponsive to be alive, but
Richard only realized that later. He tensed, ready to dive in
and rescue it, watching as it fell fifteen metres into the pool
at the waterfall's foot. It hit the surface with a splash that was
lost in the spray of the waterfall itself, and then bobbed up,
swirling towards the bank where Richard was waiting. He
realized then that it was dead, and had the presence of mind
to get his boots and trousers off before wading in after it. He
pulled its limp weight to the bank where Anastasia and Abiye
helped him drag it ashore. The others gathered round it as the
three of them rolled it over on to its back.

It was the corpse of a slim young man dressed in a sodden
white overall. His eyes were closed, but his mouth was open,
his lips blue. And yet, after a first mouthful, no water came

out of it. Richard settled down for a close examination of the corpse – as close as time and circumstance would allow. He was first aid trained to accident and emergency level for, as a ship's captain he was often called upon to perform simple medical procedures. He was experienced and insightful, fancying himself as a bit of a Sherlock on occasions. But he was not a pathologist. And even if he had been, he had neither the time nor the equipment to do anything other than to look as closely as he could and to reason as well as he was able.

The body was battered, clearly from tumbling downriver, but there were no real signs of violence – any more than there seemed to be of drowning. The pockets were empty, and the pruned fingertips suggested there had been no gloves. The blue lips and – when he looked close – the swollen tongue, spoke of asphyxiation of some kind, but there were no signs of a struggle. It seemed as though a perfectly fit young man had simply been overcome by something and had fallen, choking, dying – perhaps even dead already – into the river, which had swept him down here. But who was he? How and why had he come to be near the black river? Two questions that Richard found it easy enough to answer. But the implications of those simple answers seemed to stretch far beyond anything he could begin to imagine.

For the dead man was Han Chinese. And on the breast pocket of his white overall was a logo Richard recognized. He gestured to it, looking at Anastasia but wishing Robin was there so he could talk this over and really get to grips with the implications. It was the logo of the Chinese mining consortium whose director, *Dr Yes*, had been photographed talking to Gabriel Fola, president of neighbouring Congo Libre, and Bala Ngama, with Colonel Odem lurking in the shadows just behind them.

His eyes met Anastasia's, and although he knew she couldn't hear him over the sound of the waterfall, he mouthed the words, '*Han Wuhan!*'

Lookout

Both Anastasia's and Abiye's commands looked askance at Richard when he took the overalls off the body, before covering it as best they could. But it didn't require too much imagination for them to understand that a disguise might come in useful. Especially as the more they thought about it the more likely it seemed that Han Wuhan were already upriver, trying to get their hands on the coltan.

Richard and Anastasia didn't get an opportunity to discuss all this until well after sunset, when they broke the march for a quick rest and something to eat and drink. There was water from the vines found by Anastasia's girls and Abiye's foragers. There were the succulent hearts of some smaller palms that tasted a lot like pineapples to Richard, chopped into dripping chunks by the ubiquitous matchets. Everything left over and everything resulting from the meal went into the river in one way or another. A process that took a little time, and allowed Richard and Anastasia to crouch side by side in the darkness and exchange some thoughtful whispers. 'Looks like they've been playing games with us,' he observed.

'Looks like my stupid father may well have walked into a great deal more than just the Army of Christ the Infant,' she growled.

'If he's walked into Han Wuhan engineers then it must be a replay of the Kivu Gambit. And if he's up against the army of Congo Libre as well, then we can expect a hell of a lot more bodies to come down the river.' He nodded invisibly.

'Shit!' she spat. 'This is totally *polnyi pizdets*! Fucked up beyond repair!' And it occurred to him that she wasn't only thinking about her father. But she was being steadfast in her refusal to discuss Ivan.

'We have to get up there and see what's going on,' he said. 'That's the least we owe Max and the rest.'

'We do,' agreed Abiye suddenly, having joined them silently

and invisibly. 'It is our duty. Our country may well have been invaded. And nobody knows! This is a terrible thing!'

Anastasia stirred, clearly keen to proceed as quickly as possible. 'Wait,' said Abiye gently. 'We are blind at the moment. It is the darkest time of the night. It will be very dangerous to move too soon. In a little while the stars will be out and there will be a moon. If we remain close to the river the jungle will not steal the light. We will be able to proceed as long as we have the strength.'

'My girls are tough,' said Anastasia.

'I take your point,' said Abiye. 'We accept them not as a group of women or children but as a battle-hardened unit. And a battle-hardened unit may well be what we need if we are up against Congo Libre's regular army coming across the border under cover of the Army of Christ the Infant!'

'But,' added Richard softly, 'Congo Libre has destroyed almost all its native jungle, I understand. And that means that their army won't know how to handle this.' He gave a gesture that included the last of the forest and the first of the virgin jungle. 'Any more than Max's men seem to do.'

'That might give us an edge,' agreed Abiye. 'But whether it's enough will depend on how many of them there are.'

'And,' added Anastasia, 'the Army of Christ know all about the jungle.'

'Right,' said Richard. 'So they're the ones we go after first. Which was pretty much the plan in the first place, right, Anastasia?'

'Fucking A,' she said. And as she did so, two things happened at once. The moon came out, flooding the riverbank with cool silver light. And somewhere, deep in the nearby jungle, a leopard gave its full-throated hunting roar. Answered by another and another, almost as if they were echoes.

The next twelve hours passed for Richard like the night watches aboard a ship. He was used to keeping going with little or no sleep, but he entered a dreamlike state where his concentration on the immediate was so intense that the passage of hours went past in a flash. So that seemingly all too soon after the moon rose and the leopards gave their coughing roars, a cold

grey light filtered out of the high blue sky through a veil of
smoke from Karisoke's crest, and they found themselves
suddenly high on the mountainside, with the river in a deep
gorge on their left-hand side. And it was dawn. Though, with
the sun low on the far side of the mountain, there would be
no direct sunlight until noon.

The little group were gathered together at the crest of another
cliff, in a strange, grey-misted space between two huge trees.
One standing tall, the other lying broken. This step of the
mountainside seemed more substantial than any they had
encountered so far. And, as if to emphasize this, the tallest
tree they had come across gripped the rocky soil with a wide
reach of gnarled roots and then soared what looked like a
hundred metres straight up. Beyond it, the jungle seemed to
fall away, as though some natural disaster had warped and
stunted it. Beyond the giant tree's massive canopy, the grey,
smoke-smeared sky hung sullenly low above the south-western
slopes in a way that tricked off something in Richard's memory.
He crossed to the enormous trunk and touched it, stroking it
almost mindlessly, lost in deepest thought.

Anastasia joined him. 'What a lookout post this would
make,' she said, echoing a thought he hadn't even realized he
was thinking.

Neither team had actually reckoned on the Russians leaving
ropes and bridges for them to follow. Both leaders knew very
well that they would need to climb cliffs. Therefore both teams
were equipped with such basic climbing equipment as they
thought they might require. Whereas employing these in the
rock faces they had come up so far might have been a slower,
more difficult job, the rough bark of the huge tree presented
very little difficulty. It was at once deeply ridged and yet
sturdily attached to the trunk itself. And Corporal Oshodi
proved to be a very able climber. Armed with a pair of binoculars that communicated wirelessly with a hand-held tablet, the
twin of the one with which Mako had explored the overhanging
mangroves during Ngoboi's first visit, he went up the tree in
a way that reminded Richard irresistibly of a squirrel.

Oshodi had to climb little more than two-thirds of the way
up the tree before a broad branch gave him a perfect lookout

point. And Abiye's hand-held tablet showed a scene of devastation that spread away into the grey distance. And, although the angle was a very different one, the picture jogged Richard's memory and the whole thing fell into place. Oshodi's binoculars were scanning above the tops of the trees that had been damaged all those years ago by the combination of the volcanic eruption and the gas cloud. For there, in the distance, rearing higher than the twisted and stunted vegetation, but even more depressing in its ruined majesty, stood Cite La Bas. 'My God!' breathed Richard. 'I hadn't realized we had come so far! We must be nearly there!' Oshodi traversed right, showing the slope falling away westwards to the next valley slope, the barrier that had trapped the invisible gas, turning it into a poisonous lake for long enough to snuff out all the life in the city that had survived the terrible lava flow, whose long black scar could still be seen in the distance.

Then Oshodi traversed left, sweeping the binoculars' enhanced vision back across the dead city to the upwards slopes below Karisoke's smoking caldera and Lac Dudo. Here, it was clear that many of their worst fears were likely to be realized. For the air above the lake was busy. There were helicopters hovering there, coming and going through plumes of smoke.

Oshodi shinned another fifty or so metres upward. The new angle gave more of an idea what was going on at the lakeside. Makeshift buildings sat, their roofs just visible above the jungle down-slope of the lake. It seemed to Richard that here was where the main concentration of workers appeared to be. And maybe more than mere workers, he thought, eyes narrowing. Certainly, here was where skeletal guard towers stood. There looked to be activity all around the lake's shore, but whoever was in charge had found the thick jungle on the upslope far more difficult to clear. The last picture showed the damaged dams and sluices which had allowed the pearls that had set all this in motion to escape. There was a considerable number of workers there. Trying to effect repairs, perhaps. Certainly, what they were doing seemed important – and would therefore bear closer scrutiny – for they seemed to be surrounded by guards.

Richard looked up as the picture went blank to find both Anastasia and Abiye looking expectantly at him. 'It seems clear that we'll have to cross the river,' he said quietly. 'It may be more difficult to get up the far bank, but the extra effort should be worth it. The jungle upslope will give us better cover when we get up to the lake itself – we'll be able to get closer to whatever's going on. And the extra height above the lake will be an advantage too.'

'And,' said Anastasia, 'if we're going to cross the river, then this looks like just the place to do it.'

The second tree was almost identical to the first, except that it had surrendered its grip on the thin soil of the far bank and crashed sideways across the seventy-metre gap that separated the banks at the lip of the cliff. It had clearly fallen a little way upslope and then rolled down into its present position. Most of the upper branches, that would have formed a considerable barrier, had snapped off as it settled and lay scattered around now. The lower branches, less dense if more massive, reached outwards in shattered stumps or hung down between the sheer rocky banks almost as far as the writhing surface of the water at the edge of the fall. 'Right,' he said. 'Let's get busy.'

They used the same technique as Oshodi had to secure lines on to the bank and the rough bark of the tree. This time it was Esan and Ado who worked their way nimbly and swiftly across, getting to the far bank with the safety lines anchored firmly behind them in little more than the time it took for Oshodi to shin back down to the jungle floor. Then, one by one, they began to pick their way across the makeshift bridge. Abiye sent two of his most reliable men to join Ado and Esan at the far side and the four of them immediately set up a secure guard point. Abiye and Anastasia did the same here, and Richard stayed with them, keeping a careful lookout. The men picked their way across and the Amazons followed them until there was only Abiye, Anastasia and Richard left.

Abiye went first, then Richard followed him and Anastasia watched Richard's back while following closely behind him. The trunk was wide enough even for someone as massive as Richard to cross with relative ease, though he found that after ten metres or so he had to crouch in order to negotiate the shattered branches that stood out from the main trunk, proceeding hand over hand from shattered stump to shattered stump, grateful for the rope. He did not look down, but he could not resist looking up at the river that ran hypnotically towards him, the gorge becoming deeper and narrower like a funnel mouth gathering the water inwards towards the falls themselves. Further upstream, the river vanished round a bend into the jungle. But Richard was able to estimate that the main sluice system must begin little more than seven kilometres further upriver. They'd be there by lunchtime with luck.

Richard did not pause while making these observations but continued to work his way along the thickening tree trunk towards the bank side clearing on the opposite lip of the chasm, where the rest of the little command stood waiting for Abiye, Anastasia and him. Just as he reached the thickest part of the fallen trunk, however, where the branches stopped and there was no choice but to stand up and walk that last fifteen metres, the wood beneath him seemed to leap and shudder. Richard froze, looking upstream. The sound of the waterfall below him was so overpowering that he never really registered that there might be another clamour associated with the quaking of the fallen tree. But then he glanced to the shore ahead of him. Everyone there was looking around in consternation too. Abiye was running across the last five metres of the trunk. Even as Richard looked, the corporal threw himself through the wall of roots and into the welcoming arms of his command, trailing the end of the safety rope behind him. Richard crouched, feeling the trunk with his fingers like a doctor taking a pulse. The rough wood juddered once again.

Richard realized in a flash that what he was feeling was something greater than the power of the waterfall. He glanced upstream once again, but there was nothing. He looked back towards Anastasia. Her eyes were wide and her face sheet-white. And abruptly Richard could see why. Her end of the tree was reacting to whatever was happening much more actively than his still-rooted end. Without thinking, he turned round and began to scramble back towards her. No sooner did he do so than the tree shook for a third time – more fiercely yet. Frowning, Richard looked up into the sky, wondering whether Karisoke was erupting. But no – the smear of grey smoke was just the same as it had been. Whatever was happening here had nothing to do with the volcano.

And somewhere in Richard's head, a penny dropped. The men he had seen through Oshodi's binoculars working on the sluices. They hadn't been fixing them. They had been getting ready to blow them up. The logic was inescapable. Why had he not seen it before? The only thing standing between Han Wuhan and the black, coltan-rich mud was the water. And the only things holding the water in place were Dr Kuozumi's dams and sluices.

Five minutes or so after that first disturbing vibration, there was likely to be a wall of water coming down into that steep-sided rock funnel at more than seventy kilometres per hour.

And the tree was going to be right in its way.

Macho

Richard had never seen Anastasia so frightened. He walked towards her, using his left hand to reach for any stubs of branches that promised stability, holding his right hand out towards her, and forcing all the reassurance that he could muster into his expression. 'Come on, Nastiya, he said, although he knew she couldn't hear him. 'It's all right. We'll make it.' Her fierce gaze switched from his eyes to his extended hand. In an instant, she had attached herself to it like a limpet to a rock. He turned slowly and began to lead her on across. Since he had first realized what must be going on upstream, he had been counting at the back of his mind. It was an old habit – a childish accomplishment self-taught through seemingly endless night watches. One count per second. He was at one hundred and fifty now. If he got to three hundred and they were still out here, he thought grimly, that would be five minutes elapsed. The wave would be upon them. Then they could well be in trouble.

Richard moved slowly and carefully, however. But, as he reached two hundred, he began to feel that speed might be of the essence after all. Especially as the trembling of the tree trunk beneath him seemed to be worsening moment by moment. Still, he reached across with his left hand, steadying the pair of them against one branch after another, holding Anastasia steadily with his right and keeping a careful eye on Corporals Abiye and Oshodi – and the others who were pulling in the safety rope like a slow motion tug of war team.

It was Abiye's gesture that warned him. The gesture, for he would not have heard even the loudest shout. The roots seemed tantalizingly close at hand, the bank immediately beneath his toecaps. But Anastasia was still behind him grabbing his hand so hard that she had almost dislocated his shoulder. He followed Abiye's gesture and looked upstream. A wall of water came round the bend, exploding out of the jungle with the speed of a striking snake. The crest of the thing stood well over two metres high and seemed to be extended by a considerable mat of water hyacinth. Richard pulled Anastasia forward desperately, twisting his shoulder joint painfully as she froze, just a step or two short of safety. Richard turned to face her at last, angry and frustrated, made a little reckless by the fact that he at least was above solid ground.

Anastasia was frozen all right. But not with fear. For there, spread face-up on the approaching mat of water hyacinth, speeding towards the waterfall at the better part of fifty kph, was Ivan. Richard saw the future in a flash – the wall of water, high though it was, would not push Ivan far enough up to reach the tree. Instead he would be hurled into the branches hanging over the last of the river before the fall. But hitting those branches at that speed would be like a car crash. Ivan would be smashed against them by the force of the speeding hyacinth mat. What was needed here was quick thinking, brawn, and sheer bloody insanity in more or less equal doses.

Richard heaved his right arm inwards, simply jerking Anastasia out of her stasis and past his chest. She staggered, fell sideways, and disappeared through the wall of roots to land at Abiye's feet, holding the last of the safety line, which was now looped round Richard's waist. Still counting up past three hundred, Richard unslung his rifle and his little backpack, throwing them both after the Russian woman. Then he was securing the loop on place with a sailor's speed and dexterity, never taking his eyes off Ivan and completing his knot with the same swiftness as the Russian could strip a Kalashnikov. Then he jumped.

Abiye and Oshodi were not quite as quick-thinking as he – or perhaps they were just confused by the sheer bloody lunacy of his action. But whereas he had hoped to land on Ivan – ideally – or on the hyacinth barge at least, they jerked the line tight early and nearly cut him in half. Richard all-but upended, legs, kicking, hands reaching downwards, body swinging away downstream into the gorge towards the waterfall. His feet hit the hanging branches and he kicked off like a swimmer at the turn. Then they loosened him and he swung downwards and outwards, penduluming back upstream,

beginning to come upright once again, his vision filled with
Ivan's shocked face shouting something – as though he could
be heard amid this Armageddon of sound. At the last minute
Richard jerked his head aside so they slammed into each other
chest to chest. He wrapped his arms and legs around the
Russian and felt Ivan do the same.

The pressure of the rope around Richard's waist became
almost unbearable and they slammed back into the hanging
branches. There was an instant of stasis. Richard felt the
crushing pressure on his back and chest combine with an
agonizing pain around his waist that was sliding relentlessly
up towards his already squashed short ribs. And the most
overwhelming deluge of foul, black water that seemed intent
on drowning him, crushing him and tearing him apart all at
the same time. Then Ivan had the presence of mind to reach
one hand up and grasp the rope. No sooner had he managed
to relieve that agony around Richard's waist than the pressure
at his back eased too. The massive wash of water fell away.
The water hyacinth vanished suddenly enough to set the pair
of them swinging wildly between the vertical walls of the
gorge.

'Hang on *TIGHT*!' Richard bellowed at Ivan's shoulder, and
was rewarded by feeling the muscles crushed against his
cheek tense. He strained every muscle in his arms and legs as
though trying to crush the life out of the man he was endeav-
ouring to rescue. The rope holding them fell off the trunk and
they were pitched down towards the roaring water as the tree
itself tumbled away behind them. Richard saw the last of it
pitch-poling over the edge like a caber tossed by a giant as
he span helplessly, his toecaps seemingly just above the
writhing waters. The rope slammed sideways as well as downwards and this time it was Ivan's turn to cushion his companion
as they hit the rock wall of the gorge. But the stone had been
hollowed out by the relentless water. There was enough of an
overhang to ease the impact and no sooner had they hit than
they were swinging out again and soaring upwards as Abiye's
team stopped playing slow motion tug of war and went for
the world speed record instead.

As they came up to the lip of the overhang, there were

suddenly arms reaching down, hands grasping them, pulling them up to safety. Richard was content to be pulled over the grassy edge like a broken puppet and to lie gasping on the ground for a moment or two, simply glad to be alive. And it seemed that everyone else was happy to let him do this, for they were all grouped round Ivan. After a while, Richard lifted his hands to his waist and began to pull the knot apart. When the rope was free, he sat up and found Ivan up on one elbow, looking at him with a battered grin. The Russian looked terrible. He had clearly been badly beaten. The grin was simian – through split and swollen lips – and gap-toothed. He had been shot – just above the right hip, and just above the right ear, if nowhere else – though neither wound looked all that serious. 'You look like shit,' he said to Richard, his words slurred. And Richard realized with some surprise that he could hear. The wild rush of water had quietened.

'You look pretty crappy yourself.' He grinned. 'But it's good to see you too. What's going on up there?'

'Give me a moment to catch my breath,' answered Ivan, 'and I'll show you. It only took me five minutes or so to get down here, should be a quick stroll back up. As long as the wound in my side holds out.' As Anastasia registered this, she gestured to Ado and Esan, who vanished into the jungle.

'But they'll be expecting us,' said Abiye, clearly worried.

'I doubt it,' said Ivan. 'As far as I know they have no idea you're coming. And they've got to reckon I'm dead. I mean, how in hell's name could anyone have survived that?' He gestured at the easing spate of the river.

They formed into a straggling line and Ivan led the way, but Abiye and Oshodi soon joined him, forced at last to use their matchets and leave a trail. And not without reason. The jungle on either side was so dense that neither the soldiers nor the Amazons felt too keen to wander off and disappear into it as they had done with the secondary forest on the slopes below the city. It was as though they had really entered Ngoboi's realm now, and the deadly god lurked in every shadow, behind every tree, ready to weave his fatal magic – some of which the two youngsters were carrying when they returned. Both had handfuls and mouthfuls of medicinal herbs, which their teeth had crushed into thick poultices. These they packed on to the wound in Ivan's side, binding them in place with ribbon-thin lengths of creeper.

Richard was a little slower to move off than the rest. He was soaking. His boots were full of water. He wanted to empty them and ease his clothing or it would start to chafe before it was dry. Besides, there was his gun to check and his little backpack to collect. So it was that he found himself, unusually, at the rear of the column. And there, equally unusually, was Anastasia.

'Thank you,' she said.

'For what?' he asked gently.

'For pulling me across and for pulling that big ox up. He is too macho to say it himself, but he knows you saved his life. As I know you saved mine.'

'I was in the right place at the right time,' he said. 'Anyone who cared about you would have done the same.'

'Ah. But that's the problem, isn't it? Who else is there who cares for us?'

Lake

Richard and Anastasia quickly worked their way back up towards the front of the column. And it remained a column behind the three men hacking their way through the undergrowth. For this, at last, was the jungle proper. The trees were all as tall as the lone lookout tree on the far bank, and as the fallen giant that had carried them over here. The canopies above roofed vast shadowy spaces hung with ivies, creepers and lianas, studded with parasitic orchids as red as vampires' blood. The huge areas between were floored with bushes the size of tanks and man-high ferns, dripping with condensation as the heat went past forty degrees and the humidity past one hundred per cent. Distances became vague with wavering heat-haze and with mists as grey as the webs of massive spiders. The wind seemed to echo as though in restless caverns and there was everywhere a stirring of mysterious, invisible life. Or something other than life. Sinister, threatening, unearthly, inimical to humanity. Ngoboi's realm, filled with his lethal magic.

Richard and Anastasia arrived at the head of the column just in time to hear the details of what was going on at the lake. 'We walked straight into a trap,' Ivan said shortly. 'It was embarrassing. We thought we were chasing Odem and the makeshift Army of Christ and there we were suddenly surrounded by General Bala Ngama and half the regular army of Congo Libre. With a good deal of their air support command in back-up, once the trap was sprung.'

'Why didn't they kill you?' asked Abiye, awed.

'Two reasons,' shrugged Ivan. 'One: they wanted us as labour. That lake is a dangerous mother. Han Wuhan's Chinese workers are dying like flies and terrified of the place. But the other reason was your father, Nastia. He fronted them all off. Said *did they know who he was?* More importantly, did they know what he was *worth*? Which is why it turned out to be important that President Fola had sent the renegade Minister Ngama to oversee the project. Made him a general if you can believe it! Because the answer was *YES*! Ngama knew exactly what your father was worth, down to the last kopek. He was doing business with him right up to the moment President Chaka sacked him.'

'So he let you live and put you to work,' said Richard. 'That was lucky.'

'You could say that.' Ivan shot Richard a thoughtful look. 'There's something bad about that lake. The Chinese workers, engineers and what-have-you are all falling sick. Some of them are dying. It was the sight of one of them going over the dam that gave me the idea for my own escape attempt. This end of the lake is dammed, as you know. The floods damaged the system, so the Chinese engineers tried to fix it at first. Then, when they discovered they didn't have the equipment or the time so they started blowing the system up in series, letting the water out in a succession of surges like the one I came down on. Reducing the water level while they use choppers to get rid of the water hyacinth – choppers with grabs that heave it up and drop it into the jungle.'

'We saw choppers working on the lake,' Richard said.

'Not just working. Once they cleared an area near the dam, they brought in attack helicopters with floats. They've a regular little air force up there.'

'But you saw one of the workers go over the dam,' prompted Anastasia, bringing Ivan back to his original focus.

'Yeah. There's only the main dam left now. They have it rigged but they're waiting before they finish it off. They're still working on the down-slope side. Upslope are the old Japanese pearl fisheries and they've been told to stay clear of those while Ngama and Fola work out what half a million huge black pearls will fetch if they're released carefully on to the jewellery market. That's why they're waiting. Max is advising them on that, too, needless to say. That's where they have us corralled. But, long story short, I was working up by the dam when I saw the strangest thing. This young Chinese engineer was up there on the dam itself, laying charges or checking circuitry or whatever, when suddenly the water beside him started boiling. The air wavered, like a really intense heat haze. And he just pitched over and was washed away. The guards saw it and ran over, but he was gone downstream so fast they didn't even have time to raise the alarm. So I thought to myself: Ivan, if you're going to go, then that's the way to do it. And I started planning how to get myself up there.'

'There was no other way?' asked Anastasia.

'No. They have a pretty effective little gulag up there. Razor wire, guard towers. At least they let us sleep in tents. Feed us on what they give the army.'

'And how are they treating you?' asked Anastasia, her voice gentle at last.

'My face, you mean? I've had worse. I got worse when I was earning the red beret. But by and large if you're square with them, do what they tell you and don't talk back then this sort of thing doesn't happen to you.'

'But there's no way out other than over the dam?' persisted Richard.

'Not that we've found. And shit, the wire works both ways. Keeps us *in*, and keeps whatever's out there *out*.' He shivered. It wasn't cold.

'Whatever's *out there* . . .' said Richard, frowning.

'In the jungle. That's where Odem's men are. Odem's men and more. Ngoboi – but not just Ngoboi, you know? There's other stuff out there. Panthers. Leopards. Some of the men have seen them. We've all heard them.'

'If Odem's men can make it out there, then so could you,' countered Anastasia. 'You came up here to take down the Army of Christ and now you're scared of some tosser dressed as Ngoboi! *What the fuck*, Ivan!'

'What does Mako say?' asked Richard. 'He knows the jungle best.'

'Mako doesn't say anything,' said Ivan shortly. 'Ngoboi cut his tongue out. They have him crucified in the middle of the camp. Every now and then another bit of him gets chopped off. Or peeled off. A finger, an ear, a nostril. The skin of his forehead. But they won't let him die.'

'And none of you can help him out?' sneered Anastasia. 'Find some way . . .'

'No,' said Ivan shortly. 'Every now and then Ngoboi comes round trying to decide who's turn is next when Mako goes. Everyone has a vested interest in keeping the poor bastard alive.'

That conversation was enough to silence all of them and they remained quiet through the next couple of hours as the three men at the front slashed with brutal energy through the jungle undergrowth. While Richard walked his mind was racing, constructing, testing and discarding plans of action. And every now and then he would ask Ivan something. 'So, only one dam left standing, Ivan?' was Richard's first question. Ivan nodded. 'But they have it rigged?'

'As I say, that was what the engineer who went over was doing.'

'OK.' He added after ten minutes, 'and how much water hyacinth is left?'

'Looks like about half,' Ivan shrugged.

'But the lake is only half full now – so it's pretty tight-packed still?'

'At the far end it is. The end by the dams is clear.'

'That's where they have their attack helicopters on their floats?'

'Yes.' Ivan looked ready to add more detail. But several more minutes passed.

'Anything else? Boats? RIBs? How do they cross the lake?'

'Couple of RIBs, now you mention it. But they mostly use the choppers.'

Richard nodded. Lapsed into thought. Then, 'Where do they get the fuel?' he asked suddenly after a few more minutes.

'Bring it in over the volcano, I guess. They have engineers making some kind of makeshift road using the lava flow. That's pretty broken up down-slope but I hear its pretty smooth upslope – it's almost all in Congo Libre in any case.'

A few minutes later again, Richard suddenly said, 'But that means they have effective communications. Ours have been jammed.'

'There's a radio shack on each side of the lake,' said Ivan. 'The upslope one on our side looks the bigger. I'd guess that if they're jamming all the frequencies except their own – which is standard battlefield practice after all – then that's the one the equipment's in.'

'How do you know all this?' Richard asked at once.

Ivan chuckled and answered in fluent Mandarin, 'The guys from Han Wuhan told me. They don't know I speak their language.' He switched to Yoruba. 'And neither do the *mumu* soldiers . . .'

'I thought they were all over the other side,' said Richard in Russian after another lengthy period of reflection. 'On the down-slope bank.'

'They are. The Chinese are the ones who put us to work. It's the army that make sure we do what we're told. They're all bivouacked over there. The Army of Christ is on this side – upslope, where they can keep an eye on us. You'll be able to see for yourself soon. We're nearly there.'

Richard dropped his voice, but added intensity. 'Wait! If the Army of Christ are upslope, aren't we just about to walk into them?'

'Not at this time of day,' Ivan assured him. 'My men are at work. The Chinese are directing them and Ngama's soldiers are watching them. No one's got a chance to make trouble. The Army of Christ won't be out until after dark.'

Even so, they approached the edge of the jungle with the utmost care, moving forward in an arc that swung them up the mountainside, then down to overlook the wire-walled camp that housed the Russians at night. A little way back from the edge of the jungle itself they came across a tree that had lost some of its purchase on the sloping ground and leaned over towards the lake. Richard, unobtrusively taking command now, sent Oshodi up this with the binoculars.

Abiye pulled the tablet out of his backpack and, before long, Richard, the corporal, Anastasia and Ivan were poring over the vivid pictures it showed. Oshodi started with a slow panorama that showed the last dam standing across the northern end of the lake, its sluices wide, grey water soaring in arcs from its foot, visible behind it only because they soared out along the river valley before plunging out of sight below. The top of the dam was bustling with figures. Some were in the white overalls. Others were in uniform. The rest were in cargo pants and vests. These were obviously the Russians because everyone else seemed to be shouting at them, shoving them and hitting them.

This side of the dam, the razor-wired compound with the skeletal watch towers they had seen from the lookout tree below, stood apparently empty. Behind it, sitting on floats on the still water of the lake there were three Chinese Z10 attack helicopters, with their undercarriages adapted to take floats. All of their considerable weaponry was pointed directly at the prison camp. Oshodi focused down. The cramped and filthy space – still far too limited for the choppers to use – was packed with ragged tents around a rough square, in the middle of which stood a cross. Even from here and looking from behind, it was possible to see that there was someone standing lashed to it. And Ivan's description made it clear enough who that was.

The picture swung upward, following the line of the last dam to the larger encampment in the woods on the far side. Here the trees and undergrowth had been adapted to allow a considerable number of tents to be erected. There was more wire. But there were no guard posts – nor, as far as Richard could see, any patrols. Instead, on a long sweep of naked black mud, there were teams of men with mechanical shovels, bulldozers and eight-wheel trucks shovelling up the black mud. Then the picture swung away to their right, following the sweep of the black-shored lake. And here there was yet more movement. Three Chinese versions of the MI-26 heavy transport helicopters were swinging massive hooks into the weeds and dragging them into the jungle on the upslope, but it was clearly slow work, for the mats of water hyacinth broke up too easily. So there were more Russians on the shore beneath the labouring choppers, hooking and dragging the smaller fragments of the mat when it fell back into the black water. 'We'll go for them first,' decided Richard. 'We can take them and give your men their guns, Ivan. Double our force before sunset. Then we'll be ready for Ngoboi, Odem and the Army of Christ. The only other thing I need to know is what our radio operator thinks of their radio shack.' As he said this, the shack in question filled the screen. It was a larger tent than the others, with a tall pole sticking up out of it to serve as an aerial and a line running up to a nearby tree where it was attached to a big dish on a branch about six metres up. 'That's the jammer,' said Richard. 'Unless General Ngama's got Sky TV.'

The screen went blank as Oshodi turned off the binoculars. 'Right,' Richard concluded. 'Now this is what we're going to do . . .'

Black

There was no jungle left in Congo Libre. It had been destroyed to make room for cattle ranches, okra farms and opium fields. There were secret societies among the peoples who inhabited the country, but these were of Bantu farming origin and nothing like the Poro or the Sande. They were simple agricultural and historical organizations, using *bilumba* witch doctors to read the past with *lukasa* beaded memory boards and the future using *mboko* baskets. They required no sacrifices, blood or hearts. The Congo Libran soldiers knew nothing about the gods on this side of Karisoke, except that they were terrifying. They knew less about the virgin jungle which clothed the volcano's south-western slopes, except that it was full of creatures and spirits that would kill the unwary without a second thought. And they were afraid, even before Ngoboi appeared and began to mutilate the crucified Mako.

The group guarding the Russians dragging the water hyacinth out of the lake, therefore, were terrified when Anastasia's Amazons appeared like ghosts out of the jungle. They were disarmed, made to strip and tie each other up before Ado and Esan gagged them all, while Richard and Anastasia went after her compatriots, completing the rescue so slickly that only the most eagle-eyed pilot in the big Mils so low overhead would have noticed. Richard and Anastasia led the ten newly liberated men laden with guns and uniforms to the big radio shack where corporals Abiye and Oshodi were firmly in control. From outside, the shack appeared empty but it was in fact crowded, and it soon became more so. The Congo Libran radio operator and his assistant were on the floor beneath a table gagged with duct tape and bound with flex. Their eyes were huge and their foreheads beaded with sweat.

'Corporal Oshodi,' said Richard as the forty members of

his rapidly expanding army packed themselves in as though this were the Black Hole of Calcutta. 'We need to get a message out, but we don't want anyone near the lake to know we're here yet.'

'I can send a compressed file,' Oshodi promised. 'There would be an incomprehensible blurt of sound on one carefully selected channel, then everything would be back to normal. Unless they are monitoring very closely – and this man had neither the training nor the equipment to do so – they will suspect nothing. But where should I send it?'

'Send it to Tchaba,' said Richard. 'He knows we're here. He's waiting to hear from us. He can contact the others. Now, here's what I want you to say . . .'

Richard took a closer look around the shack while Oshodi was working on his orders. His wise eyes soon discovered the jamming equipment and his long fingers stroked it thought-fully. But he left it switched on and continued searching. After a few moments he found something that brought a lopsided smile to his saturnine face. It was a box of headsets piled on top of a central command transceiver. Richard crouched, ripped the tape from the radio operator's face and growled in Yoruba, 'I'd like you to tell me about these.'

'Right,' Richard continued a few moments later. 'Anastasia, your girls need to get into the kit we took from the Congo-Libran soldiers. Corporal Abiye's men will pass muster as they are, but you all stick out like sore thumbs. I have something else in mind for you, though, Ivan. We need to split your men into teams.' He raised his voice. 'First, are there any VDV men here?'

Half-a-dozen hands went up. Half-a-dozen faces almost as battered as Ivan's looked confused. Why would the mad *Anglican* need VDV men? 'Right. As soon as the girls are in soldiers' gear I want you back working on the water hyacinth. Will the chopper pilots have noticed you were gone?' There was a general shaking of heads. 'Back to work it is then, but what I want you to prepare is this . . .'

Five minutes later the crush in the shack eased as the VDV men and their disguised guards left, led by Ado and Esan, who had a battlefield radio headset clamped to the side of his

face. Richard continued talking Russian. 'Are there any GRU
men – boat specialists, forty-fifth regiment men?' Again,
several hands went up. The battered faces showed less surprise
now. 'Ivan. You take half a dozen of Abiye's men and go
aboard a RIB with this lot. Look as though you're under guard
and busy with something important. I need you to get across
the lake and find Max. Find General Ngama if you can – they
might well be together, knowing Max. He'll be trying to cut
a deal. I need you to bring them back here. If you hit any
complications you need to be aware that I'll be moving soon
after sunset. The signal will be when the guard towers blow
up. Then all hell will break loose if everything goes to plan.
So you'll have to be quick. Here's your headset. But hang on.
There's one more thing I need from you before you go.' He
switched from Russian to Matadi. 'So, Abiye, I'll need you
and the two men with the MANPADS, one for each tower.
And some really competent snipers. You'll be with me and in
the loop to begin with, but you'll need this headset later. Listen
for the code word GIBSON.' Then back to speaking in Russian.
'Anastasia, how do you feel about having your hair cut with
a matchet? You and I are going what they call in the trade
deep black. Disguise.'

'And what about *your* disguise?' she asked as he began to
saw at her hair.

'Don't worry, it'll be even more painful than yours. And
black on a whole new level.' He glanced up. 'Ivan, I need to
borrow one of your guys' kit.'

'A pair of Russian cargo pants and a dirty vest won't fool
anyone,' said Anastasia. 'You'll still look like one of the earlier
James Bonds.'

'Really?' asked Richard flattered. 'Which one?'

'That'd be telling. *Ouch!* Your disguise is going to have to
be *very* painful! And I know this before I even look in a
mirror.'

'Right,' said Richard. 'That's you finished. And you've still
got ears, so count your blessings. Now slip into the overall
we took from the Han Wuhan engineer who went over the
dam and try to look Chinese.'

'And what were you saying about *your* disguise?' she asked

as she stepped into the white overall. Richard was doing the
same, but he had to strip to his boxers before changing his
trousers for a pair of Russian cargo pants.

'Ivan will handle that,' said Richard, turning to face the
massive Russian as he pulled the stained vest over his head.
'Ivan, I need my face to look like yours. But I want all my
teeth and I need my right ear relatively untouched.'

'*Your* face? Like *mine*?' said Ivan, his eyes wide. 'That'll
hurt.'

'Let's just say I'm after a SPETSNAZ red beret,' said
Richard.

Mako was in a bad way. Nails had been driven through the
palms of his hands, then ropes had been used to lash his arms
to the cross at wrist and elbow. The tip of his tongue had been
cut out. Most of the skin on his forehead was missing. His
left ear was gone, as was his left nostril. His left cheek had
been slashed as though by panthers' claws. Only the index
finger and thumb remained on his left hand. Only the big toe
remained on his foot. His face was a mass of flies that only
rose when someone came to make sure he was still alive so
that Ngoboi could continue his sick games with him. Or to
feed him scraps and let him sip water while he still had teeth
and lips. Like now.

Mako raised his head to look at the Chinese engineer and
the two soldiers who were shoving yet another battered Russian
across the compound towards him. Torn, ill-fitting cargo pants
and a stained vest swam into his vision. Big, battered hands
holding a tin full of water. He looked up further, into the
brutalized face with its split lips and swollen eyes. But
suddenly, from between the fat, black lids there darted a gleam
of icy, commanding intelligence. A surge of amazement went
through Mako. And his eyes gleamed in return.

'Live or die,' said a deep voice in brutal Matadi. 'The choice
is yours.'

Mako's look was answer enough.

'Right,' said Richard Mariner slowly, his words slightly
slurred between his thick lips. 'This is how it goes . . .'

*   *   *

Bala Ngama eased back into the comfortable chair he had ordered to be carried into the middle of the jungle. His palatial tent opened westward so that he got the full benefit of the sunset and the view. The rear of the tent was to the lake. Behind the living area was a private, sleeping area, then a stout canvas wall, then the lake shore, bustling at the moment, with bulldozers, lifters, and Russian workers under the guns of Congo Libran soldiers. But ahead of him, beyond the wire of his compound, rose the jungle he already thought of as his own. Filled with animals from the menagerie he had assembled while he had been minister of the outer delta in Granville Harbour, it would one day become the greatest wildlife park on the continent. And he, with the support of President Fola, would annex it together with the lake into Congo Libran territory, rebuild the airport at Cite La Bas, fly in some rangers to control the animals and some builders to make five-star lodges like those in the great game reserves to the south or the east – and wait for the tourist dollars to arrive in their millions. It looked like a very bright future to him.

Ngama reached for a bottle of chilled Primus beer, one of a dozen or so recently unloaded from the fridge by an orderly. 'So,' he said lazily, 'let us return to business, Mr Asov.' As he spoke, Ngama gestured invitingly towards the bottles of Primus. Max would have preferred vodka. But, as the general said, this was business. And at the moment Max was in the business of staying alive. He reached for a beer. 'What had you in mind, General?' he asked. 'The world, after all, is your oyster.'

'Now that's strange,' said a deep voice. 'I have some people here who also want to discuss oysters. And pearls.' Ivan stepped out of the general's private quarters and the men who had followed him in through the slit in the tent's rear wall crowded thirstily round the table full of beer.

Five minutes later, General Ngama marched out of the front of his tent with Max Asov at one shoulder and Ivan Yagula at the other. A troop of half-a-dozen hangdog Russian workers followed behind, guarded by a smart squad of soldiers. They all marched towards a big Zodiac sixteen-seater RIB that was pulled up on the black mud bank. Had anyone in his command cared enough to look or to think, they might have been surprised to see their leader getting his exquisitely polished shoes covered with good honest mud for the first time since his arrival. But no one did. So they didn't notice the fact that the general had the point of a matchet pressed against the joint above his fifth lumbar vertebra, three centimetres above the start of his buttock cleft and three centimetres precisely from severing his spinal cord.

But as the group moved unobserved towards the Zodiac in its anchorage carefully isolated from the rest of the bustle on the western shore, they seemed to slow and stumble. The black mud through which they were walking appeared to boil briefly, bubbling and spitting ebony spicules up their legs as far as their knees. They staggered as though all of them had been caught in a sudden squall. Only Ivan's strength as a leader got them into the Zodiac. And once they were there, they sat, slumped in their seats as precious time slipped past unnoticed. But then, as the sun behind them set at last, the evening breeze swept down the mountain, and although it smelt faintly of sulphur, it cleared their heads. Ivan looked up suddenly, his mind reeling with shock, as though he were just awakening from a dream. He stared at his watch and his skin went cold. They had somehow lost nearly ten minutes. 'Go!' he shouted to the man at the motor. 'Go! Go! Go!' But he knew they were probably too late.

As the sun set and the sudden twilight swept across the mountain slopes, only the big Mil helicopters, still up in the sunshine, continued working. The last of the Russian prisoners were herded lethargically towards their gulag. And as they staggered wearily across the central compound past the listless figure of the crucified Mako, so the Army of Christ moved out of the jungle and gathered, watching through the razor wire. The evening breeze came whispering through the canopy overhead, spreading its restless sibilance down into the bushes, setting the ferns dancing as though some terrible life was in them. Ngoboi came whirling out of the shadows and into the compound behind the exhausted men. Two acolytes danced with him, keeping the raffia of his costume in place so that nothing of the man beneath the costume, of the face behind the mask, could be revealed. Led by Odem himself, the Army of Christ began to whistle and stamp in rhythm as Ngoboi leaped and capered, drawing out the performance, with his matchet whirling in the thickening shadows around him. The dark god whirled round Mako, the essence of primitive evil, embodying everything inhuman and unforgiving in the dark heart of the jungle.

At last, Ngoboi arrived at the climax of his dance. He froze, mid-caper, immediately in front of Mako, just at the point where the last of the light made it possible still for everyone to see what he was about to do. Odem held up his hands, the twilight's last gleaming reflected in his wraparound sunglasses. The silence rolled like thunder over the place. Ngoboi placed the flat of his matchet under Mako's chin and raised the colonel's face until their eyes could meet. Then the tall god turned his hideously masked face towards Mako's remaining left-hand finger and thumb. He raised his matchet and tensed for the blow.

But it never came, for there was suddenly half a metre of cold steel sticking out of the raffia costume covering Ngoboi's shoulder blades. He staggered back, and Mako stepped forward, the bonds falling away. His left hand joined his right hand on the grip of the matchet Richard had given him – and which was now rammed up under Ngoboi's sternum, through his heart and out of his back. The dead god sagged, held erect only by Mako's grip. His head lolled. The mask fell off. The face of a mere mortal was revealed, eyes bugged and mouth wide, frozen forever in the rictus of utter astonishment.

The acolytes sprang forward, screaming with outrage, matchets raised. The whip-crack of two rifle shots rang almost simultaneously out of the shadows and their heads jerked back in unison, spraying brain-matter. Odem howled something, snatching off his sunglasses to look around, his expression stunned. He looked at the guards up in the watch towers and started gesturing wildly. Even as he did so, two streaks of light soared out of the shadows behind him and the tops of the two skeletal towers exploded into flame. He ran round the end of the compound, waving his hands at the two attack helicopters whose cannons and rockets faced the prison compound in such naked threat. There was enough light to see movement in the cockpits as the pilots began to react.

But then, with an overwhelming rumble somewhere between a thunder crack and an avalanche, the dam blew up.

Dam

Richard had chosen to use the code word 'Gibson' after the leader of RAF Bomber Command's 617 Squadron. On the 16 May 1943, three months before his twenty-fifth birthday, Squadron Leader Guy Penrose Gibson, VC, DSO, DFC, led his nineteen Lancaster bombers on the raid code-named *Chastise* that earned them the name *The Dambusters*. Half an hour before the explosion, Richard had allowed himself to be shoved down from the prison compound towards the dam by a couple of irate guards and an engineer wearing a Han Wuhan overall. No one on the bridge had given them a second look as they walked into the hut from where the demolition system was controlled. There was one other Han Wuhan operative there, completing the final installation of the controls designed to take the last wall down in careful sequence. At first, when he was addressed in a gentle rumble of Mandarin, the young engineer thought it must be the other Han Wuhan operative who was talking. But then, in a double surprise of almost disorientating power, he realized that it was the huge Russian. And he registered what he was saying. 'My friends and I are taking control of this place. If you do what you are told then you might survive . . .'

The young man turned to the other Han Wuhan man and realized with a sickening lurch that the overall he was looking at belonged to the man he had last seen falling to his death over the edge of the dam. That, more than the giant's threats, utterly unnerved him. 'What do you want me to do?' he asked.

'Lock the door. Explain to anyone trying to gain entry that you cannot be disturbed. Then show me exactly how this system works.'

The explosive deaths of the watch towers was the signal for Oshodi to turn off the jammer. He had sent the coded message to Sergeant Tchaba over the one open channel while Richard was still getting his disguise battered into his face. The death of the jammer opened the channel for the battlefield headsets. 'GIBSON!' bellowed Richard's voice. And the dam went up. The Chinese engineers had placed their explosives in a carefully calculated series which they hoped would bring the structure down in sequence, level by level by level, past the foot of the dam wall itself and into the natural rock barrier that had contained the lake in the first place. Emptying out all of the water, but under some kind of control. They had never considered using the destruction of the dam as a weapon, which Richard, of course, had. On the warning shout of 'GIBSON!' therefore, the last of Dr Koizumi's containment barriers burst. And so did the basalt sill on which it had been built. What had been a wall became a waterfall with incredible rapidity, tearing a hole in the mountainside that was deeper than the bed of Lac Dudo, which proceeded to flow out as fast as the laws of physics allowed.

As planned, the two attack helicopters felt the results of Richard's explosive action first. The water beneath their floats began to thunder down into the black river's channel with incredible force, overtaking the tumbling blocks of rock and masonry in their eagerness to be free. Millions of gallons were suddenly fighting to get through the huge breach. From a standing start, currents leaped into being that raced towards the gaping fissure at incredible speed. The pilot of the WZ10 nearest the dam stopped worrying about the cannon and the rockets. He started the motor instead, hoping to lift off before his machine went over the rapidly-approaching edge. But the second chopper was sucked towards him too quickly. As the rotors began to spin, they became entangled and the pair of them went over the edge like a shooting star, wrapped together as their fuel exploded, setting off their armaments.

Ivan saw the WZ10s vanish into a cloud of fire that seemed to fall off the edge of the world. 'Faster,' he bellowed down the length of the Zodiac. They were so nearly there. The shoreline looked almost close enough to touch, illuminated as it was by the brightly burning watch towers that had been the beacons to guide him across the lake. But the seeming closeness was an illusion. The promise of safety was little

more than a bitterly ironic joke. Already he could feel the tug
of the falling water, sense that the whole lake surface was
sloping increasingly steeply down to his left. The twin beacons
of the blazing towers were sliding to his right with mounting
rapidity. And when he looked uphill to his right he could see
a wall of water hyacinth coming down on him out of the
shadows. His whole body went cold. 'Richard!' he yelled into
his headset. 'We're in deep trouble here! Can anyone help?'

'I see you!' called Richard, who was running back up from
the dam towards the camp. 'Esan! Plan B!'

What in heaven's name was Plan B? wondered Ivan, looking
around desperately. The last he had seen of Esan was when
he and Ado had taken the VDV men back on to hyacinth duty.
But then a great beam of light struck down from the sky, and
the roaring suck of the water beneath him was compounded
by a battering downdraught from above. And he understood.
Richard had sent the VDV men on to hyacinth duty because
he had some kind of a plan to get them up into the Mils. It
had to be VDV men because they were all trained to fly. And
the choppers were Russian Mils, the first of which was hovering
above him now, lowering the hook that it had used to clear
the lake. 'Get the hook,' came Esan's voice over his headset.
'We'll pull you ashore.'

'How the hell did you get aboard?' he asked as he caught it.

'Up the ropes,' answered Esan, as though it was obvious.
'They weren't expecting it. They weren't paying much attention. And they weren't armed.'

The Mil eased backwards as the hook slid under the rope
round the inflatable's side, jerking it out of the grip of the
terrible current and over towards the red-lit shore. Ivan staggered, taking firmer hold. He risked a glance around. The men
in the RIB behind him were all hanging on for dear life, Max
and Bala Ngama seemingly hugging each other with terror.
Then he looked left, and understood their fear, for the Zodiac
seemed to be sitting on the edge of the world. The sides of
the shattered dam stood high above his head. He looked to
his right and shouted with fear himself. The hyacinth was
rearing into the bright beam of the Mil's searchlight. It was
going to hit them before they could come ashore. '*HANG ON!*'

he bellowed, tearing his throat. Then the water hyacinth hit them. The Mil jerked upwards and for a wild moment the Zodiac seemed to take flight. Then it thumped on to the surface of the hyacinth, still skidding shorewards as the chopper pulled it relentlessly towards the burning watch towers. The propellers caught and the motor stalled. The solid keel of the Zodiac bumped across the heaving, sliding mat of vegetation. But the stalled propellers became tangled in the corded stems of the plant almost immediately. So that, just as the RIB reached the shore, the whole thing flipped over, spewing the passengers out into the mud.

Ivan scrambled through the lumpy slime, fighting to catch his breath in the face of the overwhelming stench of fish. It took him an instant to realize that he was plunging through Dr Koizumi's oyster beds. But then he was free and staggering up the black-mud slope to the prison compound. The Mil hovered overhead, its searchlight illuminating the crowd of Russians there grouped around the towering figure of Colonel Mako. He saw that Mako's command were drawn up into a defensive square, their guns facing out through the razor wire into the jungle. It was only when he managed to stagger up to the outer line that he realized there was no sign of Richard, Anastasia or her Amazons.

Richard and Anastasia were running side by side, with the Amazons grouped around them like a pack of hunting wolves. They had come out of the jungle now and were working their way along the lake shore, with the searchlights from the second Mil sweeping ahead of them and the guttering glow of the watch towers behind. They were in the cane forest and the tall spears of bamboo all around them were festooned with dripping clumps of water hyacinth that had been dropped here while the Mils were clearing the lake. Ngoboi might be dead. The Army of Christ the Infant might have melted into the jungle. But nothing was settled as far as Anastasia was concerned. Odem was still out there. He was, in fact, somewhere just in front of them, running for his life.

The moment the dam went up he was on the shore waving at the pilots of the two attack helicopters, trying to arrange

a deluge of thirty-millimetre cannon fire to sweep through
the Russian camp. In spite of the fact that he had been
focused on destroying Ngoboi, Mako had seen him there.
Had seen him freeze as Richard's explosion tore the dam
and the rock sill beneath it apart. Mako had watched as the
self-promoted colonel ran back towards his stunned soldiers,
clearly yelling orders to open fire. But the snipers who had
killed Ngoboi's acolytes and the soldiers who had launched
the MANPAD missiles were already busy. A fusillade of
rifle fire came in out of the jungle that the Army of Christ
normally assumed was its own territory. Caught in a perfect
killing field around the exposed razor wire, Odem's soldiers
were in no position to listen to him – even had they felt any
inclination to do so after the spectacular demise of his own
private god.

Mako saw the self-styled colonel stop, look wildly about,
and run into the fringe of the jungle. He was on the point of
sending some of his own men after the renegade when Richard
and Anastasia arrived.

'He has to be heading for the highway,' gasped Richard as
he and Anastasia ran, the Amazons coalescing around them.
'If he can get through the belt of jungle here, then he'll be on
the lava flow from Karisoke that the Congo Librans are using
as a road. It's his fastest way out. Or it would be, except that
I warned Tchaba to tell Kebila about it. I'm surprised the
Benin La Bas air force hasn't been up here yet.'

But, 'There!' she called, and Richard saw a movement in
the cane forest ahead. The Amazons went after him, swinging
out around him, racing to cut him off from the last strip of
jungle that might allow him access to the makeshift highway.
The frightened man saw their movement, for his course veered
towards the shore of the lake itself. The pack of women swung
west as well, driving him into the open even as Richard and
Anastasia burst on to the lake shore. But the shoreline stretched
out into the blackness, and where there had been water there
was now only lake bed – a wilderness of black slime stretching
away to the far shore where the army of Congo Libre stood
hesitant, rudderless and leaderless; out of their depth and far
away from home. And the engineers and executives from Han

Wuhan stood beside them, equally at a loss and far further away from home.

And that was the moment the lake bed chose to adjust to the sudden absence of thousands of tons of water that had been pressing down on it until just now. The basalt bowl which had been forced down for aeons on the great bubble of carbon dioxide trapped beneath it moved fractionally now that the weight of the water was gone. The pressure, building sufficiently to be forcing the gas out in bursts and clouds strong enough to kill the Chinese engineer and gas Ivan's men aboard the RIB, exploded into freedom now. And, just as had happened twenty years or so ago, a great bubble of deadly vapour exploded up out of the mud and went rolling downhill into the long-deserted graveyard of Cite La Bas. Everyone on the down-slope bank was swept away with it. The fittest lived for four minutes, choking as their lungs filled with pollution. Everyone else was dead long before that. Some of the deadly carbon dioxide rolled back into the bowl of the empty lake bed, filling it invisibly for a while before it followed the water out through the shattered dam and down the black river valley.

But none of this was obvious from the upslope shore where Odem came running full-tilt out of the cane forest, finally threw away his precious AK-74 and went slithering down the bank into the black mud of the empty lake bed. Had there been water there he might have turned to fight like a cornered rat, even though his matchet was long gone – discarded in the jungle somewhere together with his beret and his wraparound sunglasses. But the lake bed stretched away before him, seemingly offering yet another chance of escape. And so he blundered on. Calling instructions to the Mil, Richard ran down the slippery black silt slope just behind Anastasia. The Amazons were in an arc on either side of them now, all of them focused on the floundering apparition at the heart of the searchlight beam. Richard slowed, his nose twitching, watching the black spectre heaving and falling, apparently trapped by magical toils of the glittering mud he was wading through. He caught at the stem of his headset. 'STOP!' he bellowed. '*Nastia!* HALT!' On his word, the girls froze. 'Fall back,' he called. 'There's deadly gas here.'

Odem already knew that. His whole face was on fire. His eyes and nose were streaming. His adenoids and throat were alight. He could feel the strength being sapped out of his body as the black mud wrapped itself around him as though it was made of nets. He grasped at the mud as it twined itself around him and pulled against great ropes of blackness while his consciousness reeled. He felt himself sinking into the suffocating, icy ooze. It was every one of his nightmares rolled into one overwhelming dreadfulness. He would have screamed at the horror of it but he could not catch his breath to do so. Richard watched as Odem fought, shaking his head in amazement at the way the mud seemed to gather itself into a great tangle of vines festooned with huge black grapes. And then he realized. It looked like nets because it *was* nets. Dr Koizumi had used nets to hold the oysters in place. The whole bed of the oyster farm was made of webs of indestructible nets to which the oysters were attached. Odem was getting himself tangled in them and the more he struggled, the deeper he sank, so that it was a race between the black mud and the caustic gas as to which one would choke the life out of him first. 'Nastia!' he called. 'Here's what I want you to do . . .'

Odem was dying. The acrid gas was burning the insides of his lungs now and the more he choked in the more he felt as though he was drowning. How could the whole of his chest be on fire inside while his entire body was freezing in icy slime on the outside? Had he been capable of rational thought he might have dwelt on the irony, but his brain was spinning into primal, howling panic. Then, suddenly – utterly unexpectedly – someone threw themselves across the mud towards him. A huge man with a battered and bloodied face reached out towards him. He grasped the massive hands and his grip was returned. 'NOW!' bellowed the giant and the pair of them were slowly dragged free of the clinging mud and back towards the cool, sweet, life-giving air of the shore.

Ironyen

Ten minutes later, Richard was watching the puking wreck hanging between two of Anastasia's biggest Amazons come whimpering back to life. They had dragged Odem out of the mud and halfway to the compound before there was any real certainty he would survive. And now that he was showing signs of life, Richard broke into a trot while the Amazons carried their captive towards the brightness of the camp. 'Right,' he choked into his headset. 'Check in. Esan. Have the Mils got enough fuel to get us all down the mountain as planned?' He paused as Esan confirmed. Anastasia and the Amazons were all accounted for. 'Abiye? Mako and your men OK? Good. We'll be with you in a minute. Ivan, what about your Russians?' He paused again, listening for Ivan's reply. But then he was interrupted as the radio operator cut in. 'Oshodi? What? Kebila's jets are on the way in? OK. One run with cannon and bombs to close the road to Congo Libre. That should do it. We'll keep an eye out. Keep us informed.' He began again. 'Ivan, what were you saying? All Russians accounted for. Except for Max! *Max!* Where in hell's name's Max?'

Bala Ngama had not been clutching Max out of fear as the Mil dragged the Zodiac across the mat of water hyacinth. The general was inexperienced but he was no fool. And Ivan had been his usual overconfident self too. For Ngama carried a weapon that the cursory search did not reveal. It was a Walther P22 in an ankle holster on his right leg. Through most of the voyage, its barrel was jammed into Max's ribs. Ngama reckoned that the Russian billionaire should ensure that anyone thought twice before acting too hastily when they came to deal with Ngama himself. Like Max, when the positions had been reversed, Ngama was looking to cut a deal. In furtherance of which, he was not sitting idly but was searching with his spare hand amongst the equipment boxes beneath his seat.

There were all sorts of useful things in there, and at the very least he stood a good chance of finding a torch. And so it proved. He felt the familiar icy column of a Maglite's handle. He pushed it into his capacious pocket, his mind racing with plans to make best use of it, his gun and his hostage.

But then the RIB flipped over. When the two men were spilled out on to the lake shore, Ngama kept tight hold of both his gun and of Max. Whereas everyone else ran towards the camp as soon as they had picked themselves up, Ngama pushed Max towards the shadows, then on towards the darkness of the strip of jungle separating the work areas from the road across Karisoke into Congo Libre. The roaring of the vanishing water and the battering bluster of the Mil's downdraught made it impossible to hear anything else. So the two men staggered away and nobody noticed they were gone.

Ngama's desperate need for speed ensured that they stayed as high on the bank as possible – where the roots of the cane forest kept the soil solid. So they avoided the nets that were already wrapping themselves round Colonel Odem up ahead. And they also stayed clear of the deadly gas. The shoreline formed a series of little bays with outcrops of bamboo thick enough to conceal the two parties running this way and that from each other. They passed one another unobserved and unaware – one set dragging their whimpering captive towards the light and the other pushing his towards the darkness.

But the darkness was not absolute. The moon had been waxing for the last few nights and tonight it was full, casting its beams over the two men running along the lake shore. It was even bright enough for Ngama to make out Odem's discarded AK74. 'Stop!' he yelled at Max, who was at least able to hear him now that they were away from the dam, most of the water was out of the lake and the Mils were both hovering down at the far end. The Russian obeyed and stood gasping as Ngama stooped and grabbed the rifle. He pocketed the Walther and swung the AK up into his armpit, using it to gesture Max forward into the jungle. Only when it was towering oppressively above them did Ngama dare get out the Maglite and switch it on.

Max was ready to explode with frustration and anger. To

have been within millimetres of rescue and then to watch it slip away! But he could see no alternative other than to obey for the moment and keep an eye out for a chance to turn the tables. He did as ordered, therefore, and plunged forward along the beam of brightness Ngama's torch laid down. He was unknowingly following in the footsteps of Mizuki Yukawa when she had come stumbling this way more than forty years earlier with the pictures of Dr Koizumi's death replaying in her mind. Prodded by the barrel of the AK whenever his footsteps faltered, Max pushed through the ferns, tripping over roots and stumbling into bushes. 'Keep going!' snarled Ngama. 'You will soon see the lights from the roadway, then we will be safe.'

Max pushed through a jungle wall into a kind of path. He did not recognize it as an elephant trail any more than Mizuki Yukawa had done when she too discovered it. The trail had become overgrown but it still led down to the massive barrier of the fallen tree, then it turned to one side and now led out on to the wilderness of the lava flow with its makeshift road running up to Congo Libre. 'Hurry up!' snarled Ngama, made impatient by the nearness of safety and the hope of escape. 'We're there! We're nearly . . .'

The panther leaped out of the bushes and hit the general from behind. It was a huge beast, raised on the carefully balanced diet that the zookeepers in Granville Harbour had calculated would make it grow strong and healthy. It did not occur to them – for they did not know what its ultimate fate would be – that it would come to associate human scent with that of the food they brought it. Since its release into the wild, it had starved. And Ngama smelt like a good square meal as far as it was concerned. It measured more than two and a half metres from nose to tail-tip and, even half starved, it weighed more than ninety kilos. It was moving at nearly fifty kph when it hit him. Ngama hurled forward, losing his grip on the AK and throwing it towards Max. The gun hit the Russian on the back as the general vanished under the bulk of the massive predator, his torch beam only serving to show the beast's face as it sank the huge white blades of its canine teeth into the screaming general's throat. There was a choking gurgle, a pulsing hiss, a sound of ripping. A sharp crack as though a big branch had been broken. The deep purring growl of a feeding cat.

Max grabbed the gun and took to his heels with the sounds pursuing him down the elephant path. He had no thought except to escape, so he pounded down the trail blindly, shadows gathering impenetrably in front of him as the torchlight died and the last of the moonlight was swallowed by the canopy above. But then, through the pallisade of utter blackness which was the stand of trees to his left, he saw the promise of some brightness. He remembered what Ngama had said about a road over the mountain to Congo Libre. He turned, following the illusory beams, grateful that the dreadful sounds coming from behind him were fading. A wind came through, fanning his face, bringing with it a faint rumble of motors and the welcome stench of diesel exhaust.

But then, seemingly immediately above his head, there gathered the screaming howl of a squadron, its jets going into the attack. What had been flickers of brightness like fireflies in front of him exploded into a thunderous magnesium-white inferno so intense that he wondered for a moment whether the volcano had erupted. But then he understood. The Benin La Bas air force had just closed the road to Congo Libre. 'NO!' he screamed.

Suddenly the darkness etched before him by that massive wall of sheer white light coalesced into a familiar shape, and Max found himself screaming profanities into the face of an angry gorilla. It came out of the undergrowth without giving any warning at all. Like Max, it was overwhelmed and terri-fied by the air-raid on the nearby road. Like the panther, it had been raised in the zoo and was a superb specimen. It towered two metres high and weighed two hundred and fifty kilos. Its arms extended two and a half metres, ending in hands nearly thirty centimetres wide – and they reached for the screaming Russian as it charged. Without any thought at all, Max started firing the AK74. Its bullets smashed into the huge creature's abdomen, but they missed its spine and pelvis so they did not slow it down. It reached for the gun and tore it out of Max's hands. Then, holding it by the barrel, it smashed Max's face open. All the Russian billionaire's cunning, planning, deviousness and ambition were bludgeoned out of his head along with his brains. If there was one last thought, it was simple astonishment at the overwhelming irony. *Ironyen.* It was actually funny, in a twisted Russian sort of way. After all he had been through – put Nastia through in one way and another – that it should come to this. *Simian Artillery.* He was actually being killed. By an ape. With a gun.

His body fell back on to the elephant path without even twitching and lay there, less than twenty metres from the remains of Mizuki Yukawa. The gorilla rose up and drove the stock of the assault rifle down on to Max's head one last time. And the gun went off. The rest of the clip emptied itself automatically into the gorilla. Twenty rounds of five point four five millimetre ammunition went up under its massive chin and out through the top of its skull at nine hundred metres per second. The gorilla stood still for a second, as though hardly able to believe that it, too, was dead. And then it fell forward to bury the body of the man it had just killed with its own mountainous black bulk.

Black Pearls

R ichard and Robin always preferred to stay at the Kempinski
  when they were in St Petersburg. They loved its combination of old-world charm, courteous service and fine dining.
Their favourite suite overlooked the Moika River, had a decor of
restful blue and was full of photographs of 1930s sailboats. When
they visited in the summer they always ate out on the balcony of
the Bellvue Brasserie on the top floor. Not only was the food
exquisite, so was the view which overlooked the back of the
Hermitage. They had eaten there yesterday evening, soon after
their arrival in the city. But the view had proved less than uplifting
because it also included the golden onion domes of The Church
of Our Saviour on Spilled Blood, which was where they were
bound for today for Max's long-delayed memorial. It was just as
well that there would not be a coffin. It had been Richard and
Ivan who dragged the gorilla off Max's corpse the next morning
when they found what was left of Ngama and his hostage, though
it had been Anastasia who had seen the irony and laughed with
a mixture of bitterness and hysteria until Ivan half carried her
back to the camp. That had been at the end of last summer and
now it was spring, with even St Petersburg thawing under an early
heat wave. Max's will had mentioned his wish to have his memorial at the Church of Our Saviour on Spilled Blood; an unexpectedly romantic gesture that had cost a good deal of extra time. It
was the church he had promised that Ivan Yagula and Anastasia
would be married in – in the days before his own Ivan died.

As usual, Richard was up and about first. He showered and
shaved – a process that took longer these days courtesy of
Ivan's over-assiduous help with his disguise. Then, wrapped in
one of the hotel's dressing gowns, he crossed to the bedside
phone and dialled 914. 'A cafetière of Blue Mountain,' he said,
rubbing his still-tender jaw, testing a still-loose tooth. 'Robin,
do you want tea?' Robin grunted in the affirmative and rolled

over. 'And a pot of English Breakfast tea, please.' He hung up. 'Mind if I take a look at the news?' he asked. Robin grunted.

Richard picked up the remote handset and scrolled through the channels until he got the BBC World News. He was just in time for the four o'clock news GMT – which made it five a.m. in London and eight a.m. in Moscow and here. 'Better shake a leg, darling. We're meeting Felix at ten. Service is at eleven.' He didn't quite catch what she said in reply but he heard the word, 'tea'.

He was distracted by the news report. '. . . And in a surprise announcement from Granville Harbour, Julius Chaka has conceded defeat. President Chaka will be succeeded by his daughter, the freedom fighter and political activist Celine Chaka. All the negative stories about her campaign have been proved to be groundless and the final count is decisive. Her first priority is likely to concern the long-running border dispute with Congo Libre which led to the tragic confrontation at Lac Dudo last year.'

There was a gentle tapping at the door and Richard crossed to open it and accept a tray laden with the coffee and tea he had ordered and turned back.

'. . . associated story,' the anchorwoman was saying as he slid the tray on to the bedside table nearest Robin and let the scent of English Breakfast tea work its magic on her. He straightened with his cafetière in one hand and his coffee cup in the other, listening as he poured. 'The Russian consortium Bashnev/Sevmash is continuing with its assessment of the bed of Lac Dudo, in spite of the upheavals at head office resulting from the death of its co-founder Mr Maximilian Asov, ex-CEO of Bashnev Oil and Power. Initial estimates of the worth of the coltan in the discovery now seem to have been inflated, but a spokesman for the consortium has informed our Moscow correspondent that the new government in Benin La Bas is fully committed to continuing the project with them. The Bashnev/Sevmash share price as quoted on the Moscow and London stock exchanges remains at an all-time high.' Richard sipped his coffee as Felix Makarov's face filled the screen.

'What's the time?' asked Robin sleepily.

'It's gone eight,' he said. 'Felix will be outside in just under two hours.'

'Oh my *GOD*! Why didn't you tell me, you *bloody* man?'

10.15 a.m.

Felix was waiting outside the Kempinski at ten in one of Bashnev/Sevmash's St Petersburg fleet of Bentleys. 'This is a bit excessive,' observed Robin. 'We could walk. What is it? Five hundred metres?'

'My dear girl,' said Felix, 'nobody walks. Nobody who is anybody. Certainly not today!' He reached into a capacious briefcase as they climbed in and handed them their ID badges. Like everyone else attending Max's memorial, they would only be allowed into the church if their lapels announced clearly who they were.

Robin settled into moody silence, fiddling with the pin on the ID badge she did not want to push through the cashmere of her outfit, still flustered from having to get ready in what she considered to be a brutally short time. Though the effect, thought her indulgent husband, could hardly have been bettered, even though black was not really her colour. 'You looked good on television this morning,' he said to Felix, looking up from his own badge. 'Talking to the BBC.'

'I'll have to talk to more than the BBC, and you know it,' rumbled Felix. 'I'm booked on the first flight to Granville Harbour tomorrow. Even so, I'll be well behind Han Wuhan. Doctor Chen is going himself, hoping the president will succumb to a Chinese charm offensive.' He too lapsed into silence.

The radio on the car was tuned to Voice of Russia news. The report filled the confines of the passenger compartment. 'The sudden death of Fydor Novotkin, millionaire music producer and ex-guitarist with Simian Artillery, has thrown the music business into turmoil, as our reporter Ludmilla Sokolova explains.' The voices changed. 'It's as though Simon Cowell had died unexpectedly,' breathed excitedly tones. 'Fydor Novotkin was discovered in his suite at the Petrovka hotel. He apparently died of an overdose . . .'

'That's strange,' said Richard.

'You think so?' asked Felix and Richard couldn't tell whether the Russian's mind had been elsewhere or whether he just knew a lot more than he was saying. Richard frowned, his mind racing. Robin hadn't reacted at all. She really was lost in thought. And her Russian wasn't quite as fluent as Richard's.

'And in international news,' the radio continued to whisper, as the first voice resumed control. 'Funke Odem, self-styled colonel of the Army of Christ the Infant, appeared before the World Court in the Hague yesterday. Colonel Odem is accused of crimes against humanity including rape, torture, mutilation and murder. He is accused of using black magic rituals, sex trafficking, employing child soldiers and attempting to invade the sovereign state of Benin La Bas, whose new president, Celine Chaka, has already said she will be giving evidence against him in person. Colonel Odem has been compared with the notorious Joseph Kony, leader of the Lord's Resistance Army who was famously the subject of a viral video in 2012.'

11.00 a.m.

It took the Mulsane the better part of half an hour to ease its way through the traffic down Moika Embankment, along Nevsky Prospekt and back up Griboyedova Embankment to The Church of our Saviour on the Spilled Blood, even though, as Robin observed, it would have been easier and quicker to walk. But at last the limousine whispered to a halt outside 2A, Kanal Griboyedova and the three passengers in the back were able to climb out. Richard looked up at the dazzling frontage, wrestling with the irony that had Max Asov laid out on the spot where Tsar Alexander II had been assassinated by guerrillas rather than gorillas – and with a bomb, not a gun.

The roadway was packed with congregation moving under the golden awning into the side of the beautiful building. As well as the mourners with their ID badges, there were hoards of well-wishers, onlookers, tourists and TV crews. It was a considerable crowd and Richard could see why. Max had been a social animal and a big beast in all sorts of jungles other than the one he had died in. The sober-suited men were world-class politicians, business leaders, media and sporting personalities. The women in beautifully fashioned mourning were film stars, TV stars and models. Almost all of them were young and breathtaking – many of them ex-girlfriends of the man who was desperately trying to replace his dead son. Richard saw the lovely Irina Lavrov in the crush, star of one of the most popular and long-running Russian TV shows – and now a considerable film star on the international stage – the next Milla Jovovich, perhaps. Beside her was Tatiana Kalina, the last of the late mogul's girlfriends. All of the mourners were worth looking at – independently of the fact that the fairy-tale church was St Petersburg's most popular tourist attraction after the Hermitage. All well worth interviewing.

Or, it seemed, they were until Felix and the Mariners arrived. Then the TV crews gathered round the three of them with an eagerness that bordered on frenzy. Richard was the first to feel the camera lights on him as he was asked to retell the story of Max's last few hours and how he had found the body. His version was nothing less than the truth, but it glossed over certain elements, playing down his own role and emphasizing Max's, Ivan's and Anastasia's. It was a version of events agreed between the survivors in the days after the Battle of Black Lake as it became popularly known. In this version, Max died heroically pursuing the traitor Bala Ngama on behalf of the peoples of Benin La Bas. Ivan and Anastasia had done much the same with Colonel Odem. And the destruction of the dam, the road, and the invading army from Congo Libre with their Chinese associates, were all part of a quick-thinking reaction to the crisis on the part of Colonel Laurent Kebila, the president's chief of staff. Coupled with the repetition of a natural disaster similar to the one that wiped out half the population of Cite La Bas just after the turn of the millennium.

Richard had just reached the end of this story when a long black limousine with diplomatic plates drew up. A smart driver in a military uniform jumped out and ran round to open the passenger door. And another man in uniform stepped on to the pavement, came to attention and marched up towards the church but turned aside when he saw Richard. For once in his life, Richard was absolutely astonished. The man approaching so smartly was Laurent Kebila. Under one stylishly uniformed arm, where he habitually tucked a swagger stick, he carried what looked like a roll of parchment. Richard was so surprised to see Kebila in the first place that it took him a second to register that the medal ribbons on his breast had been updated and the pips on his epaulettes, together with the gold braid on his cap, had received attention too. All of which was confirmed on the ID label he wore on his lapel just above his campaign decorations. 'Captain Mariner,' said the punctilious officer.

'General Kebila,' returned Richard. 'This is an unexpected honour.'

Kebila half turned so that he was addressing Felix and Robin as well as Richard. 'Captain Mariner, Mr Makarov,' he said formally, 'I have come at the express orders of President Chaka to represent the people of Benin La Bas at the service. And the president has asked me to pass this to you, Mr Makarov. It is the award of our nation's highest honour to your deceased associate.'

Felix took the proffered scroll, moving like some kind of a puppet. He unrolled it, apparently without thinking, and held it up to the cameras. General Kebila announced in a loud, formal tone, 'Mr Maximilian Asov is hereby made a Companion of the Legion of Honour of Benin La Bas.'

And under the brightness of the TV lights, Richard could see the signature above the presidential seal. *CELINE*, it said. Now that was a confident woman, Richard thought. Confident of victory, carefully planning ahead. What a president she was going to make!

There was a moment of silence, then someone started clapping. Then someone began to cheer, and the whole of the roadway and the canal beside it was filled with a kind of standing ovation, so that Richard didn't even hear the engine growl as the final car arrived. And it would have been quite a growl, for the last car was a Bugatti Veyron. Its wings were black and its bonnet red. The windshield and the side windows were tinted. It prowled up to the kerb and simply crouched there, reminding Richard of his Bentley Continental, which was also full of feline grace – like a black panther. But the Veyron could go fifty miles an hour faster even than the Continental, which could top 200 mph.

Richard crossed to Felix. 'Isn't that Max's?' he asked. 'Or are there lots of Veyrons in Bashnev/Sevmash?'

'It's Max's,' nodded Felix. 'Or it *was*.'

The driver's door opened and Ivan folded his massive frame out, stretching to his full height and testing the seams of his perfectly tailored black suit and cashmere overcoat with its Persian lambskin collar. Gone was the rough and ready soldier-boy who had helped carry Max's corpse back to the compound with Mako's cross. This was every inch the shark-smooth *biznisman*. A fitting successor to his godfather. Ivan caught Richard's eye and came up towards him at once, raising his hand to Felix as he did so, and blowing a kiss to Robin. The coat billowed wide as he shoved a black-gloved hand into its pocket.

As Ivan came up to face him, Richard read his ID badge. *Ivan Larentovitch Yagula, Head of Security, Bashnev Oil and Power*. 'Richard. I have something for you,' said Ivan, pulling his hand out of his pocket. It was a roll of red felt. Richard looked down at it, frowning. Then he understood, even as Ivan unrolled it and gave it to him. 'Me and my Spetsnaz guys had a talk,' he said. 'We agreed you'd earned it.'

It was a red beret. Richard took it, overcome. For once in his life he was speechless.

'That's quite a car,' said Robin disapprovingly. 'Max's babe-catcher.'

'I don't need a babe-catcher,' said Ivan easily with a wide grin. 'Anyway, it's not mine. It's the boss's. I just get to drive it once in a while.'

'The boss's,' echoed Richard, looking up from the red beret.

Ivan nodded once and stood aside. 'The boss's,' he said emphatically.

There behind him, standing tall in a black business suit that looked to be Chanel, with a sable wrap and a cloche hat boasting a half veil, stood a woman whose simple beauty took Richard's breath away. As with General Laurent Kebila, the change was so unexpected, the transformation so absolute, that it took a moment before he registered who he was actually looking at. Then the little half smile gave it away. That and the ID badge beneath the sable and the rope upon rope of lustrous black pearls: *Mme Anastasia Asova, Chief Executive Officer, Bashnev Oil and Power.*